For Dan, wh
the F

For my mum, wi
s

And for my dad, whose love for books
encouraged me to read.

EMILY & PETER

by C. L. Sharples

I AM IN LOVE WITH A BOY CALLED PETER

Emily

Hello there. I'm Emily. Emily Clarke.

If there is one thing you should know about me, it's that I am in love with a boy called Peter Woods. Maybe it's the only thing you need to know, but I like to think there's more to me than that. I'm pretty mature for my sixteen years of age. Just ignore my mum when she calls me giddy and childish because I am neither of those things. I like listening to music and going to school, and I have a cat named Blondie, who is, in fact, ginger.

If you thought the school part was weird, I only like it because I get to see my friend, and Peter, every day. I don't classify Peter as a friend because he is much, much more than that. He also likes to frequently remind me that he's not my friend, but who is he trying to kid?

Peter is the most important person in my life. And I'm not saying that to be dramatic or anything. This isn't just some young, childish, high-school kind of love. It's also not the 'temporary' kind, either, as I've heard before. As though my love for Peter could ever be temporary. No, my love is the pure kind. The eternal kind. The kind that doesn't go away no matter how much rejection I receive. And believe me, I know rejection.

Because Peter Woods does not love me back.

But that's okay. My love doesn't demand reciprocation, at least not immediately. It is patient. Not only is it patient, but it is also hopeful. Hopeful that he will one day recognise my charms and fall madly in love with me back. I can wait for that.

A little background on Peter. First, he's the most popular boy at our school. Everyone wants to be friends with him. It's kind of funny because he doesn't seem to want to be friends with anyone back. He's the aloof type. Me, I'd love to be friends with everyone, but I only have the one. Why does it work like that? Anyway, the second thing: he's insanely smart. I don't understand why he's in set 2 because I know he knows the answer to everything. He's also funny in his quirky way. Adorably funny. And the third thing, he is mind-bogglingly gorgeous. Picture the cutest guy in your school and double - wait, triple it. That's him.

Don't get me wrong, I don't like him for his looks or popularity. I'm not that shallow. Actually, his popularity sort of irks me because it means I rarely find him alone. And his cuteness... damn his cuteness. Almost every girl in school has a crush on him, *including* the cheerleaders. I don't need that competition.

But I'm different. I've liked him ever since I saw him, way back in primary school when he hadn't had his growth spurt yet and still wore braces. Back then, he never said a word. He was the introverted, mysterious type. The one who sat alone in the corner while the other children played. He still doesn't say a lot now, but it's part of his charm. I like that about him.

I, on the other hand, talk a lot. Maybe too much. I only say this about myself because I sometimes see people space out while I'm talking. When I speak to Peter, I wonder if he's listening or thinking about some intelligent scientific thing because his brain is so smart. What matters is that I can speak enough for the two of us.

I used to worry that we were too opposite to be compatible. You know, the old introvert vs the extrovert. Now, I don't worry at all, because whatever you are, when it comes to love, it doesn't matter. I can easily sit in silence if that's what Peter needs. And Peter, all a person needs to do is be patient with him. Sure, there are a lot of his walls baring me from entry

- but if he's taught me anything, it's the importance of perseverance. Last year, he rarely acknowledged my existence. Now he says good morning to me when he sees me outside. Progress.

"Emily! You are going to be late for school!"

That's my mum calling. She tells me I'm going to be late every morning, even when we both know I'm not. I have Peter to thank for that, too. If it wasn't for the incentive of seeing him before school, I'd probably be late every day. Oh - Peter is my neighbour. He lives across the street from me. He also likes to get to school early, so I need to make sure I'm ready to leave on time for him.

Peeking across the street, I check to see if his bike is still there, and it is. My heart does that little flip it likes to do every time I see it, chained up against the railings.

"Emily!" My mum calls again. Her voice is nearing that scary sound when she's about to storm upstairs. "Come down for breakfast or you are going to be late!"

"I'm coming!" I grab my purple school bag and pause to look at myself in the mirror. I'm smaller than the other girls in my year, with brown hair and a plain face. My mum keeps saying I'll have a growth spurt soon, but I no longer believe her. Everyone else had theirs over the summer. Not me. I'm the walking dwarf among a crowd of giants. Even my best friend, Natasha, grew a few inches. Not that I'm complaining. While I don't have any remarkable features to make me stand out, I only need to stand out to one person.

And it's my personality that will win him over.

Downstairs, my mum is standing by the sink and rinsing a cucumber. I scan the table for food, but there isn't a crumb in sight.

"I thought you said breakfast is ready?"

"No, I said to come down and get it. You need to make it yourself."

"Okay." I open the cereal cupboard and eye my mum sideways. I can never wager her mood anymore. She might be okay... or she might bite my head off for breathing. "Where's dad?" I ask. This question usually helps me determine what I'm working with.

"In bed." She answers - without a sigh. "Try not to wake him when you leave. You're such a noisemaker."

"No, I'm not." She's definitely okay.

And if you're wondering why my dad's still in bed, well, he's sort of going through a mid-life crisis. He quit his job two months ago. The place was a soul-destroying, money-obsessed, corporate dump. His words, not mine. We've been waiting for him to get another job ever since. My mum has been pretty good about it all because she wants him to be happy, but it means she's been working extra hours. I'm still deciding what my dad enjoys more, looking for something new or spending his days watching Netflix.

I wolf my food down, afraid I'll miss my important meeting with Peter.

"Have you done all your homework?" My mum asks.

I gulp. "Yes."

I'm a terrible liar, and she sees right through me.

"Emily, you've been off for two weeks. Why haven't you finished it?"

Hmm. Why haven't I finished my math and science homework over Christmas break? Well, because it sucks, and I've had better things to do. Like staring at a wall. Or watching paint dry. And why do teachers set homework over breaks, anyway? This is a question I'd like answered because it does not equal a break.

I don't say this to my mum. I'm smarter than that. "I've nearly finished it. Like 90%."

"Well, make sure you get it to one hundred. I don't want you falling into set 3 again."

I shiver because neither do I.

My school splits classes into sets. Set 1 means you're smart; set 2 means you're also smart but not quite smart enough for set 1; set 3 means you need to work on yourself, and set 4 means why do you even bother coming to school. Me, I'm set 2 across the board. You might think this means I'm smart, but I have to work hard for it. Really, *really*, hard. During class, I'm usually the last to know the answer. And that's if I even get to it. But Peter is in set 2, and class would be boring without him. So I put in the effort.

"Okay, I'm leaving." Hopping to my feet, I plant a kiss on my mum's cheek. "Love you, mum."

"Okay, sweetie, have a good day."

I'm a little early. Peter's bike is still outside. I pretend I need to tie my shoe and take a while doing it. His front door opens, and I see his little brother run out. His mum is next, followed by Peter himself. He looks cute, as usual, and I smile involuntarily. I notice that his mum doesn't say bye to him as my mum does to me. She just throws him a set of keys and leaves with little Sammy.

He locks his front door and unties his bike. I leave my garden, waiting for him to notice me. When he doesn't, I walk across the little patch of grass that separates us and greet him.

"Good morning!" I grin.

He glances briefly at me before turning his attention back to his bike. "Morning."

"Did you have a good Christmas?"

As I wait for him to respond, I get the sense something is off. He's not usually chatty, but today he seems... gloomy. Did he have another argument with his mum?

"It was fine." A pause. "Yours?"

I haven't seen him or spoken to him for so long - *an entire two weeks* - that I explode into a tirade of speech. I detail everything I did over the break, from visiting a Santa's Grotto with my mum to eating a giant bag of Doritos's while having a movie night with Natasha. He has a patient look in his eye that encourages me to continue.

"So that's it," I say, huffing out a breath. He stares at me for a second, and I worry I've said too much. Feeling a sudden chill, I pull my coat tight around me, and his eyes dart to my fingers.

"Sounds good." He swings his leg over his bike. I move away so he can wheel it onto the path, taking a step after him.

Still sensing that gloominess, I pull the flapjack my mum packed for me out of my bag and hand it to him. I know they are his favourite. "This is for you. My mum, um, gave me two."

He clears his throat and takes it from me, slipping it into his pocket. "Thanks."

Pushing his bike into momentum, he rides away. His dark hair blows gently in the wind, holding my attention for a moment.

With a sigh, I start walking. I regret that I don't have a bike.

WHY DOES
HER MUM PACK
HER TWO?

Peter

T hank God it's school again.

While I'm not a school fanatic - most of my classmates are annoyingly loud - my house is like my personal purgatory, so school makes for a blissful escape. And if you think that's twisted, it is.

Over the Christmas break, we visited my aunt in her 2-bedroom cottage down by the coast. You can imagine how cramped we all were, what with there being me, my brother, my mum, my aunt, my cousin, and their three dogs. My brother shared rooms with our cousin, who's also seven, which meant I got stuck on the couch. Lucky me. I wouldn't have minded so much, except I was right next to the kitchen, and my mum and aunt stayed up most nights drinking wine and *talking*.

Their conversation was always the same, and I couldn't drown it out, no matter how much I tried. Not even a pillow to the ear worked. This is how it went: my mum complained about my dad, who was supposed to be there with us, and my aunt complained about her ex-husband, who wasn't. That was it, every night. Every. Single. Night.

My mum complains about my dad to me all the time, so you'll excuse me when I say I've heard enough of it. Sure, I was annoyed at him too, if only for my little brother. He was excited to see him, and my forever-letting-us-down dad called last minute to say he had to stay at work. He works away a lot, and I appreciate him for doing that, but you'd think he'd want to be with his family at Christmas. Next time I'm going to demand I stay at home.

I throw my legs out of bed and head to the bathroom. I can hear my mum on the phone downstairs, arguing with someone. Most likely, it's my dad. My little brother is poking his head out his bedroom door, looking worried. I ruffle his hair with a smile and push him back inside. It's not fair on the twerp.

When I finish in the shower, I change into my school uniform. It's an elaborate costume our school forces on us to show the world they mean business. I fasten the shirt and then cover it with the blue blazer, something I'll remove later on. It's restrictive and retains too much heat. My pants show a bit of my ankle, and I change into navy socks, wondering when I'll finally stop growing.

Downstairs, I find my mum in the kitchen. She's slicing fruit and placing it on top of some pancakes. They smell good, but I know they aren't for me. I pour myself some cereal and go to the fridge as my brother comes down for his breakfast.

I sigh. "We're out of milk."

"I used it for Sammy's pancakes." My mum replies. As if that helps.

I suck in a calming breath and close the fridge. I don't want to argue. I do not want to argue.

"Do you want some of my pancake?" Sammy asks in that sweet voice of his.

My mum is quick to shut that offer down. "No, honey, those are for you. You need them to grow big and strong."

"Then what will Peter have?"

"There's some bread in the cupboard," she says to me.

"But no butter," I reply.

Her frustrated sigh tells me the argument is about to begin. "What do you want me to do about it, huh? I have to make sure Sammy is fed and ready for school, and on top of that, I have to make sure I'm ready to leave for work. And all this without your dad being here, so forgive me for not finding the time to buy butter."

She always finds a way to mention my dad. Always. "It's fine, mum. I'll have it without butter." Yum.

She gives me a look that makes me think she'll say sorry or something, but she doesn't. I just want to get out of the house. I finish eating my far too dry breakfast and get to my feet.

"We're leaving now, too." My mum says. "I have to be at work early. Don't forget your lunch bag - I've made you a tuna sandwich, so I'm not a complete waste."

I don't even like tuna, but I'm not going to remind her again. "Thanks. And I don't think you're a waste."

She nods her head with a distracted look in her eye. "Come on, Sammy, brush your teeth so we can leave."

Sammy hops to his feet and runs upstairs. I follow behind to do mine. In the bathroom, I stand next to him. I look like a tower next to his tiny figure.

"Are you glad to be back at school?" I ask him, wondering if this house is as much of a prison for him as it is for me. I hope not.

"Hmm, I guess so."

"You guess so?" I jab him in the ribs, and he makes this giggle sound. "If anybody gives you any trouble, you come to me, okay?"

"I can fight my own battles."

"Wow. I respect you for that."

We go back downstairs. My mum pulls me to the side when Sammy isn't looking, and I already know what she's going to say. "I can't pick him up today, mum. It's the first day of basketball practice."

"Please," she begs. "I forgot to ask Tammy, and I can't get out of work early today."

"Can't you message her? What about my practice?"

"Is your brother not more important?"

That was a low blow.

"More important than what?" Sammy's round face peeps out beneath her arm.

I sigh because I don't want to argue in front of him. "Fine. I'll do it."

My mum smiles and rubs Sammy on the head. "Your brother is going to pick you up from school today."

The only thing that makes it worth it is the beam now on his face.

It's freezing outside. I feel the cold before I've even left the house because Sammy's opened the front door and is running out.

"Ooh, there's Emily!" He squeals.

My head snaps up. I tell myself it's because I'm afraid Sammy might fall in his excitement. Emily. For a brief moment, I wonder what she's been up to over the Christmas break. But then I remember she'll probably force every detail on me later because that's what she does. I smile.

Emily is my annoying neighbour. I don't use the term annoying to be harsh. It's just a fact. She'll probably admit it herself if anyone asks her. The thing about her is that she can talk. For hours. I really don't know why she wastes her breath on me because I never say much back. I prefer silence over talking. She's the opposite, and it drives me insane. She also has this habit of appearing out of nowhere. There was this time at school when this girl asked me out, and she just... appeared. Like that. Annoying, right?

I don't look up at her as I unlock my bike. Maybe if she thinks I'm ignoring her, she'll leave me alone. Of course, that's too much to ask.

"Good morning." She greets. A glance tells me that she's somehow right beside me. There she goes again - appearing out of nowhere.

"Morning," I say back.

"Did you have a good Christmas?"

I wonder how she always manages to sound so cheerful, especially at this time in the morning. And why does she leave this early for school, anyway? Does her mum annoy her as mine does me, forcing her to escape? I'd ask her, but it's not for me to pry.

I realise I haven't answered and say, "it was fine." And then I pause because I really don't want to ask her this question. "Yours?"

And off she goes. Seriously, how does this girl talk so much? She's saying something about Santa's Grotto, and I wonder if she's got a younger sibling I didn't know existed. No. She means herself. Dorito's? What is she talking about? I space out. I don't mean to do it, but it doesn't seem like she's going to stop talking any time soon. She's blocking my way out of the garden, so I can't even try to escape.

"So that's it," she says. Phew. It's over. She pulls her coat tight around her, and I look at her fingers. They are red from the cold. Doesn't she own a pair of gloves?

I consider giving her mine, but no. It's her own damn fault for not wearing them.

"Sounds good," I say and swing my leg over my bike. Luckily, she moves out of my way, or I might have run her down.

"This is for you." She holds something out to me before I can make a safe distance. Seeing the familiar blue wrapping, I hold back a groan. "My mum, um, gave me two." She adds.

Why does her mum pack her two? I don't even like flapjacks. I can't tell her this now because I've already accepted too many, so it will probably upset her. Damn it. I clear my throat and stuff it into the pocket of my blazer, making a mental note to give it to Sammy later. It looks like she's about to say something else, so I make a move.

The day that Emily gets a bike is the day I will stop riding mine.

PLEASE SAY NO

Emily

I always meet Natasha outside of our local convenience store. We meet here for one simple reason: the snacks. I have my lunch money safely tucked away in my pocket, something my mum gives to me every morning for the school cafeteria. Little does she know I spend it before I even get there. If she ever finds out, I think she might kill me. Either that, or she'll start making me a packed lunch, and I'm not sure which one is worse. If I don't have my giant bag of Wotsits to get me through the morning, I may cry.

For this reason, I walk to Natasha like a vigilant ninja, keeping an eye out for my mums' red car in case she drives past on her way to work. She almost caught us once, and we flew behind a bin to avoid her line of sight. That day, I walked around school with gum stuck to the back of my skirt until the last bell rang, and it's safe to say that it scarred me. Natasha claims she hadn't seen it, but the memory of her mysterious, randomly-timed giggles tells me otherwise. Peter is the one who pointed it out to me. My vigilance is a direct outcome of that.

Natasha grins when she sees me. I swear I only saw her the other day, and she's grown. Darn it, would she please stop? She's like a head taller than me when I stand next to her now.

"Hey tiny," she says as if she can read my mind. She likes to say this because I can no longer say it to her.

"Have you gone for a style change?" I ask, flicking one of her loose curls.

Natasha has beautiful light brown hair that falls to the top of her waist. She usually ties back, but today she's wearing it down. In my not-so-biased opinion, it makes her look like a model.

"Yep." She gives me a twirl before we enter the shop. "If I don't change my style over break, when can I?"

"Should I have done the same?" I tug at my limp brown hair and twirl it in my fingers, wondering how she got hers to curl like that.

When she sees what I'm doing, she laughs and throws her arm over my shoulder. "I'll bring my curlers around to your house this weekend," she says, patting my head. "Let's see what we can do with you."

The thought of luscious, thick curls - the kind I see in those magazines at my mums' hairdressers - excites me. In my head, I imagine myself turning up at school

17

looking like the next top model. Everyone turns to look at me as I walk across the schoolyard, but I don't care about them - I search the ramp and find Peter by his usual spot next to the railing. His mouth drops open when he sees me. He walks over to me; he bends his head, he-

"What on earth are you thinking about?" Natasha's question snaps me out of my reverie.

I look away before she can see how red I am. "Nothing."

"You're thinking about Peter." Her voice has that teasing edge as she pokes me with her fingers.

"No, I'm not." I lie, but I'm smiling despite my effort not to. Peter's name has that effect on me.

"Did you see him this morning?" Natasha throws two bags of crisps into our basket as we move down the aisle. "Wait, let me guess. You waited until you saw him leave his house, and then you pounced on him."

"I actually left the house first," I tell her. "But I did see him," the smile creeps back onto my lips.

She turns on me, blocking my path to the chocolate aisle. She's so abrupt that I walk straight into her. "Tell me everything. Did you speak to him? Did he say anything to you? How was it after being apart for two weeks? Is he in love with you yet?"

"Yes. Yes. Amazing. And no." I move past her and drop a Twix into the basket.

"Well, what did he say to you? Did he tell you what he did over Christmas?"

"Just that it was good."

"That's it? Does he ever say more than two words to you?"

I shrug. "Sometimes."

"I've said this before, Emily - I don't think Peter Woods is the guy for you."

"Yes, he is."

She continues like I didn't say anything. "He's cold and silent, whereas you're warm and bubbly. It's like he's an ice-cube, and you're a toasty flame."

I fold my arms. "Maybe my heat can melt him." As soon as I say the words, I regret them. Natasha makes a barfing sound, and I laugh because I have to admit - that was cringe even for me.

With our snacks purchased and hidden safely in our bags, we make our way to school. It's only a ten-minute walk from here, but for us, it takes twenty. We see Harvey Morris across the street, and I call him over because I know he has a crush on Natasha, and I'm rooting for the two of them. As he crosses the road, her face turns red, and she pushes me into the bush before speed-walking ahead.

"Where's she going?" Harvey asks, watching after her.

I glare at her back as I pick a leaf off my shoulder and say, "She needs the toilet."

"Oh." He pushes his glasses up his nose. As I watch, I have a sudden urge to hug him. If I were Natasha, I'd give Harvey a chance. It's a shame on him. Maybe it's because I know what unrequited love feels like, but he's also one of the sweetest boys in our year.

"She'll come around," I tell him, giving him a consoling tap on the shoulder. "I know she will."

I'm surprised to see him grin. "Actually, I'm over her."

"You're *what*?" I'm so shocked that I stop walking.

His grin widens. "Yep. I met a girl at a temp job over Christmas, so Natasha doesn't need to avoid me anymore."

"Wow." I don't know whether to be sad for Natasha or happy for Harvey. I think I'm both.

We reach the school and follow a swarm of students through the gate. I'm still mind-blown by Harvey's admission that I almost pass by Peter's spot on the ramp without waving at him. I remember just in time and turn to find Peter staring at me. My heart does a little flip, but when I wave, he turns away, so maybe he hadn't been staring after all.

Natasha is waiting for me inside the school entrance. I can see her checking for Harvey, but he's already left for his locker.

"You don't need to worry," I tell her, "he doesn't have a crush on you anymore."

Are my eyes deceiving me, or does she seem disappointed? No, it can't be. Not Natasha.

"Good," she flicks her hair over her shoulder in an uncharacteristic manner. "Because he never stood a chance." Her eyes freeze. "Emily, don't look. Peter's on his way in."

"What?" I turn my neck so fast I feel a spasm of pain. "Is that Hannah with him?" My voice raises an octave when I ask this because Hannah Pierce is the most popular girl in our year. She's the one who looks good without ever trying, the one who makes girls like me feel like we missed puberty.

I've never seen Peter show an interest in her before, so I always assumed he was immune to her charm, unlike the other boys in our year. But now...

"I told you not to look," Natasha spins me back to face her with a frown. "Do you want to seem desperate?"

I'm too panicked to care. "Why is he with her?"

"I don't know. Maybe they're friends."

"What?" I turn again, but she grasps me by the shoulders, pinning me in place. "I need to go speak to him."

"You will do no such thing." She warns.

I know she's right, but I'm not sure I can help myself. My legs start to jiggle. "I don't think I stop myself."

"Yes, you can."

"Are they near?"

She peeks around me. "They're coming in. Don't look."

I have every intention to listen to her. But not looking when Peter is near is an impossibility. When I see Hannah batting her lashes at him, I can't stop myself from wriggling my way free, ignoring Natasha's sigh as I do so.

"Hey, Peter!" I say, jumping in front of him. He looks down at me with an unreadable expression. Hannah's eyes are a little more comprehensive. It looks as though she wants to stomp on me.

"Emily," Peter says.

What now? I say the only thing that comes to my mind. "Did you enjoy the flapjack?"

No. No. No. No. I want. To bury. Myself. In the ground.

"I-," He stops speaking. What does that mean? "I did."

Before I can say anything else, Hannah tugs him by the arm. Just the sight of it causes my throat to go dry.

"Come on, Peter." She says. "We'll be late for English."

He walks with her. He's walking with her, and there's nothing I can do to stop it. I feel Natasha's hand on my arm, and I turn to see her looking at me with sad eyes.

"Oh, Emily," she says, cupping my face in her hands. "You really don't know how to get a boy, do you?"

My lips jut into a pout. "No. No, I don't."

She sighs, pulling me into a walk. "And Peter Woods at that. Mr Impossible-to-win-over."

"Not for Hannah." A lump rises in my throat. I try to swallow it down.

Come on, Emily. You're better than this.

"I told you, now is the time you need to get over him. This is good. It gives you a reason."

Maybe she's right. No, she isn't right. I don't want to get over Peter. But right now, I wish I could hit a pause button on my feelings.

I take my seat at the back of English class, passing

Peter's table without looking at him. My desk is two behind his, to the left. For the first time, I notice that Hannah sits two desks in front of him. Has he been looking at her this whole time? I don't want to know. Natasha takes her seat beside me, pulling out our first bag of crisps. I shake my head when she offers me some because I'm no longer in the mood. When the teacher comes in, she assigns us a group project. We have to get into groups of four. I look at Peter because I always ask him to team with us, but something stops me this time.

"Are you seriously not going to ask Peter?" Natasha whispers. She knows as well as I that it's always my first thought.

I shake my head when I see that Hannah is already turning to look at him.

"Do you want to team with us, Peter?" She asks, smiling that perfect smile.

Even though I've already decided to stay silent, I can't help but think, *please say no.* He doesn't answer her at first, and part of me thinks he might. But then I see him open his mouth, and he says,

"Sure."

IF SHE ASKS ME NOW, I'LL SAY YES

Peter

I t only takes me five minutes to ride to school. Five minutes, and I am within the gates of my second purgatory, a hell-hole that isn't quite as bad as my first.

Nobody is at the ramp yet. That's just how I like it. It's the only part of the day when I don't get pressured to make small talk or pretend something interesting is happening in my life when it's not.

The ramp is where the popular students go to hang out if you care to know. For this reason, I have no idea why I'm here. To be more precise, I have no idea why *they* want me here. It's not like I fit in or contribute to their day in any way. Part of me thinks I must meet some generic description of the word *popular* because I can't think of any other reason why they badger me to stay.

I lock my bike and walk over, taking my usual spot by the railing. I chose this spot for one reason: it offers a quick escape. It was a strategic decision, and you should never underestimate the importance of having a quick way out. Believe me.

Leaning my arms against the railing, I look out at the basketball courts. It's currently a ghost town over there. Last year, the courts got hijacked by school smokers. Since nobody has been brave enough to claim them back, the guys who play for sport use the ones inside now.

Seeing the courts reminds me that I need to miss practise after school. Heaving out a sigh, I find myself hoping the coach doesn't throw a fit again. It's happened before. He probably would have kicked me off the team if I weren't as tall as I am. Not that I blame Sammy for any of this - bless the kid. I blame my mum. But what can I do? Under no circumstance can I allow Sammy to know how screwed up our parents are, so my only choice is to do this.

"If it isn't Peter Woods, back from the grave."

I hear the voice behind me and brace myself for the social talk. And so the quiet time is over.

"Matt," I say, turning to greet him.

Matt's on the team, too. I wouldn't call us friends, exactly. We're more like two people on speaking terms. I haven't seen him since before Christmas. He's shaved the sides of his head off since then, leaving just a tower of black on top.

"Where the hell have you been hiding?" He asks as if I haven't already told him.

"My aunts."

"Was it good? Never mind, I have some big news for you." He glances to the side before leaning in closer. "Over the break, I overheard a girl saying she likes you."

Out of all the girls, Emily is the one who springs to my mind. It must be because she's told me she likes me before. But I rejected her then, so I doubt it's still the case. Sure, she still talks to me an awful lot - more than any other person does - but she's just that type of person. Come to think of it, how would Matt know anyway? As far as I'm aware, the two have never spoken a word to each other before. They could have bumped into each other over winter, but I doubt Emily would confess something so personal to a guy like Matt. Who-?

"Hannah Pierce," Matt answers my unspoken question.

Ah. Hannah Pierce - the school Queen Bee. Whenever I see her around the school, she's being followed around by her pack of cronies. I use the term *crony* instead of *friend* because they're always a step behind her, trailing as if she's their leader with them her subjects. The worst part is that Hannah is egotistic enough to allow it.

Why do I feel so disappointed?

When I refocus on Matt, I realise he's waiting for my response. Up here, someone is always waiting for me to say something, and it's never on a topic that interests me. "I don't like her back," is all I can give him.

"What, man, are you serious? She's the hottest girl in our school." He says this like it's the most important factor.

While I can't argue with the hot part - Hannah *is* a good-looking girl - the fact that she walks around like she owns the place is reasoning enough to put me off.

"If you like her so much, why don't you ask her out?" I say and then turn away. As I look out, I spot Emily walking through the gate. The sight of her tiny figure tottering in among the tall people makes me smile. She's basically half the size of everyone else coming in with her.

Today, she isn't walking in with Natasha, as she usually is. She's with that Harvey guy. While I'm not surprised the two of them get along - it makes sense, considering they're always getting into trouble in class together - I do wonder what it is they talk about. Not that it's any of my business.

If there is one thing I envy about Harvey, it's that easy way of his. The way he talks - so freely - it's something I can never achieve myself. It crosses my mind that if Emily did like someone, it would be him, not me. Not that I care.

I'm still watching her as she passes me. She usually waves, but she doesn't today. Oh wait, she's doing it now. I turn away, embarrassed at being caught looking, and then I feel like a jerk for ignoring her.

"I'll see you at lunch," I say to Matt before I swing beneath the railing to catch up to her.

My eyes are on Emily as I walk, but I feel someone tug on my arm, making me lose her in my distraction. When I turn, I find Hannah beside me. Her cronies aren't far behind, and I have to hold back a groan because the way they're looking at me means Matt might be right.

A little background on Hannah and me: we aren't friends. We barely speak - and, if ever we do, I get the sense she's not talking to listen. We're opposites in a very bad way. I continue walking and notice that she is now walking in with me.

"Did you have a nice break, Peter?" She asks. Before I have a second to answer, she continues, "mine was just *awful.* My dad took us to his lake house, and my sister annoyed me the entire time. Aren't younger siblings the worst? You have a younger sister, don't you? I bet she's annoying. And being back at school is such a *drag-*,"

I keep my eyes ahead as she continues talking. Emily is somewhere inside those doors, and I need her magical ability to appear out of nowhere now more than ever. She's probably the only one with enough nerve to interrupt a conversation, even if it's with Queen B.

We enter the doors, and I see her standing by the wall with Natasha. I almost sigh in relief. The problem is, she isn't looking our way. She still isn't looking. We continue walking, and the opportunity for her to see me is gone. I'll have to find some other way to-,

"Hey, Peter!" Somehow, Emily is right in front of me. I am looking down at her face, and I want to laugh. She really does appear out of nowhere. It baffles me enough that I want to hug her for doing it. I would if I weren't afraid of how she'd take it.

"Emily," I say, holding back a smile.

"Did you enjoy the flapjack?"

"I-," I clamp my mouth shut before I can admit to hating them. "I did."

She doesn't say anything else. Why isn't she saying anything else? She always comes up with some excuse for stopping me - one time it was to ask me to listen to a song, of all the things - I might not always say yes to it, but she asks.

"Come on, Peter." Hannah says, "or we'll be late for English."

Give me an excuse to stay, I beg with my eyes, but Emily isn't looking at me. Her eyes are on something further down. I start walking. When we get a few steps ahead, I realise that Hannah is holding my sleeve, and I tug my arm away.

"God, isn't that Emily girl annoying?" she says.

I stop walking. "I don't find her annoying at all."

"Oh." Hannah blinks. It satisfies me to see she didn't expect me to say that.

I do, of course, find Emily annoying, but I'll be damned if I let Hannah Pierce call her that.

In English, I take my usual seat by the window. I look out at the cloudy sky and wonder if I've done anything to annoy my neighbour. She doesn't seem like the type to get annoyed, but I wouldn't put it past myself, either. I've annoyed people before.

My suspicions intensify when she enters the room and walks straight past my desk without so much as a glance. I'm still wondering what I've done wrong when the teacher asks us to get into groups of four. Surely she'll ask me to be on her team. She always does. I wait for the question, but it doesn't come. I twist my head slightly, still expecting it, and I'm surprised that I can't hear her voice at all. Isn't she always talking? Maybe she's been abducted by aliens. Only something that insane can silence that girl. I'm about to turn to see if she's okay when I hear someone say my name.

It's Hannah asking me if I'll be on her team.

I really, really, don't want to pair with Hannah. Not only because I don't much enjoy her company, but I also don't want to give her even the slightest reason to believe I like her back. But how do I say no without sounding like a complete ass?

I need Emily to ask me. If she asks me now, I'll say yes. But her silence remains, so I feel forced to say,

"Sure."

I'M GOING TO GO FULL EMILY ON HIM

Emily

I've been sulking for the past thirty minutes, and I'm not proud of that. But every time I look across the room, all I see is Peter with Hannah. Talking, sharing notes, getting all cosy together. Okay, I may be running away with myself on that last point, but my brain can't help it.

Sighing, I sit up straight and hold out my hand. "Natasha, pass me the Wotsits."

No more sulking. No more looking across at Peter with sad eyes. It's time to fight. Because I am not Emily

Clarke if I am not a fighter.

"I'm not passing you the Wotsits." Natasha's refusal somewhat ruins my fighting spirit. Looking across the table at her, I see that she's still annoyed with me. I'm not entirely at fault, but I am part of her problem. When the teacher asked us to get into groups of four, there weren't enough students to go around, and our team ended up being a team of three. Natasha's problem is that our team includes Harvey and me. Put mine and Harvey's brainpower together, and you've got yourself a person. We may as well be a team of two.

I grab the Wotsits myself and stuff a handful into my mouth. We're sitting with our teams, and Harvey joined us, so we still have our table at the back of the room. This is good. It means I can hide behind the students in front of us while I eat my snacks.

"It's like the mess corner over here," Harvey complains, brushing orange powder off his sleeve. The powder leaves a horrible orange stain on his shirt, and I feel bad that I've done that to him.

"Do you want some?" I hold the bag out to him as a peace offering, but he pushes it away.

"Eating crisps this time in the morning is just wrong. And can you at least cover your mouth when you talk?"

"Sorry," I put a hand over my mouth and swallow.

"Could you two focus?" Natasha snaps. "We have a project to do here."

One look at her face moves Harvey and me into action. I pull a textbook toward me as Harvey does the same, but I've already forgotten what the teacher told us to do. Not wanting to ask Natasha *that* question, I look at the board in the hope it's been written down.

Peter is within my line of sight, and my eyes lose focus as I watch what he's doing. He taps a pencil against his lips, and I can't help but wonder what it would feel like to kiss those lips of his. He moves the pencil to his head, and my eyes move with it. Most of the boys in our year wear their hair slicked back, but not Peter. He lets his fall in perfect waves. I wonder if his hair feels as soft as it looks...

"You two have the attention span of a five-year-old." Natasha's curse snaps me back into the room. I look at Harvey, and I think he may have been falling asleep. He looks like my dad when my mum has control of the TV.

"Not true," he says, but he's wiping drool from his chin as he says it. Maybe this is why Natasha has never liked him back. I, at least, appreciate someone who falls asleep in class. If it's not me doing it, I'm glad somebody else is. It makes me feel better knowing I'm not alone.

"I wish you asked Peter." Natasha sighs again. It's funny how she's okay with my feelings for him when it suits her. Everyone knows he's the smartest one in class, and, on the occasions when he does say yes to me, it shows on our grades.

"Why the hell would Peter say yes to being on our team?" Harvey asks.

Natasha shrugs. "For Emily."

I like how Natasha says for Emily. I do not, however, like how Harvey is laughing at it.

"Yeah, because Emily asking will make Peter's answer any different." He chuckles. I throw a Wotsit at him. Unfortunately, he dodges out of the way, and it flies across the room.

"Emily Clarke, I saw that."

Oh no.

I duck my head as the teacher gets to her feet. Maybe if she can't see me, she'll assume I've apparated from the room.

"Come and put it in the bin." She orders.

With reluctance, I push my chair out and get to my feet. I keep my head down as I make the small steps over to the little orange Wotsit, which has fallen closer to the front than I realised. My cheeks burn as I near Peter's chair, but a glance tells me that he's not looking. His eyes are still concentrating on his work. Throwing the Wotsit in the bin, I turn back to my desk, but the teacher stops me.

"Would you like to tell your classmates what it is you threw across their class?"

How humiliating to be saying this. "A Wotsit."

Hearing a few of my classmates laugh, I duck my head lower.

"And are we allowed to eat Wotsits in this class?"

"No, miss."

"Go back to your seat. And don't let me see you doing it again."

"Yes, miss." It's hard not to run back to my seat. It's

all I want to do so I can bury my face in my hands.

"I'm sorry," Harvey apologises as I sit down. "If I knew that would happen, I would have taken the hit."

"It's okay," I sigh. "I've experienced worse."

It's true. Throughout my sixteen years, I've come across enough embarrassing moments to last a lifetime. Like the time I walked around with gum on my skirt. Or the time I attempted to dye my hair blonde, and it came out ginger. Not a nice ginger, either; more like the colour of my Wotsits ginger. I brush it off quickly if it's not in front of Peter. If it is in front of Peter, I feel the urge to cry. At least he hadn't been looking.

Although we work hard on the project for the rest of the hour, I feel bad for Natasha having to pair with the two of us. We try, but we still don't get very far. On the upside, I know what we're doing now. We're creating a flyer and poster for a book event. The class is supposed to vote on the best one at the end, and let me tell you this now, it's not going to be ours.

I'm happy when the bell rings to mark the end of class because I have a new plan ready to put into motion. My happiness lasts one whole second, and then the teacher crushes it by telling us to bring our homework to the front.

"I didn't know we had English homework," I whisper to Natasha in horror.

She just shakes her head at me like this is something she expected. "The first day back, and she doesn't have her homework. Tut. Tut."

"I don't have it *because* it's the first day back." I defend. "What person remembers to bring homework on their first day back to school?" Even as I say this, my heart rate is picking up. *Why do they set homework over Christmas break?*

"Every student in the class," Natasha retorts.

I look around. She's right. Not a single person is having that awkward conversation with the teacher about how their dog ate their homework. Or, in my case, my cat. At least I have Harvey to rely on for not doing it. I follow behind him as we make our way to the front, letting him be the one to go first. Then, of all the treacherous and horrifying things, I see Harvey pull a sheet out of his bag and toss it onto the teacher's desk. I'm so shocked at what I see that my mouth drops open.

"Your homework, Emily?"

"I, um-," Peter steps beside me, and I lose my thought process for a second. He's close enough that warmth radiates from his skin onto mine. I catch his eye and look away lightning-fast. "I don't have it," I admit, cringing as Peter drops his homework and walks out.

"First, you throw a Wotsit in my classroom, and now you don't have your homework." The teacher sighs. "I'm sorry, Emily, but I'll need to see you after school in detention for this."

"That sounds fair." I duck my head as I walk out of the room. Detention on my first day back - that's a record for me.

Natasha pounces on me as soon as I'm in the hallway.

"I have news for you," she says, looping her arm in mine. "Peter and Hannah are not a thing."

Suddenly, detention doesn't seem so bad. I bite my lip as the smile creeps in. "Don't mess with me, Natasha. How do you know that?"

"Because I just asked him."

"You *what*?" I pull her to a stop. "Why did you do that? What did you say? What did he say?"

We start walking again. I lean close to her as if this will somehow help me hear better. "Well, I asked if he's going out with her, and he said no. And then I asked if he liked her, and he said no. And then I asked if he likes anyone else, and he said no to that, too." Her lip pulls down at this last part, but I don't mind. It's okay that he doesn't like anyone – it means there's room for me.

"I think I know how to win him over," I say, letting the smile surface now.

"How so?"

"I'm going to go full Emily on him."

She stops. With my arm looped in hers, I stop with her. "I don't think that's a good idea."

"I have to agree with Natasha here." Where on Earth did Harvey come from? "I don't know what 'full Emily' is, but it's not a good idea."

"But full Emily is me releasing my inner charm," I say, wounded by the double rejection. "You know, I'll talk to him more, let him see how funny I am. Ooh, I'll get a bike so we can ride to school together!"

37

"Let me stop you right there." Harvey holds a finger up to my face. "As a man, I know the way into a man's heart, and that is not the way. But, since I like your determination, I'm going to help you win him over."

"*You're* going to help her?" Natasha scoffs.

"I got myself a girlfriend, didn't I?"

Before Harvey can see the colour rising on Natasha's cheeks, I quickly ask, "what do you think I should do?"

"First, tell me who the guy is, so I know what we're working with."

"Peter Woods."

"Oooft." I don't like *oooft*. What does *oooft* mean? "Peter Woods might be a challenge since his heart is colder than the average males-"

"No, it's not!"

"-But I think we can do it. What you need to do is act like you're not interested. Don't say hi, don't wave, don't make eye contact. If he passes you in the hall, you turn the other way. You got that?"

I exchange a look with Natasha. We both know that what he's asking is close to an impossible task for me.

But I do it. At least, I try to do it. It goes pretty well at first. In math, I don't look at Peter once. Not even a glance. I'm really proud of this feat because he looks double cute when he concentrates, and math makes him do this a lot. I don't wave at him when he enters the cafeteria at lunch, and I don't stop him on our way to p.e. - something I usually do to ask how his day has been. It gets difficult around this point. As I walk down the hall, I bump into Peter. He looks down at me with this expression which makes me think he wants to say something, but he doesn't. I somehow manage to pull myself away, but it is a very close call. So, it all goes well. Until the bell rings for the end of school and I see Peter leaving.

"Isn't it basketball practise after school today?" I ask Harvey, frowning at Peter's downcast face as he leaves the school doors.

"Um, yeah, but I don't play. Why?"

"Because Peter's going home." I'm still watching him, but I notice Harvey and Natasha exchange a look from the corner of my eye.

"I overheard him tell the coach he can't make it," Harvey says. "But remember what I said, Emily. You can't show any interest in him."

"Don't do it, Emily," Natasha adds.

"But he loves playing basketball," I say, looking at them both in turn. When I see their disapproval, I decide at that moment that Peter's happiness is more important to me than winning him like this. And I make a run for it.

"Hey, Peter!" I call, chasing after him. He stops still. His back is to me, so I run around to face him, momentarily bedazzled by that face of his. This is not the time to be dazzled. "Isn't it basketball practice today?" I ask. "Why aren't you going?"

"I'm picking Sammy up from school."

I can tell that he doesn't want to do this, and I wonder why his mum can't do it instead.

"Let me do it," I say.

He shakes his head. "You can't."

A feeling that I rarely feel suddenly rises to the surface. He always does this. Whenever he receives an offer to help, he rejects it. Not just from me, either. His mum once told my dad that their shower broke, and my dad offered to fix it. Peter said no. He had to do it himself, even though it was clear he had no idea how. And I'm angry about it.

"You know what, Peter? If you keep rejecting kindness from others, you're going to end up unhappy and alone." I say. "I only offered because I know you love basketball. And why can't I do it? What's so wrong with accepting my help? Is it really that horrible?"

I wait for him to respond, still reeling from my unexpected anger. I just wish he'd let me - or *anyone* - help him. Because sometimes it's okay to not go at it alone.

As my anger still boils, I'm surprised to see his lips pull up at the corner. My breathing hitches as he places his hands on my shoulders, bending his head so that his eyes are level with mine. I watch as the smile appears again, and then I look back at his eyes. Before I can think about what's happening or get lost in them, he spins me around.

"You have detention, remember?" He says, and then he gives me a little nudge back to the school.

HAS SHE
FORGOTTEN
SHE HAS
DETENTION?

Peter

I f you can send help, please do.

Maybe that's a little dramatic. I guess this is not as bad as it could be, depending on how you look at it. On the one hand, I have to sit with Hannah, and her lead crony Jenna, for the next few weeks of English class. And they like to talk. A lot. Our fourth team member, Jim, also likes to talk a lot, except in his case, he tells jokes that aren't at all funny. Do you know how hard it is to sit and listen to an unfunny joke? Am I supposed to laugh or do I tell him to stop? I'm leaning toward the latter, but I think I'd be a jerk if I did that.

On the other hand, at least my team does the work. Even with the talking and the joking, I can see that progress has been made. We're currently designing posters for a made-up book event. I'm on leaflet duty, Hannah and Jenna are working on the poster, and Jim is writing down the key details we need to include. Boring, I know.

If I look around the room, I can see that not all teams are making progress. Liam, for example, is making a paper aeroplane. Sasha is on her phone. And Emily is- staring at me. I pause with my pencil on my lip. Is she daydreaming? She must be, or she would have looked away in embarrassment by now. I move the pencil up to my head, and her eyes follow. What is she thinking about? I realise I may not want to know and flick my eyes across to Harvey. It looks as if he's falling asleep.

A daydreamer and a sleeper. If Emily ever asks me why I say no to being on her team, I'll give her this reason. They make my group seem like a golden ticket.

"So, Peter," Hannah says, bringing my attention back to the table. "I'm thinking of watching the basketball practice after school. Do you want me there?"

For a second, I wonder if I've missed the last few minutes of conversation because why would I want her there? Then I realise she's hoping I'll say yes, and I shake my head.

"I'm not going. I'm picking my little brother up from school." I can't help the sigh that comes every time I think or say this.

"I thought you had a little sister?" She asks.

"No. He's a brother."

She looks unconvinced, and it annoys me. Does she want me to convince her otherwise?

"I have this funny joke," - oh no - "about little brothers," - please no - "it goes like this-"

"Emily Clarke, I saw that."

I sigh in relief as the teacher interrupts Jim's would-be little brother joke. And, of course, it's Emily Clarke who does the interrupting. I swear there isn't a day that goes by where she isn't getting into trouble about one thing or another. I look across at her, wondering what she's done this time, but she's disappeared. Lifting my head, I find her crouching low in her seat. Does she really think that's going to save her from Miss Gardner?

"Come and put it in the bin." The teacher orders.

I watch as Emily gets slowly to her feet. I do feel for her. Then again, she's done this to herself, whatever it is she did.

As she nears my desk, I notice how embarrassed she is, and I look away. From experience, whenever Emily catches me looking at her, her cheeks turn a deeper shade of red. I think I might have caught her crying once, so I do this - pretend to concentrate hard on my work - as a precaution. Still, it isn't easy keeping my eyes away as she bends to pick up this mysterious object.

I'm glad when the teacher asks my burning question for me.

"Would you like to tell your classmates what it is you threw across their class?"

"A Wotsit."

It takes a lot of effort not to laugh with the rest of the class. A Wotsit? And I'm not even surprised.

When she goes back to her seat, I finally look away from my work.

"Who throws Wotsits in class?" Jenna laughs. I hate that sound. It's that fake, unpleasant laugh people use to cover up the fact they're being mean.

"She's so embarrassing, isn't she?" Hannah joins in. "How childish of her."

"Did you see her face? I think she had orange around her mouth."

They both laugh. I clench my fist. It pisses me off when people feel the need to say mean things behind a person's back. At least Emily would have the guts to say it to their face. Actually, scrap that. I don't think Emily would say this at all.

"If the two of you have done prattling, could we get back to the project?" I say. It shuts them up, at least.

When the bell rings, I let Hannah leave first. I take extra long packing my bag just to make sure she isn't waiting for me outside. I can't be sure Hannah would do that, but I'm not taking any chances. As I unpack my homework, I spot Emily as she passes me, and I jump to my feet because I'm still not sure if I've done something to annoy her. I step beside her and look down. When I see how close I am to her and that she's looking back at me, I shoot my eyes away.

"I left it at home." She says. It takes me a moment to realise she's talking to the teacher, telling her about her homework. It takes me another moment to realise she sounds embarrassed by it. I drop my homework and walk out, just in case she doesn't like that I'm here. I hear the teacher give her detention and sigh. Ah, Emily. You're always getting yourself into trouble.

"Peter?" I jump at the sound of my name. It isn't Hannah, as I feared. It's Natasha. What could Natasha want with me?

"What's up?" I ask, stepping closer. She looks out of her comfort zone, and it doesn't surprise me. Even though Natasha is often round at Emily's, and I bump into her on our street, we've never actually talked. She's different from my neighbour. She's... well, a little scary.

"Are you and Hannah dating now?" She asks.

I blink in surprise. Why this question? Wait - has she heard something? "No," I answer.

"Do you like her?"

Easy. "No."

"Do you like anyone?"

I pause. It's not because I have someone in mind. It's because I'm wondering why on Earth she's asking me these questions. "No," I say. When it doesn't seem like she'll ask me anything else, I turn and walk away.

We have math next, and I like math. You probably think this statement is abnormal. In a way, it is, but there's just something about problem-solving that feels therapeutic to me. When I'm concentrating on a problem, nothing else is going on in my mind. It's just me and the sheet in front of me. As a person who thinks a lot and about things he doesn't want to think about, having this distraction is a good thing.

The rest of the day passes by uneventfully. I have my tuna sandwich at lunch - my least favourite part of the day - and then I walk over to the locker rooms to change for p.e. We're running the track today, even though it's freezing outside. Just another example of how grown-ups can make questionable decisions.

"What are you thinking about?" Matt asks while we walk.

I hadn't been aware that he was walking beside me. "Me? Nothing. Why?"

"It looks like you're thinking about something."

It had actually just crossed my mind that Emily hasn't stopped to talk to me since this morning, but I'm not about to tell him that. I need to snap myself out of this, anyway. What does it matter if she's talked to me or not? What does it matter if I've annoyed her? I'm struggling to understand why I care because it's good if she's finally decided to leave me alone.

"You're definitely thinking about something," Matt says again.

I shake my head, more to shake the thoughts from it, and then enter the locker rooms. It's easy to find a quiet corner in here, but I need to do something first. Heading over to the coach's office, I knock on the door and enter, bracing myself to tell him about practice.

"We have a match in a month, Peter." He says after I break the news. He's sat behind his desk and looking at me with disappointment in his eyes. "You told me this wouldn't happen again."

I didn't think it would. "I'm sorry. I wish I could say it this time, but-,"

"You can't." He sighs. "I am sorry, Peter, but it's not fair on the other boys. If this happens again, I *will* bench you."

"I understand," I say. And I do - but it still sucks.

When I leave, Harvey is standing right outside the door, and it looks as if he's been listening. We stare at each other for a second before I swoop around and pass him. Just like Natasha, I haven't exchanged much more than a word with Harvey in the five years we've been here. It's not that I haven't wanted to. I'm just not good at starting a conversation.

Part of me thinks it's good that we're out in the cold. As I run around the track, the icy air helps quiet my mind, and things become clearer. If I'm honest with myself, I am bothered that Emily seems to be ignoring me. I don't want to be a cause of annoyance for her like my mum is for me. Being annoyed sucks.

I decide to confront her. I don't know what I'm going to say, but I want to make sure we're fine. I see her leave the gym and walk up to her, only to do a full swivel at the last moment, running a hand through my hair as I walk in the opposite direction. I hope no-body saw that.

Why is this so hard? The next time I see her, I walk up to her, but I can't think of any words to say. She just looks at me with these wide eyes and then walks away. I wonder how she does it. I mean, out of all the years that we've talked, how many of those times has it been her coming up to me?

When I walk out of school, I have two things on my mind. First, missing basketball practice; second, missing the chance to find out what I've done wrong to Emily. It's too late now since she'll be in detention. It's probably for the best, anyway. I am not a good friend for her.

"Hey, Peter!" I freeze. Was it all in my head? That's Emily's voice - and it sounds like it always does. Maybe she isn't annoyed with me after all. She appears in front of me, and I have this feeling when I see her face, but I can't put my finger on what it is. I've never felt it before. "Isn't it basketball practice today?" She asks. "Why aren't you going?"

Ah, basketball practice. "I'm picking Sammy up today," I tell her.

"Let me do it."

Has she forgotten she has detention? "You can't."

A look crosses over her eyes. A look that makes me want to take a step back because I've never seen this look on this face before.

"You know what, Peter?" She says, and I know I'm not mistaken - she's angry. Angry enough that she's now drilling into me about how I'll end up sad and alone. I can see where she's coming from - I do have an issue with accepting help from people. But, when my dad isn't around, I've learned that it's important I can do all that stuff myself.

I don't think I have ever seen Emily Clarke angry before. For some reason, seeing it brings a smile to my lips. I bend down and grab her shoulders. They feel so small in my hands. Small, but not fragile. When I see that the look in her eyes isn't angry anymore, I smile again and turn her.

"You have detention, remember?" I say, and then I give her a little push back to the school.

I LOOK LIKE HAGRID

Emily

By the time Sunday arrives, I'm exhausted from all the homework I've needed to catch up on. At least Natasha is coming over today. I'm excited because she's bringing her curlers with her, and I'm about to achieve that super-model hair. Harvey will say that I'm doing this because of him, but I'm not. He's actually taking this make-Peter-fall-for-Emily mission more seriously than I thought he would. After I failed to follow his first advice – avoid Peter – he gave me a second tip. Try to be "hotter".

Answer me this – why would I want Peter to fall for me because of how I look? Is that even possible? What will happen when I have one of my pimple break-outs, or I stand next to a girl like Hannah? Will Peter stop loving me then? He will do if all he cares about is how I look.

I don't want any of that. I want Peter to think I'm cute even when I have pimples on my face, just like I think he's cute when I catch him taking the trash out in his *Super Mario* onesie. Catching Peter in the *Super Mario* onesie is probably the only time I've seen him blush, and it was the cutest thing. Now I know that embarrassed Peter should not be allowed to exist in this world. The adorableness of it causes the heart to explode.

No. I'm not having my hair curled because Harvey said I should. I'm having it curled because I want it curled.

"Emily, Natasha is here!" My mum calls, and I feel a jolt of excitement.

"Coming!" I look down at my lap, where Blondie is currently curled up asleep, and I wonder for a second if I can leave Natasha waiting. No, she'll probably leave if I do. She's fierce like that. "Sorry, Blondie," I say, pushing the ginger fur-ball off me. I give her a quick scratch behind the ear before leaving, just to make sure she doesn't hate me for doing this. She can be temperamental.

Natasha snaps her curlers at me when I reach the front door. "Ready?"

"I'm so ready," I pull her inside and drag her straight upstairs, taking two steps at a time. I can hear my mum mumbling something downstairs, and I remember she hates when I do this. It makes her think I'm up to something devious when I'm not.

"Wow, I feel like I haven't been in your room in forever," Natasha says, dropping her stuff on my bed as I close the door.

"I've only been grounded for a week," I say. Grounded. Doesn't that word make you want to barf? I've been under house arrest ever since I got detention on Monday. The joke is on my mum, though, because I don't have a social life on a school night anyway. All I want to do on weekdays is eat, listen to music, and sleep.

Thinking of detention reminds me of my moment with Peter, and I have to swallow down my giddiness. I can still feel his hand on my shoulder from when he touched it. And his eyes. Wow! Those eyes-

"Has Blondie put on weight?"

I shoot Natasha a dirty look and bend to cover Blondie's ears. "Do you mind? She's right here."

"It's not like she can understand what we're saying."

"She's a very intelligent cat, for your information."

She rolls her eyes. "Get on the chair, Emily, before I decide to leave."

I do as she says because Natasha does not kid.

It takes her a while to curl my hair, something she does with a look of intense concentration. I admire this look because I can never seem to concentrate for this long myself. We take a snack break halfway through and find my mum in the front room, scrolling on her iPad with a plate of melon. We don't want melon. My dad is sitting next to her and has control of the TV again.

"Do we have any chocolate in?" I ask either one of them.

Of course, it's my mum who answers. My dad's too busy being absorbed in Netflix. "No. I told you I'm not buying that stuff anymore. You eat far too much of it."

"But mum-," I start to complain before she cuts me off.

"But nothing. If you want to eat that rubbish, you buy it yourself."

"Fine. We'll go to the corner shop, then."

"Ooh, could you get me a pot noodle?" My dad asks. Only food can capture his attention.

My mum hits his arm with a "Paul!" and that's my cue to pull Natasha from the room. "You are not a good influence on our daughter," we hear her continue, "don't get him the noodles, Emily!"

"Don't listen to your mother, Emily!"

I'll decide which parent to listen to when I get to the shop. Probably mum, since she uses the 'grounded' word more often.

The shop is up a hill. I gasp when we reach it because my fitness level does not meet the demands of uphill, and my keen-eyed friend notices.

"I'm sorry to say this, Em, but you need to exercise more. You look a right state."

Thanks, Natasha. I'd say this out loud, but I haven't caught my breath yet. I hold my rib with one hand and suck in a deep breath as someone leaves the store.

Oh my Goodness.

"Peter!" I'm so excited to see him that I manage to half-rasp, half-shout his name.

He stops still in the doorway and looks at me. He's wearing his grey hoodie - it's my favourite - with headphones around his neck, and his hair is scruffier than usual. What would it take to get him to keep it this way?

"Oh - um-," he moves his eyes to the side without saying anything else.

Understanding this awkwardness of his, I smile and try to help. "Have you had a good weekend?"

"I-," before he can say more than this, I feel Natasha's hand on mine, and she pulls me into the store with a, "sorry, Peter, we're in a hurry!"

"We aren't in a hurry!" I say, shooting her a wounded look as I lose sight of him. She pulls me to a stop in the toilet paper aisle.

"Do you want him to see you looking like this?" She indicates my face with her hands. My cheeks drain of colour.

"How bad do I look?"

"One side of your head is curly, the other is in a ponytail, and your face is as red as a beetroot." I cover my face as she adds, "and those are the oldest pair of sweats I've ever seen."

"Do you think he noticed?"

As she sighs, I peek through my fingers to find her storming ahead. She zigzags through the aisles and then makes her way to the checkout before circling back to me. "Let's go make you look like the Queen you are," she says, flicking my hair with a smile. I follow her out with a grin. I love this girl.

The good thing about the shop being uphill is that the way back is down. No gasping this time around. We pass Peter's house on the way to mine, and I look at the light in his hallway, wondering if I'll get to see him again tonight.

"Do you think Peter catches you gawking at his house?" Natasha asks.

Crap, does he? I divert my eyes to the house next door as if I'm interested in this one, too. Just in case this doesn't work, I look up at the sky and nod my head like I've noticed something interesting. Saved it.

Back at my house, I throw the pot noodle to my dad and then drag Natasha upstairs again. She spends the next half-hour curling the other side of my hair while she nibbles on a bag of cookies and drops crumbs on my floor. I eye them with evils.

"Do you think Harvey actually has a girlfriend?" She asks suddenly.

"I don't see why he'd lie," I say and then narrow my eyes. "Why?"

"Nothing," she shakes her head, but I sense there's more.

"Natasha Painter, do you like him?"

"Ew, Emily, gross." She swats my arm, and I have to laugh at her.

"Come on, Harvey isn't gross." He may pick his nose from time to time, but I think everyone does that, so I won't hold it against him.

Natasha finishes with the curls and then sprays them with something sticky.

"Do not touch it." She warns. "I'll know if you did."

"I wouldn't dare," I say, admiring myself in the mirror. It never looks this way when I do it myself.

She leaves before her dad can call her, and I finally start the last of my homework. I'm still doing it when my mum pokes her head around my door.

"Privacy, mum," I complain. She *never* knocks.

"Are you doing your homework?"

This is one of the rare times when I'm telling the truth. "Yes." I glance at her, wondering when she'll leave, but she comes and sits on my bed instead.

"Your hair looks lovely. Did Natasha do this?"

I grin. "Yep. It looks good, doesn't it? I can't wait to show it off at school tomorrow!"

"But won't you lose the curls by the morning?"

"Will I?" I look down at them and frown. I don't want to lose them - I just got them.

"Trust me on this, honey. My girlfriends and I used to curl our hair all the time, and we-" whenever my mum starts to tell me about one of her *back in the day* stories, I sing a song in my head. I do this now until I realise she's pulling my chair toward her and is touching my precious curls.

"Natasha told me not to touch them," I protest, dodging out of her way.

"Trust me. I know what I'm doing. The curls will still be there in the morning." She looks so happy as she plays with my hair that I can't bring myself to tell her to stop, but I really want her to stop.

I should have told her to stop.

My hair does not look good when I take the plaits out in the morning. I look like the book version of Hermione Granger. No, I'm wrong. I look like Hagrid. On his absolute worst day. My hair is so bushy it may as well be a nest. Maybe a bird will see me and take a seat on it.

I enter the kitchen and catch my mum's eye. She puts a hand to her mouth and steps back, confirming how bad I look. "Your hair-"

"Please don't speak to me today," I say. "I am very unhappy with you."

"Oh, Emily-,"

I grab a breakfast bar and turn away. I'm already running late, and that's because I've been failing to sort this hair out. Peter has probably already left. Then again, that's a good thing. I can't have Peter Woods seeing me like this! At least in class, I might be able to hide behind the other students.

I leave the house and see him wheeling his bike out of his garden. My heart soars when I see he's still here, and then it sinks in mortification. I quickly turn and bend to tie my shoe. My heart is pounding. It doesn't help that I don't have shoelaces, so I'm just making knot shapes in the air.

"Morning," I hear him say.

Wait, is he saying that to me? I turn my head, unable to stop myself, and grin when I see that he is. Progress! "Good morning!"

His eyes are on my face, but they slowly move up to my hair. He blinks, and then the best and worst thing happens. Peter Woods bursts out laughing.

DO WE HAVE ANY CUTE NEIGHBOURS?

Peter

I 've been babysitting Sammy all weekend. It hasn't been as bad as it sounds, either, because as far as little brothers go, I got pretty lucky with mine.

Sammy is a sweet kid. A kid who doesn't deserve the hand he's been dealt. If there is one saving grace to it all, it's that he has no idea how bad things are, and I'm holding onto the hope that my mum and dad sort their crap out before he finally realises. Don't get me wrong, he can annoy the hell out of me at times, and I'm far from being a good big brother. Sometimes I get annoyed with him for the wrong reasons - like when my mum does something for him that she'd never do for me - and I hate myself when that happens. It isn't his fault, and he doesn't deserve to get snapped at for it, so why can't I help it? Those times, Sammy goes out of his way to make sure *I'm* alright. Me. Like I say, sweet kid.

He's been no trouble at all this weekend. Believe it or not, he's spent most of the time either doing his homework or playing with his toy robots. Now and then, he's asked the awkward question of when my dad will be home. My answer is always 'I'm not sure'. But I wish I did have the answer to that one, Sammy.

It's been good getting to spend some time with him. Even so, there are times when a person just wants to be alone. That's why I'm glad my mum is finally home. She may be nursing a hangover, but at least she's here. She went out last night with one of our neighbours - some woman who's just moved here - and don't ask me how those two met because I don't want to know myself. At least she asked me if I was okay with looking after him this time. I said yes because I think it's a good thing she has a new friend, but I do wonder what she would have done if I'd said no.

I throw on the first hoodie I can find and go downstairs, finding my mum led on the sofa with a bag of frozen peas on her head. I smile when I see Sammy sitting next to her. He won't admit it, but he's missed her. I close the door on them and head to the kitchen.

After gulping down a glass of water, I check the cupboards. We need food. While I don't want to interrupt my mum when she's like this, I don't have any other choice if I want us to eat tonight.

"Mum?" I ask, approaching with caution. A groan tells me she's listening. "We need some food in." Another groan. "I can go to the shop if you want."

She waves her hand in my direction, and I realise I'm not going to get much from her. "Ask me later. My head is splitting."

"Fine," turning away, my eyes fall on one of my spare basketballs wedged between Sammy's bike and a pile of bags. May as well get some of that alone time in.

A good thing about my house is that it's around the corner of a basketball court. It's nothing special, basically an outdoor hoop with some running space - but it's always empty. I come here when I need to clear my head or just get some practice in. Today is the perfect day for it. While it's cold, it hasn't rained for days, so there's no longer any ice on the ground.

When I say it's always empty, there have been some exceptions. I find Emily here from time to time, trying to play. Seeing her here surprised me at first, but then I realised she needs practice more than I do. More than anyone, even - because I can't even describe how bad she is at it. Her shots go *way* past the mark, and I sometimes find it fun just watching her try.

As I start bouncing the ball, the relief is instant. It's easy to forget everything when I'm out here and pretend like everything is normal. Whatever normal is. I make a shot, and I'm glad to see I've still got it, despite not getting any practice in over Christmas. If I play good in front of the coach, there's a chance he won't bench me.

I go for about an hour when I notice someone walking toward me. It seems like he may go around at first, but then he gets too close, and that possibility disappears.

"Hey, man," he says, smiling as he stops in front of me. I hold the ball under my arm as I analyse him. He's not someone I've seen around here before, but it looks like he might be my age - a few inches shorter, with hair trimmed close to his head, and a face that screams 'let's be friends'.

"Hey," I say.

"Can I join you?" I hold back a groan. *Definitely* the friendly type. Not that being friendly is a bad thing - I just don't know how to be around people like this. But then, it might be good having someone to practice with. I toss him the ball.

"I haven't seen you around here," I say as he starts dribbling it. Good hand.

"I've just moved here. I live around the corner - you know Queens Street?" - I do, it's the street next to mine - "I live there. I saw you out here, and I thought I'd come and introduce myself. I'm Ben."

"Peter." He passes the ball back to me, and I shoot.

"What school do you go to, Peter? I'm about to start Woodshaw tomorrow. Do you know that one?"

"I do. I go there."

His face splits into a grin, making me panic that he's going to want to walk in with me. "What year are you? I'm in my last one. Not a great time to move, right? But my mum got a new job, so here I am."

"I'm last year, too. We could use someone like you on the team."

"Really?" His grin somehow widens even further as he takes a shot. "I'd love to be on the team." After a few minutes of silent play, he asks, "What about the girls? Are there any cute ones who go there?"

I almost sigh at the typical question. "You'll have to decide that for yourself."

"Oh." He seems disappointed by my answer, but he only has a day to wait before he can find it out. "What about around here? Do we have any cute neighbours?"

I pause with the ball in the air. "Not that I can think of."

"Sounds about right," he sighs. "I move a lot, but I never get a cute neighbour. Damn it."

I can't help but smirk at his colossal disappointment. "We do have a chatty one, and she's alright."

"What's her name?"

"Emily."

"Emily," the way he says it, it's like he's tasting her name on his lips. "I can't wait to meet her."

I take the shot, but it goes wide this time. It doesn't matter. I'm ready to leave now. "Well, it was nice meeting you, Ben. See you tomorrow."

"Oh, okay. You too, Peter."

I nod my head. He seems alright, and I can't see him

having any problems making other friends at school tomorrow.

When I get home, I realise just how hungry I am. I check the fridge and groan when I remember we still need food. My mum is still in the front room, suffering from her hangover, but at least now she's in a sitting position.

"Where's Sammy?" I ask.

"In his bedroom."

I make my way over to it and knock on his door. "What do you want for tea, Sammy?"

"Um... potato waffles and chicken dinosaurs?"

That's what you get for asking a seven-year-old. "Coming right up." I go back to my mum. "Can I have some money? We need food."

"There's some change in my bag," she nods her head, and I turn for it until she stops me with my name. I glance back, and I'm surprised by the some-what tender look in her eye. "Thanks for watching Sammy this weekend. I appreciate it."

For a second, all I can do is stare at her. "You're welcome, mum." *And thanks for saying thanks.*

The shop isn't far away. I listen to music as I walk, and it's actually kind of nice. Inside, I grab Sammy's requested items, and then I grab a fizzy drink because I know my mum likes these when she's not feeling well. I take them to the checkout before I head back out, where I come face-to-face with Emily.

"Peter!" She pants. Did she run here? I look down at her beaming face, and I wonder again how she manages to look this happy all of the time.

"I - um-," I realise that her hair looks a bit weird, but I'm sure she knows this already. After living across the street from her for several years, I no longer bat an eye at this stuff. Has your neighbour ever run out in fluffy pink pyjamas before? Mine has, just to chase the ice cream van.

Noticing Natasha's eyes on me, I look away.

"Did you have a good weekend?"

"I-"

"Sorry, Peter, we're in a hurry!"

I can't decide whether or not I'm grateful for Natasha's interruption. They go inside, and I catch a final glimpse of Emily's desperate face as she gets pulled away. I can't help but smile at that. It makes me think she wants to stay out here because it's me. No. What kind of thought is that?

The rest of my night is spent in my room studying. I've already done the homework stuff, so I move on to whatever I think will crop up next. People often tell me that I'm naturally brainy. They're wrong about this. I spend most of my nights doing this - burying myself in schoolbooks - and that's so I can one day take care of myself. And Sammy, if he needs it.

In the morning, my mum complains to me about how her hangovers now last two days instead of one. I help her with Sammy's lunch and then get ready to leave. I'm running late, but I don't mind it so much today.

Outside, I spot Emily in her garden, crouching

down with her back to me. I wheel my bike onto the path and pause, looking over at her. She's taking a long time. I give it a few more seconds before I shrug it off and leave. But then, she's always the one to approach me first.

I turn back. "Morning."

"Good morning!" She spins to face me so fast that it takes a second for my eyes to focus. When they do, I notice that her head looks bigger than usual. I look up at her hair and blink. Forget the pink, fluffy pyjamas - now *this* is a look I haven't seen before. Emily's hair usually falls flat against her head, but today it's five times the size it usually is. The best way to describe it is that it looks as if she's been electrocuted.

But it isn't the hair that makes me laugh. It's the look of sheer mortification I notice on her face as if she forgot her hair looks like this. Is this why she spent so long crouched over her shoes - because she didn't want me to see it? I laugh again, and then out of no-where, Ben's question replays in my mind. *Do we have any cute neighbours?* I guess we do have one.

I'M GOING
TO BAKE HER
A CAKE

Emily

There is a chance that I may never move from this spot. Peter left some time ago, and my eyes are still glued to where I last saw him.

He called me mini-Hagrid. Right after he laughed, that's what he said. I am mortified.

Before I can convince myself to run back inside my house, I force my feet into a walk. Natasha will hate me if I leave her alone with Harvey in English, and I couldn't do that to her. I think of Peter as I walk, of that amused chuckle I heard as he wheeled his bike away. My mind is so preoccupied with this that I don't realise what I'm doing until somebody points it out.

"If you keep kicking those stones, you'll end up taking somebody's eye out."

I glance to the side and find a boy standing a few feet away from me. I've never seen him before, but I notice he's in my school uniform. This is enough to pique my curiosity.

"Who are you?" I ask. "I don't think I've seen you at school before."

"Today's my first day." He tugs on the straps of his backpack with a smile. "I'm new. Just moved onto the street next to this one."

A new neighbour! Yes!

I swallow down my enthusiasm as I say, "oh, that's cool," because I don't want to come across as too 'Emilyish' on our first meeting. Too 'Emilyish' is what my mum likes to call it when I supposedly scare someone away for being my energetic self. I don't think I've actually scared anyone away before, but I don't want to risk it with this guy because we rarely get any new neighbour's around here. My last one was Peter, and I hit the jackpot with him.

"I'm Emily," I tell him, holding out my hand. He shakes it with an odd look in his eyes, and I realise that people our age don't actually shake hands.

"Emily. I'm Ben."

"Would you like to walk to school with me, Ben? I have to meet my friend, Natasha, but she won't mind."

"I'd love to," his grin tells me that I like him already.

"Are you sure she won't mind?"

"Oh, she definitely won't." At least, I think. Natasha is as temperamental as my cat.

We start walking. As I peek at Ben, I can't help but think how scary this must be for him. I'd hate to join a new school this late in the year. I glance at him, and he doesn't seem nervous, but you can never be too sure.

"How are you feeling?" I ask. "Nervous?"

He shrugs. "Not really. I move a lot, so I'm used to it. My mum has to relocate for her job," he adds, seeing that I was about to ask.

"Well, you don't have to be nervous at all. It's a good school. At least, I think it is. I'm sure many will disagree. Not to scare you off," I add quickly. "You can sit with Natasha and me at lunch. This guy Harvey recently joined us, too. Natasha isn't happy about that, but I don't mind. You'll like Harvey, I think. he's-," I see a smirk on his face and stop talking. "What?"

"Nothing," he laughs. "It's just, you really are chatty, aren't you?"

"Who told you that?"

"This guy Peter-,"

"You met Peter!" The burst of enthusiasm comes out before I can stop it. And it's not just any enthusiasm, either - it's Peter enthusiasm - the only enthusiasm that may well scare someone away. I bite my lip. "Sorry. Continue."

"Yeah," he looks at me with a frown, "I met him at the courts yesterday. He doesn't say much, does he?"

"Not everybody does," I say, hoping he hasn't judged

Peter too quickly, "but that doesn't mean they aren't great people."

He gives me a long look before he agrees with me. Maybe mine warns him that this girl doesn't tolerate anything anti-Peter. We are pro-Peter around here.

Natasha's eyes are like two snipers aimed at Ben when we reach her, and I try to flag her down. Not now, Natasha. She gives him a long, inspector-y glance that makes me fear for him. Luckily for Ben, he tells her that he wants in on the snacks, and I know he's going to be okay. Snacks are the way into Natasha's heart.

"I think I'm going to like you, Ben," she tells him with a smile. As she turns to face me, her smile disappears. "What the hell happened to your hair?"

What? Oh. Crap. My hair. I've been so excited about getting a new neighbour that I forgot about what a complete mess it is. The bad thing is that Ben hasn't said a word about it, which means he must think that I always look like this. Great first impression, Emily!

I lower my head and mumble, "my mum did it."

"What?"

I can see this amused smile on Ben's face as I mumble once more, "my mum did it."

"I can't hear you."

"My mum did it!"

Ben snorts out a laugh as I storm into the store. Natasha follows me inside. "You could at least have put it into a bobble," she says, turning me to face her. After running her fingers through my hair, she ties it back. "Honestly, sometimes I have no idea what you're thinking. There, that's better. Right, Ben?"

"Right. Although I also liked it before."

I narrow my eyes at him. "I was told I look like Hagrid earlier."

He laughs. There's this look in his eyes that tells me he was thinking it, too.

After our customary morning shop, we set off for school. Natasha goes twenty questions on Ben, but I'm glad she does. It means I get to learn more about him. He hasn't settled in one place for more than two years, which means he doesn't have many friends. If I hadn't already made up my mind to be his best friend, I would have done so in a heartbeat. Everybody should have a friend, even if it's only one.

We're almost at the school when I notice a commotion across the street. Stopping still, I realise that three stocky boys are harassing a smaller boy from our school.

"Hey, leave him alone!" I shout. The three assailants step back in alarm, giving the fourth boy a chance to pick up his bag. Darn stupid bullies. "I'm over here," I tell them, seeing their stupid faces search around.

They laugh when they see me. "What's it to you, shortcake?"

I step forward, but Natasha holds me back.

"Who are you calling shortcake?" She yells.

"Come over here and say that to my face."

"I will," Ben steps forward. While I like that I have another spunky neighbour, this isn't what I wanted.

I don't want a fight. I just wanted to stop them from bullying.

I hold up my phone and show it to them. "If you don't leave in five seconds, I'm calling the police."

It only takes three, and then they run like the cowards they are.

"Bully's," I mutter, crossing the street to make sure the other boy is okay. Thankfully, he is, and he joins us for the rest of the walk. The bell rings just as we get there. This makes me sad because I can see Peter already going inside, and I'm too far away to catch up to him.

After taking Ben to reception, we plod our way to class. I stop by Peter's desk as I pass it to give him one of my Snickers. It was a two-for-one offer, and Natasha doesn't like them. Okay, I bought the Snickers on purpose.

"This is for you," I say, dropping it in front of him with a smile. Hannah gives me a dirty look that I ignore. I mean, between her and Peter, I prefer to focus on the cuteness of Peter.

"Thanks," he drops it in his bag. As I start walking, pleased with myself, he adds, "Hagrid."

I step back. "Do I still look like him?" He meets my mortified eyes, and I can see a little smile on his lips. This smile - I'm pretty sure it means he's amused, so he must be having me on. "Very funny, Peter," I say before I walk over to my table. I look over at him as I sit down, and he's still smiling. That makes me giggle.

"What are you laughing at?" Harvey asks. He actually has a textbook open in front of him. Wow.

"I'm just madly in love," I tell him.

"Barf," Natasha twists away as the teacher walks in.

"Settle down, class. I have an announcement to make." She motions with her hand, and Ben walks in, eyes darting around the room like he's nervous after all. I wave my hand so he can see that he has a friend here, and he relaxes. The teacher gives him a short introduction before she sends him over to our desk.

"Good to see you again, scary girl." He grins, pulling out our fourth chair.

I think he means Natasha at first, but then I realise he's looking at me. "I'm not scary."

"You were when you scared those three gangsters away."

I open my mouth to say that they weren't gangsters at all when Harvey turns to me with a frown. "Wait, you said something to those guys, Emily? I saw them on my way in here. They look like trouble."

"They're just a bunch of bullies," I say, and then lower my voice, "anyway, what I really need to know is this third tip of yours."

"What, this hair didn't win Peter over?" He laughs at the look I give him. "I'm kidding. Okay, the third tip-,"

"No, no, no, no, no," Natasha waves her hand out in front of us, silencing him. "Tell her after class. I need her to concentrate."

I pull my books toward me with a pout. She's right, but group projects just aren't as fun if you can't chat with each other. I notice Ben watching me as I take out the leaflet, and I realise that there's now another person who knows about my crush on Peter.

When the bell finally rings, I turn to Harvey, ready for his next piece of advice. "Third tip, please."

He opens his bag and starts packing his books away - slowly. Too slow. I tap the table in agitation. "My third tip," he says, pausing as if he needs dramatic effect, "is to win over the mum."

I frown. "His mum?"

"His mum."

I glance at Natasha, who doesn't seem convinced. "How stupid," she mutters.

"It's how my girlfriend won me over," he bites back. "Trust me. The mum is the way into any guy's heart."

I rub my arm, turning to Ben. "Is this true?"

He gives Harvey a slow look before shrugging his shoulders. "I don't see how it can hurt."

As I leave the room, I ponder over this. Will winning Peter's mum over really help me with him? My only problem is that Peter's mum is the one neighbour I haven't been able to get friendly with. I always wave when I see her, but she never waves back for being too busy. Maybe I can somehow catch her when she's not.

I start planning what I'm going to do throughout the rest of the day. This means I get in trouble for daydreaming in math class, and I get hit by a dodgeball about twenty times in p.e. By the end of the day, I know what to do.

"I'm going to bake her a cake," I tell Natasha on the way out. Her eyes light up at the word *cake*, and I make a secret plan to bake two. "Think about it. Who doesn't love food?"

"Do you even know how to bake a cake?"

"It can't be that hard, I-,"

Someone pulls the hood of my coat up from behind me, covering my eyes with fabric. I shove it down and search angrily for Harvey because he's the only one I can think of who would do this. My eyes, trained as they are, fall on Peter, and the anger disappears.

He has his back to me, walking a few metres ahead with his hands in his pocket, but something about him makes me suspicious. Did he do it? As though to answer me, he glances back with a smile.

My heart skips a beat at that smile. It goes into overdrive when I hear him ask,

"Do you want to walk home together?"

I exchange a look of shock with Natasha, and then I nod my head with the most enthusiasm I've ever felt.

DO YOU WANT TO WALK HOME TOGETHER?

Peter

Sometimes, Emily Clarke is just the person I want to see. This is far from always the case, and my old self would be shocked if he heard me say it - because it wouldn't be an understatement to say that I avoided my new neighbour like she was the plague when I first moved here.

I didn't know how to deal with her at first. I was

awkward, and she was... anything but that. All of a sudden, I had this girl knocking on my door every day, asking me if I wanted to play out. I didn't. Worst, my peaceful morning walk was now ruined by this random person's constant talking. I didn't ask for her to walk with me - she just did it, and it annoyed the hell out of me. That's when I got the bike.

Back then, I thought if I ignored her enough, she'd leave me alone. That's what most people do. If it isn't my silence that scares them away, it's my obvious social discomfort. How it comes so naturally to one person and so difficult to another is beyond me. Not that I'm going to beat myself up over it - I actually like being alone. It might sound strange to most, but I'm fine with sitting in an empty classroom, staring out the window at the chaos outside, feeling no pressure at all to join in. I feel at ease when I'm by myself. But that's not always the case.

Sometimes I need to be with someone, even if it's only for a minute. Like when I'm feeling down, and I can't seem to pull myself out of it. This is where my neighbour comes in. Unlike most, she hasn't become fazed by my silence. It amazes me that she still says hi to me every morning. What amazes me more is that she never shows any awkwardness around me, even though I'm an awkward person to be around. I guess this is why I no longer feel awkward around her.

And I'm glad I don't. While her unceasing cheerfulness used to make me uneasy, it now has the power to make me feel better. Not only her cheerfulness but her quirkiness, too. Take this morning as an example. Who goes out with their hair like that and then seems to forget that they went out with their hair like that?

I laugh to myself as I wheel my bike across the road, not seeing what's in front of me until it's almost too late. I manage to skid to a stop before I make an impact, but the sound my back wheel makes as it scrapes across the concrete makes me wince. Looking up, I find three guys standing in front of me. Three jacked-up teens who obviously blocked my path on purpose.

I look around me. Are these guys idiotic enough to do this in a place so busy, or are they really that fearless?

"Careful," I say, "I have a lot of witnesses."

"Yeah?" the meanest of them snarls. "And all they're going to see is you handing over your bike to us."

I bark out a laugh. "What makes you think I'll do that?"

"Because you won't like what will happen to you if you don't."

I stand up fully. I'm taller than all three of them, and it's clear from their expression that they were expecting someone shorter. Fearless, my ass.

"Get out of my way, or I'll make you regret ever stopping me."

They exchange a look between them. I don't give them a chance to decide what they want to do. Instead, I straighten my bike and ride off, not taking a single look back at them. People like that don't deserve it. They live off of fear, and if they see you aren't scared of them, they start to lose their nerve.

At school, I lock my bike and head straight for the principal's office. I'm lucky that he's sitting behind his desk and isn't in some unknown location like he usually is.

"How can I help you, Peter?" He asks, smiling as I enter.

"I just thought you should know that I ran into some street thugs on my way into school. They'll probably try to harass some other student, so I think they should get reported."

"Ah-" he looks lost for a second as he searches his desk. "Right, um - thanks, Peter. I'll call the authorities straight away." I nod my head and turn. "Peter?"

"Yes, sir?"

"I've had a few teachers tell me how impressed they are with you in class. If you want, I can budge you up into Set 1."

"Don't you have to get a certain mark to move up a set?"

"Well, I can make an exception for you."

I shake my head. "Thanks, sir, but I'm happy where I am."

"Very well," he smiles, but his eyes tell me he doesn't understand why I'd turn the offer down. I'm not sure I do, either.

Thanks to this detour of mine, the ramp is now crowded with people. This isn't how I like it because it means I have to walk through everyone to get to my spot, and I'll get stopped on the way. Nah, I'd prefer not to go through that. I turn, but some guys on the team spot me and drag me back with them.

"Peter, my man!" Jimmy says, throwing his arm over my shoulder.

"Whoa, Peter's my man," Dec snipes back. When did I become either of their men? "Hey, so the coach told me to tell you that practice is now tomorrow. You can make it, right?"

"I'll try." It's the best I can give him at this moment in time.

When I reach my spot, I turn away from the commotion behind me and focus my eyes on the gate. Our school holds many people, and it's impossible to recognise all the faces. I do recognise one girl. When Emily walks in, I realise I was looking forward to seeing that wild hairstyle again, and I'm disappointed to see she's tied it back. It's probably for the best. I smile and move my eyes away, remembering that expression of hers this morning.

Wait-

I glance back. Is that Ben with her? It is. See, I told you my neighbour is chatty. But does she have to be so chatty with *everyone*? No. I shake that thought away. Ben is her neighbour now, too, and it's good he's met Emily. She'll make sure he's fine on his first day.

"Peter, are you coming?"

I turn at Matt's voice and notice everyone is heading inside. The bell must have rung. I follow them in, stopping by my locker to pick some books up. Hannah and Jenna are already sitting at the table when I get to class, prattling about something I'm sure I don't care what. I keep my head down as I sit, hoping to go by unnoticed. That, of course, is impossible.

"Hi, Peter," Hannah says. I find her leaning toward me, her arm brushing against mine. The smell of strong-scented perfume hits me, and I wrinkle my nose. I prefer a softer scent. Something like- "I was just telling Jenna about how my dad is renting me a Rolls Royce for prom this year. Isn't that great?"

I edge away, pulling my arm back. "Lucky you."

"Whoever asks Hannah will get to ride in it, too," Jenna adds, giving me a not-so-subtle look. "Obviously, everyone is going to ask her, so they better be quick if they want her to say yes."

"I'm not going," I say as Emily appears in the doorway. Seeing her makes me straighten in my seat. I don't know why I just did that. Slumping, I pretend to work - a hard thing to do when Jim hasn't arrived with our project yet.

A chocolate bar appears before me, forcing me to look up.

"This is for you," Emily says, smiling as usual.

My lips twitch. "Thanks," I drop it into my bag, wondering why she gives stuff like this to me. But, between a Snicker and those flapjacks, I'm happy I got a Snicker. She starts to walk away, and I have a sudden urge to say something else to her. "Hagrid" is the first thing I can think to say. Damn, that's embarrassing.

But it works. She steps back. "Do I still look like him?" This look on her face - it resembles the one she wore this morning - I can't help but smile at it. "Very funny, Peter." She says before walking off.

I chuckle to myself as Jim pulls out his seat.

"That was a good one." Hannah snorts. My laughter dies with her words.

"I wasn't saying it to be mean," I say, turning away to face the teacher.

Turns out that Ben is in my class. There's only one team he can join - the three-squad at the back. He walks past my desk with a grin on his face, not batting an eye at me. I glance to the side, stopping myself before I turn fully.

"Good to see you again, scary girl."

Scary girl? God, who says that. I turn my attention back to my table, grabbing the leaflet from the pile of paperwork in front of Jim. Eavesdropping is not something I ever want to do. Besides, I have too much work to be getting on with for that.

Still, despite my effort to focus on my work, I can't help but overhear what Ben says next.

"You were when you scared those three gangsters away."

I shiver. Does that mean Emily bumped into those douchebags? The thought of them being near her makes me angry. I realise my hands are clenched and tell myself to calm down. It's not like she's hurt.

"They're just a bunch of bullies," she retorts. I shake my head at the word *just* as if they aren't three guys capable of causing trouble.

When class ends, all I want to do is head straight to

the principal's office to see if he has any updates. I have to wait until lunch break before I can do it.

"Nope, I've had nothing," he says, taking a large bite out of a sandwich. "But they said they'd ring if they find them causing trouble again, so I'll let you know."

If they cause trouble again? So we have to wait for it to happen before it's stopped?

I shake my head as I walk out and bump into Ben for the first time today. We stare at each other for a second, and then he smiles.

"Oh, hey, Peter. Good to see you again."

"You too. How's your day?"

He shrugs. "Not bad. As first days go, I mean."

I nod, not quite knowing what to say next. "Well, if you need anything, you can come to me."

"Thanks," he taps my shoulder, "but I think I'm alright. I've got Emily's help."

I look down at his hand still on my shoulder and wait for him to remove it. When he does, I ask, "will you be walking home with her today?"

A smirk appears on his lips. I have no idea what that smirk means. "I would, but I've got a meeting after school, so I can't."

Damn it. I watch him leave as a feeling of unease settles in my stomach. I don't like the thought of those three guys being out there.

When the last bell rings, I go back to the principal's office to see if there's an update from the police. He isn't inside. After searching for him for five minutes, the panic kicks in. I set off at a run back through the school, afraid that I'm now too late to catch up to Emily. My heart pounds up until the moment I see her. I slow down, forcing myself to appear calm as I lift the hood of her coat and walk ahead. When I look back, I hope the smile on my face seems casual and doesn't give away the thumping in my chest.

For a second, I almost don't ask her. For a second, I remind myself that I like to travel alone. But then I think of those three guys again, and those thoughts are gone. "Do you want to walk home together?"

Yep, I'm going to regret that one later. Emily stares at me for a long second. Her eyes flick across to Natasha, and then she nods her head. This nod - the energy of it - gives me this feeling that I might not regret asking after all.

PETER HAS A GIRLFRIEND

Emily

My walk home with Peter was everything I ever expected it would be - utterly perfect. So perfect, in fact, that I didn't feel the need to say anything at all. I was happy to walk in his silence. His perfect silence. I did, of course, glance at him now and then, if only to remind myself that he's real. How lucky am I that he is? He wheeled his bike next to him as we walked, his long legs taking small steps to match mine. I mean, I could have walked faster, but I wanted the walk to last as long as possible. Can you blame me for that?

Right now, I feel giddy at the thought of seeing him again. I can't keep the grin off my face as I peek out my window and see his bike outside because I expect he'll want to walk with me again today. I've already told Natasha to go ahead in anticipation of it.

And I have more exciting news. I got a bike! I don't have it right this second, but my aunt is bringing one over for me this evening. My cousin Penelope's grown out of hers, and I couldn't be happier about receiving her hand-me-down. I can't wait to show it to Peter.

I get ready at super speed and hug my mum goodbye, grabbing the cake I baked for Natasha on my way out. I made two of them last night. The one for Peter's mum is sitting lovingly away from where my dad might find it. I'm planning on giving it to her when Peter next has basketball practice. They aren't perfect, but you can tell they're homemade, and homemade shows you care.

"Morning, scary girl."

I turn to see Ben walking up to me with a big grin on his face. I smile back. "Morning, Ben. That's not my nickname now, is it?"

"It is since I've forgotten your real name. I'm kidding!" He laughs as my smile disappears. "What are you doing out here, *Emily*? Are you waiting for someone?"

I nod. "Peter should be out soon."

"Cool." He leans his back against the gate, dropping his bag to the floor. "Then I'll wait with you."

I scratch my nose. While I'd prefer to walk alone with Peter, I wouldn't want to make Ben feel like he isn't welcome. It would be rude to send him away.

We talk about random stuff while we wait, and I learn that Ben has interesting hobbies, the Taekwondo one being the coolest. He says he'll show me some moves one day, which will be interesting since I can't seem to lift my leg higher than my hips. After more time passes, we exchange a look.

"Maybe he's already set off?" He suggests. I frown at Peter's door. He isn't usually this late, and if we wait much longer, we'll be late ourselves. I sigh. The last thing I want is to make Ben late when he's new.

"Let's go," I decide, setting off into a regretful walk.

Unfortunately, we're late anyway, and Ben's too nice to accept my apology. Since we both have p.e. first, we speed-walk through the empty schoolyard together, parting ways at the changing rooms.

"Finally!" Natasha breaths, her hawk eyes zoning in on me as soon as I enter the room. "What took you so long? I thought you might have kidnapped Peter or something."

"He didn't show," I pout, following her to our usual corner.

"He didn't?" When I shake my head, a thoughtful look crosses over her face. "You didn't do anything to annoy him yesterday, did you?"

Annoy him? That thought never even crossed my mind! "I don't think I did. Do you think I did? Wait - is he avoiding me because I did?"

"Calm down," she commands, fanning my face with her gym shirt. "I only said it because I've never known Peter to miss school before."

This doesn't help. If anything, it makes me feel worse. I'm in full panic mode as we make our way over to the field. If Peter is missing school because of me, I'll throw up. But what did I do? I think back to our walk, which still seems so utterly perfect to me, and I can't think of anything annoying at all. But if it isn't me, is everything okay with him? I hope he isn't sick, or worse-

"*Emily*," Natasha jabs my ribs, causing me to stumble.

"What?"

She nods her head at something in front of us. I turn, hoping that it's Peter, but it's not. It's just Alice and Lily.

I give Natasha a questioning look, and she whispers, "Alice just said she's going to ask Peter out."

Alice? Not another girl!

In my panic, I blurt out the first thing that comes to my head. "Peter has a girlfriend!"

Stupid fart brain, when will you learn to think before you speak? Alice turns, and I gulp down my take-back because I'm not ashamed to admit that she scares me. Scares me because this is someone who will snap if you look at her in the wrong way, and I have no idea what the right way is.

"How would you know?" She snarls.

"I-,"

"Peter's her neighbour. That's how she knows." Natasha locks her arm in mine, and I see Lily do the same for Alice. It looks like we're having a stand-off. Are we having a stand-off?

"Girls, keep moving!" The coach yells. I'm more than happy to oblige her.

That is until I see the boys are out on the field, and I consider running back. I don't know why the coaches do this to us - throw us all in together - because it's beyond humiliating. I don't need the boys witnessing how bad I suck at sport. Not any more than they already have. Maybe it's a good thing Peter isn't in today. As I think this, I see his tall figure within the crowd of boys. My heart doesn't know how to react. To make matters worse, I now spot the equipment lined up behind the coaches, and it looks like we'll be practising for Devil's Day today.

By Devil's day, I mean Sports Day - but I think my version is more accurate. It's a day where everyone goes outside and competes against each other in their selected sport. My school hosts it every year. I usually sit out because I find it more fun to watch. But this year, we all have to join in. The joys of being in your last year of high school.

"I'm going to kill it this year," Natasha says. She's already stretching her muscles. Oh, how I envy my friend and her athletic abilities.

Natasha is a track runner, just like Peter. They both come first place every year, to my extreme pride. Well if I have to choose one sport, I guess it should be track. At least then I can be with my two favourite people. Yep, that's a great idea. I grab Natasha's hand and pull her with me, spotting Peter at the front of the track line. He gives me a questioning look as we approach, making my heart rate quicken.

"Emily, you suck at running," I hear Natasha say, and Peter's lips twitch, "why are you doing this? Seriously, we'll need to call for an ambulance for you if you do. Your endurance levels are zero."

When Peter turns to cough, I take the opportunity to pinch Natasha's arm.

"Ouch! Why did you-" she stops, her eyes suddenly glued to something in the distance. I turn to see what's caught her attention. When Alice comes into my vision, I choke back my panic.

Oh crap.

She approaches the front of the line, stopping by Peter. "Hey. So I hear you have a girlfriend now, huh?"

Oh double crap.

Peter looks at her in confusion, giving me a sudden urge to run. "Girlfriend?"

"That's what I heard."

"By who?"

Please don't say me.

"The girl who claims to be your neighbour."

Oh double, triple crap.

Peter's eyes flash over to mine, and I see a crease forming between his brows as I half-hide behind Natasha. "My neighbour is wrong."

"*Sorry*," I mouth, but he shakes his head slightly. Somehow, this feels worse than a scolding.

"Well, that's good," Alice continues, releasing me from Peter's piercing stare, "because I was wondering if you wanted to go out with me sometime?"

Please say no!

"I can't, sorry. I, um, like someone else."

As he turns his back, I exchange a look of surprise with Natasha. This look means: *who on this Earth is blessed enough to be liked by Peter?* At least for me, it translates to that. For Natasha, it's probably: *wtf*.

When Alice stalks off, I hear Matt ask, "who the hell are you crushing on, man? Is it who I think it is?" and I listen with more interest than I have ever felt before.

Say, *Emily*, say, *Emily*.

"Nobody. I just said it to get her off my back."

I sigh. It's not our time yet.

I have to admit, now that I'm here, looking at the others in line, I think this may be the worst decision I've ever made. I'm seriously going to die out there.

"You know," I hear Peter say, "I think girls who choose Javelin are impressive."

"Do you?" Matt tilts his head, and I look over at the Javelin poles with him.

So Peter likes Javelin? Should I do that instead? Yep, that's a great idea. "Good luck," I say to Natasha before I run over to that line.

I'm not sure if I'm good at Javelin, but it has to be easier than running track. I watch how the people in front of me do it first, and then I copy the technique Ben uses because his pole went the furthest. Mine doesn't go so well. My pole does this weird thing where it catches the ground when I throw it, and it falls straight away.

"Nice try, Emily," the coach sighs. "You can sit the next one out if you want."

"Thanks," I turn, and my foot hits something solid. The next thing I know, my knees are hurtling toward the floor. My only hope is that Peter is now out on the track. If he's not, he may be witnessing the catastrophe that is Emily Clarke.

"You okay, scary girl?" as Ben lifts me by the arm, I brush the grass from my knees.

"Thanks. If you need me, I'll just be hiding in a hole somewhere."

I walk over to the water cooler and sit down. *This* is why I hate outdoor sport if anybody needs an example. At least it wasn't as bad as when we did long-jump together. That time, my short legs didn't make it past the first marker, and even the coach laughed.

"Are your knees okay?"

My head snaps up at the sound of my favourite voice. Peter is standing in front of me, looking more like a sportswear model than any p.e. student has the right.

"My knees are fine," I say, rubbing them as proof. "Have you- have you already run the track?" What I mean by this is, did you see me fall?

"Yup. I came second." His eyes flick away, and I wonder if it's because he's feeling bad about not coming first. While he usually does, second place is still great.

"You should still be proud of that, Peter. I mean, look at me. I always come last, and I'm okay." His lip twitches as I add, "were you late in today? I didn't see you this morning, but your bike was outside."

"Oh, yeah. I dropped Sammy off at school, so I got in early - why are you smiling?"

I'm smiling because this means he wasn't avoiding me. "I thought- nevermind." I notice the smile now on his lips and ask, "why are *you* smiling?"

"Nevermind." His smirk deepens as he reaches down for a water bottle, his shirt brushing against my skin in a way that makes my heart race. Does he know how close he is to me? He turns his head, and I swear making my heart race is what he's trying to do because his eyes are now delving into mine. I look down at his lips, and the shape of them causes my brain to scramble. Before I can descramble it, he taps his water bottle on my head and stands. "Oh, and Emily?"

"Y-yes, Peter?"

"Don't tell people I have a girlfriend unless I do."

WHAT THE HELL HAS GOTTEN INTO ME

Peter

Do you remember when I said I no longer feel awkward around Emily? Well, that wasn't the case yesterday. My walk home with her felt awkward, to say the least.

Not at the start. At first, it was fine; good, even. I was happy I wasn't riding my bike for a change - the slow pace delayed me from getting home. And it was peaceful, even if I did need to keep half an eye out for those douchebags the entire time. Maybe this preoccupation is why I didn't notice it at first. But when I did, it was as if a red flag went up in my brain, and Emily's silence became loud.

Now, when I say I'm comfortable with silence, I mean it. I can be in a room full of loud people, and my silence won't bother me. I can be in a room full of quiet people, and their silence won't bother me. Why, then, did I feel so bothered by Emily's?

Her silence set my brain into panic mode, and my panic mode went like this: she usually talks - why isn't she talking? I should say something first - what should I say? Does she regret saying yes to walking with me? What if she never says yes again? Overthinking sucks. Only when I was within the safe confinements of my bedroom, with the door firmly closed, did my panic finally subside. And then I started to wonder why it got to me in the first place.

It's back now that I'm about to see her again. In fact, I don't think I want to see Emily today at all. Or do I? Maybe if I ask her to walk with me again, I can make up for yesterday's fiasco. Does it even matter if I do? So what if it was a fiasco. I prefer to walk alone anyway.

What the hell has gotten into me.

I hear my mum shout from downstairs, and all other thought vanishes as I make my way onto the landing.

"No, you listen to me, David. If you're not back here tomorrow like you said you would be, I'll- *what am I supposed to tell the kids?!"*

What's she supposed to tell us? How about 'your dad's bailing on you again, but I know that's no surprise'. I sigh as I turn. My stomach drops when I see Sammy's little figure standing by his door.

"Are mum and dad fighting again?"

I force a smile onto my lips, but it takes a lot of effort to keep it there. "It's-," am I supposed to lie to him? "It's nothing they can't work through." I see his chest heave out as he inhales, and I have a sudden urge to hug him. "Hey, how about I walk you to school today? Would you like that?"

My question has the desired effect. Sammy's face splits into a grin, and I smile with him. I have no idea why me taking him to school excites him so much. It's the same as when I pick him up - he loves it, and it makes me think I'm doing something right in the big-brother department.

We leave the house after I indicate to my mum that I'm taking him. My eyes drift across to Emily's front door, and I wonder for a second if she'll notice my absence this morning. I shake my head. That isn't something I should be thinking.

I drop Sammy off at his school gate. Unlike me, he's good with other kids, and it's nice to see. I smile as I turn, but it drops when I see who's now in front of me. You just can't escape people.

"Is everything okay with your mum, Peter?" Tammy asks. Tammy is my mum's *mum* friend, and she has this way of making you feel like you're not as good as her kid.

"My mum's fine."

"That's good. It's just your dad-," she stops whatever she was about to say.

"My dad, what?"

"Nothing. Well, it was nice to see you, Peter." With that cryptic message, she disappears, and I'm left questioning what the hell it is she was about to say.

I'm still trying to figure it out when I arrive at my school. I could ask my mum, but she'll probably lie. I could ring my dad, but he lies all the time. Maybe I should-

I blink. Where's my neighbour today? I see Natasha heading in, but no Emily. Is she sick? Maybe, but I wouldn't put it past her to skip school even if she's not, like that time I caught her dancing in the garden when she was supposed to have the flu. She ran inside when she saw me looking, and it was pretty funny.

When the bell rings, I force my neighbour out of my head because it's none of my business if she's in today or not. I'm halfway between swapping my shirt in the changing rooms when I see Ben rush in, looking like he just ran here. He freezes when he sees me.

"Oh, you're here."

Did he expect me to be somewhere else? "Yep. I'm here."

He shakes his head as he walks away, chuckling at something. I remember that I'm not yet sure what to make of him.

We're practising for Sports Day today. Good. As

school events go, this is one I can get behind.

"And the girls are coming out too," Matt says, rubbing his hands together in excitement.

I turn to look at them with him, my eyes searching for one in particular. When I realise I'm doing this, I turn away because once again, I'm not sure what the hell has gotten into me.

"At least you'll get to spend more time with Hannah," Matt says, nudging my arm in that irritating way of his. How many times do I need to tell him I don't like her?

I open my mouth to tell him *again*, but someone cuts across me.

"So, you like Hannah, do you?" It's Ben. For some reason, I do not want this guy getting the wrong idea.

"No," I clarify, "Matt doesn't know what he's talking about."

If I thought that would put an end to it, I forgot what Matt's like.

"Hey, new kid - you've seen Hannah, haven't you? Will *you* tell Peter how crazy he is for not making her his girlfriend?"

"My name isn't new kid. It's Ben," he retorts, and I hold back a smile because Matt had that one coming. "And yeah, Hannah's good-looking, but that doesn't make her girlfriend material." With this comment, he smiles and walks away. I have to give it to him. He's got nerve.

"That cocky son of a-"

"Actually, his name's Ben," I laugh at the look on

Matt's face and make my way over to the track line. He follows behind. While we wait, I move my eyes across the field, doing a double-take when I spot Emily. Seeing her - my heart does something weird, and I frown because this feeling confuses me.

And then I see that she's walking over to this line, and I'm more surprised than anything. Does she realise she can't even walk to our corner shop without losing breath? I don't need to tell her my concerns because Natasha does it for me.

"Emily, you suck at running," - she isn't wrong - "why are you doing this? Seriously, we'll need to call for an ambulance for you if you do. Your endurance levels are zero."

I bark out a laugh, somehow managing to turn it into a cough. Still, I need to turn away before the look on Emily's face can force another one from me.

"Hey. So I hear you have a girlfriend now, huh?"

What?

I turn to see Alice in front of me. It looks as if her question is aimed at me. "Girlfriend?"

"That's what I heard."

What jackass is spreading rumours about me now? Crap like this annoys me because if the wrong person hears it- I keep my eyes firmly on Alice. "By who?"

"The girl who claims to be your neighbour."

What? I look across at Emily, not sure what to believe. When I see she's half-hiding behind Natasha, wearing this sheepish look on her face, I realise it must be true. "My neighbour is wrong." She knows she's wrong, doesn't she?

Emily mouths the word *sorry*, and I shake my head because I'm still unsure if she said that thinking I do have a girlfriend or if she said that knowing I don't. If it's the latter-

"Well, that's good," I flick my eyes back to Alice, "because I was wondering if you wanted to go out with me sometime?"

Damn it. And now I can't even use the girlfriend card to get out of this. "I can't - sorry. I, um," - how else do you let someone down gently? - "like someone else."

That works. I turn away, and something crosses my mind. Did Emily somehow know that Alice was going to ask me out? Did she pull the girlfriend card to help me, or was it for another reason? I hear Matt ask something, and I mutter some half-assed response because I'm more concerned with something else.

I need to test something.

I have no idea if this will work - or how idiotic I'll feel if it doesn't - but I need to test it anyway. I turn back to Matt. "You know, I think girls who choose Javelin are impressive." And just like that, Emily disappears. I tilt my head as I watch her join the Javelin line, wondering if this means what I think. Does she still have that crush on me?

"Okay, Peter, out on the track!" The coach's yell forces me to pull my eyes away from Emily. I walk over to the first line. When the horn blows, I set off into a sprint, but my mind is only half on the run. The other half is now whirling over the possibility that Emily still likes me. *Does* she still like me?

I reach the halfway point, and I spot her at the front of her line. Her pole seems to land at her feet. I'm not surprised, but I do feel bad that I'm the one who sent her there. When she walks away, she falls, and I stop still. Is she hurt? I step forward, but then I see someone help her back to her feet. Is that-

"Too slow, Peter," Matt says, overtaking me into first. With a groan, I set back into a run, but I can't catch back up to him. Second place isn't something I'm used to.

With the race over, I search the Javelin line for Emily. My eyes link with Ben's instead. He gives me this funny look, and I turn away, sure that he has something against me. Spotting Emily by the water cooler, I head towards her. She has green stains on both her legs. "Are your knees okay?" I ask.

Her head snaps up. "My knees are fine," she rubs them as if she's trying to prove it. "Have you- have you already run the track?"

Good. So she hadn't been watching. "Yup. I came second," I move my eyes away before she can guess the reason.

"You should still be proud of that, Peter. I mean, look at me. I always come last, and I'm okay." My lips twitch as I try not to smile. It's true, yet she somehow manages to stay cheerful about it. "Were you late in today?" She continues, her voice unusually quiet, "I didn't see you this morning, but your bike was outside."

"Oh, yeah. I dropped Sammy off at school, so I got in early-" I stop because I notice the look on her face, "why are you smiling?"

"I thought- nevermind." She shakes her head, and something crosses my mind. If she thought *I* was late in, then maybe she waited for me long enough for *her* to be late. And if she did that- "why are *you* smiling?" She asks.

"Nevermind." I feel my smile deepen, so I reach down for a water bottle to hide it. When I turn, I find she's closer to me than I thought, and the proximity catches me off guard. For one wild moment, I find myself wanting to kiss her. But then I remember that something has gotten into me today, and I tap her head with the tip of my water bottle before I can do anything rash. "Oh, and Emily?"

"Y-yes, Peter?"

What would I have said if it had been *you* asking me instead of Alice? **"Don't tell people I have a girlfriend unless I do."**

IT WAS A HUGE MISTAKE TO COME HERE

Emily

We have career counselling this afternoon. While I currently have zero clue about what I want to do with my life, I'm happy we get to skip math class for it. Anything is worth skipping math class. Another plus is that Peter is in our session, which means I'll get to see him while we wait for our turn. That's if I even want to see him. I'm still a little scarred from this morning. 'Don't tell people I have a girlfriend unless I do'. This phrase keeps replaying in my head like an unwanted song lyric. *Why* did I have to tell Alice Peter has a girlfriend? What must he think of me? And Alice, why did *you* need to tell Peter that I said it?

"You're making that face again," Natasha says. The face she's referring to is my 'this is so embarrassing it's actually painful' one. Because on top of the Peter incident, my brain keeps replaying what happened at javelin practice.

"Am I an embarrassment?" I groan.

"If you are, it's one of the reasons why I love you," Natasha gives me a wink as we join the students queuing outside the counsellor's office.

"If being embarrassing means I'm lovable, Peter would have fallen for me already," my eyes search for him as I say this, but he isn't here yet. My shoulders slump.

"I still can't believe he came second," Natasha has said this about five times today. Yes, it is news, but Peter's human too, so he can't be expected to come first place all the time.

"It was only practice. Cut him some slack."

She shrugs. "I know that, but it's just the way he stopped still, like something-," she cuts off, turning away suddenly. Realising why this must be, I swivel with her. A glance back tells me Peter's joined the line.

"Do you think he overheard us talking about him?" I whisper. I don't need that after the girlfriend incident. She shakes her head slightly, and I peek back again. "He looks concerned to me. Does he look concerned to you?"

"I bet he's more bothered about coming second place than you think."

As I contemplate this, the counsellor's door opens, and she calls the first person into the room. When I remember I haven't filled out the form she needs, I quickly twist my bag to the front.

"Let me guess. You left it at home." Natasha rolls her eyes, and I pull the sheet out with a hint of smugness. Instead of looking impressed, like I thought she would, she looks disgusted. "What's all that brown stuff on it?"

"What brown stuff?" Oh no. Oh no, no, no. Please don't tell me that's what I think it is. I rummage through my bag, letting out a shriek when I see the squished mess at the bottom of it.

"Is that cake?" Natasha sounds offended. "Emily, why didn't you tell me you have cake? Were you keeping it for yourself?"

"It was supposed to be a surprise," I sulk, "but I forgot I had it in there." Picturing all the books I've thrown in since this morning makes me wince. It's best not to mention that bag fight I had with Harvey at lunch.

"Well, thanks," Natasha looks half-grateful, half-concerned as she pulls out the beaten box. My favourite pencil is poking out of the mushed-up cake, and I take a second to mourn for it.

"I'm not going to make you eat it," I sigh, taking it back from her. "I'll just go clean this up."

"I'll hold your place for you."

I look away from the sympathy in her face as I head for the girl's bathroom. While there, I do my best to clean the cake out with wet toilet paper. It's somehow gotten *everywhere*. On the plus side, at least my bag smells good now, and it's my turn next in the line when I get back.

"Oh no, you don't," Jim steps out in front of me, blocking my path. "I'm next."

"But I was here. You heard Natasha say she'll hold my place for me."

"Is she here now?" He looks smug as he says this, and I know I don't have a good comeback for that. Seeing my defeat, he thrusts his thumb over his shoulder, "back of the line."

I still need to fill my form in. This is the only reason why I turn on my heel and make my way to the back, but not before I pull a face at him. As I'm on my way, someone holds their arm out, and I stop before I walk into it.

"Peter-," I blink up at him in surprise. He nods his head, and it tells me he wants me to join him. I can't stop the smile that spreads across my face. "Really?"

His lip pulls up at the corner. "Yes. You can take this spot."

I step in front of him, turning my face as I try to control my smile. When I glance back, I see that he's looking at me, and the smile creeps in again.

"Are you alright?"

"I'm perfect!" I bite down hard on my lip as my Peter enthusiasm escapes. Luckily, he doesn't seem to notice it.

"About before-," he says, just as I say,

"I'm sorry-,"

"Go on," we say together, and he laughs. His laugh is the most beautiful sound in this world.

"I'm sorry I told Alice you have a girlfriend."

"It's fine. If you thought I did-,"

"That is what I thought! Sorry," I chew on my lip. I'm just so relieved he doesn't know the real reason why I said it. But then he chuckles, and this time the sound disarms me. "Why are you laughing?"

"I'm not," he covers his mouth with a cough, but I know what I heard. "Your form is looking empty," he observes.

"Shoot! I still need to fill it in." I pull a pen from my bag, blushing slightly at the cake crusting on it, and use my knee to lean on. This makes my scruffy hand-writing even scruffier than usual.

"Use this," Peter's textbook appears in front of me. I take it with shaking fingers, feeling as if I'm holding a winning lottery ticket in my hands. When I see his name scribbled at the bottom, I try not to freak out.

"Thank you, Peter."

I write as quickly as possible because I don't want to waste any of this precious time. I'm on the last box when I feel a tap on my shoulder.

"We need to move," Peter's lips are next to my ear, and my breath hitches. When I look to the side, I see his face next to mine, eyes focusing ahead, and I lose all functioning of my brain. How is it possible someone like this exists in my world? I don't think I'll ever be able to look away from him again. He straightens, and I use this moment to regain control over myself.

I don't want to leave him, but the counsellor calls me in next, giving me no choice. My session goes like this: I get asked what I want to do when I leave school, and I answer that I have no idea. The counsellor gives me a worrisome look, and I feel a wave of panic that my life is going nowhere. And all the while this is happening, I'm thinking about Peter. We reach the end of the session, and I jump to my feet, eager to see him again.

"Before you go, I need to tell you something." I step back. "The teachers have been talking, and we think it's best if we move you down to set 3."

"But I don't want to do that," I choke. "I like it where I am." The thought of leaving Natasha and Peter, and even Harvey and Ben, sends a wave of dread through me.

She must see it on my face. "I might be able to help you, but you'll need to get a B on your next mock test. Your grades have been slipping, Emily."

"Thank you!" I race to the door before she can go back on her word. Even though a B in math is nigh on impossible for me, I have faith in myself that I can do it.

"And I want to see you doing some extra-curriculum!" She calls after me. I give her the thumbs up before I turn to face Peter.

"Do you-," I suck in a steadying breath. "Do you

want to walk home together again today?"

A look passes behind his eyes, and I worry about what this look means. "I have basketball practice."

Oh. That sucks. An idea crosses my mind. Maybe this means I can take the cake around to his mum while he's not home. Yes.

After school, I race home, saying a quick hello to my dad before I grab the second cake from its hiding place. I'm not sure if Peter's mum is home yet, but it's worth a shot. Taking the small steps from my house to his, I knock on the door. Footsteps sound behind it.

"Can I help you?" Mrs. Woods asks.

"I-," don't feel nervous. You've got this. "I baked some cakes yesterday, and I wondered if you wanted one?" I hold the box out to her, but she doesn't react the way I want her to.

"Why would you-?"

"Emily!" Sammy's little face peeps around his mum, and I sigh in relief. In my opinion, Peter has the best little brother.

"Hey, Sammy," I bend down to face him. In truth, I don't have to bend much - I'm almost as small as him, and he's seven. "Would you like some cake?"

"Yes, please!"

I look back up at his mum, remembering how Peter had to miss basketball practice the other day. "You know, if you ever need someone to pick Sammy up from school, I'd be more than happy to help."

"Well, thanks," her face brightens at my words. "Emily, is it? Why don't you come in with that cake?"

"Thank you," I grin as I follow behind her, peering around with curiosity.

"Is Peter still at school?" She asks, stopping to pour herself a glass of wine.

"He has basketball practice." How does she not know this? My mum always knows where I am.

She takes a seat by the kitchen table, and I sit down opposite her, feeling the pressure to impress kick in. "I never know what that boy's up to," she sighs, "he's a mystery to me."

Are my ears deceiving me, or does it sound like she's complaining? "Peter's great," I tell her, shocked that I even have to say it, "you should be really proud to have a son like him."

She waves her hand in dismissal, sipping her glass of wine as she does so. "He's too moody. But at least he's not his dad. Now *he* is someone who annoys me."

"Oh?" I don't know what else to say to that. All I can think is at least Sammy isn't in the room because I'd hate to hear my mum say this about my dad.

She complains to me for a while, and I realise this may have been a bad idea. But when I try to change the topic - try to impress her like Harvey said I should - she doesn't let me. All I can do is listen while she slates Peter's dad.

Relief floods through me when I see Peter in the doorway. I straighten in my seat, hoping he'll want to join us.

"Emily-," his eyes widen. For a second, he seems almost as happy to see me as I am him - but it's gone in an instant, and I wonder if I imagined it.

"Oh, you're back," his mum says. "I was just telling Emily here about how your dad-"

"You need to leave."

I'm so surprised to hear Peter say this to his mum that all I can do is stare between them. I look back at Peter's face, and my stomach drops when I realise he's saying it to me. The warmth in his eyes is no longer there.

"Peter, I-,"

"Out," he steps back, opening the door wide. "Now."

I realise my mouth is hanging open, but I don't have it in me to close it. With shaking legs, I get to my feet, shrinking at the look now on his face. I walk past him in silence. There is an alarm blaring loud in my brain, telling me that it was a huge mistake to come here.

A RAY OF SUNSHINE

Peter

I have something on my mind. That something is a five-foot chatterbox that goes by the name Emily. Yup, for some reason, I can't seem to get my neighbour out of my head today. Maybe it's because I've been finding her a lot less annoying recently. Come to think of it, out of all the girls in our year, Emily is someone I can tolerate the most. When did that happen? Better yet, how did that happen? That's what I've been trying to figure out all morning - especially since p.e. Because I can't deny that I felt something earlier.

The strange part is that she hasn't changed all that much. She's practically the same person I met all those years ago. What has changed, then? She still talks a lot, she still gets herself into trouble, and she still has a knack for appearing out of nowhere. Yet, when I give it thought, I don't think I mind it as much anymore. Is it me that's changed? Maybe - because somewhere between then and now, I think I started to care about her.

Exhibit A - when I saw her fall earlier, it felt as if someone threw a bucket of ice over me, and I wanted nothing more than to help. It's not like I haven't seen her fall before, either - you can add clumsy to her list of tendencies - but it's never hit me as hard as it did today.

I guess it's because we've been neighbours for such a long time. Neighbours care about each other, don't they? Especially ones who have known each other for as long as we have, right? But that doesn't explain why I wanted to kiss-

"Peter, are you coming?" Matt's voice interrupts my thoughts. "We have that stupid career's counselling, and I wanna be out of there pronto."

I nod my head before I remember that I've yet to fill that form in. See, my mind has been so preoccupied with Emily that I forgot something I wouldn't usually forget.

"You go ahead," I tell him, "I'll be there soon."

As the students around me filter inside, I pull the form from my bag, using the railing to lean on. It's a rushed job, but at least it's done. The bad thing is my delay means there's a bunch of students in line when I get there. I roam my eyes over them, stopping on the girl who's been in my head all day.

My hand goes into autopilot when I see Emily is looking at me, and I wave at her. Again, this isn't something I usually do, so I'm at a loss when she turns straight away without waving back. I scratch the back of my head and look at the floor. Did she see me wave and ignore it? Or was she not looking at me in the first place? Maybe I was wrong earlier. She might not still have that crush on me. Not that it matters either way.

I try to keep my head clear for the rest of the wait, but it's hard when there is nothing else to do but think. I'm doing alright, up until the moment I hear a shriek come from the front of the line, and my heart tightens like it did when I saw Emily fall. But then I hear Natasha say something about cake, and I step back into place with a smirk. When is it not about food? When I look back over at them, I see Emily walking my way, and I turn to the person in front of me without thinking.

"So, what do you want to do when you leave here?" I ask Sasha. I'm not surprised to see her mouth drop open. I've never spoken so randomly before.

"I- I-," she swallows hard, and I feel bad for engaging her in this awkward small talk. "I want to be a teacher, I think."

I nod, but my mind is half-focusing on the girl now passing me. "Me too."

"Oh, you also want to be a teacher? Peter?"

"Sorry, what?"

"You - you want to work in teaching, too?" Sasha's

cheeks are turning crimson, making me wonder what the hell it is I just said to her.

"Oh, um, I'm not sure what I want to do."

It looks as if she wants to say something else to me but decides against it. I have to admit that I'm relieved she's turning away. Let's not do that again.

By the time Emily strolls back past me, her friend has already gone inside. I watch Jim as she makes her way back to the front, curious to see how he'll react. On top of telling unfunny jokes, he can be a bit of a jerk. Yup, there he goes, sending her away like the jerk he is. I shake my head. Would it kill him to let her go in front?

A glance back tells me the line has gotten long. I can't let her go all the way to the back. Can I? It's what I'd usually do. But today, I seem to be going crazy. I hold my arm out.

She looks at it expressionless for a second before her eyes move up to my face. "Peter-," I hold back a smile at this reaction, nodding my head as an invitation for her to join me. "Really?" Her surprise brings the smile out. I guess this is a surprise for both of us.

"Yes. You can take this spot."

She steps in front of me, tilting her head away so I can't see her face. I find myself wanting to see it.

"Are you alright?" My question causes her to turn again, just how I wanted.

"I'm perfect!"

My lip twitches at her enthusiasm. I remind myself that if she is perfect, it has nothing to do with the fact she's with me. Or maybe I should test out that crush theory again?

"About before-" I'm about to ask if she thought I had a girlfriend or not because this will probably provide the answer, but she speaks at the same time as me.

"I'm sorry-,"

Oh? Why is she sorry?

"Go on," I say, just as she says it herself. A laugh rises in my throat.

"I'm sorry I told Alice you have a girlfriend."

Well, this is easier than I thought.

"It's fine. If you thought I did-" before I can say anything further, she cuts across me.

"That is what I thought!" The energy with which she says this, paired with the look on her face, confirms one thing to me - it's not what she thought, and my crush theory still stands. "Sorry," she bites down on her lip. If I had to guess, it's probably to stop herself from talking. "Why are you laughing?"

"I'm not," I cover my mouth before I can laugh again, but she's onto me. Searching for something to distract her with, my eyes fall on the blank sheet of paper in her hands. "Your form is looking empty."

It works.

"Shoot! I still need to fill it in."

I watch as she pulls a pen from her bag, frowning at whatever the hell that brown stuff is on it. She twists away slightly, but I can still see it. After a second, I notice she's struggling to write - not surprising since she's trying to balance on her knee - and I pull a textbook from my bag.

"Use this," I say, handing it to her.

"Thank you, Peter."

I smile to myself as she starts writing. Strange how I used to find it annoying whenever she said my name, and now I don't mind it. Still, that's not as strange as the fact I no longer mind if she has a crush on me. Better than Hannah and Alice, that's for sure. When I think of those two, something dawns on me. Maybe it's not that Emily's changed - maybe it's that I've seen enough of her good sides that her annoying one no longer matters to me. Her tongue pokes out as I think this - something she does when she concentrates - and I smirk before I move my eyes away.

Matt catches my eye. I see him nod towards Emily with a questioning frown, and I take an automatic step closer to her. Emily isn't the type of girl *he'd* stand beside. Sucks to be him.

The line moves down fast. So fast that I start to wonder when she'll finish. When the last person leaves, I tap her on the shoulder. And then I get this sudden urge to tease her.

Giving in to it, I bend down, making sure my mouth is next to her ear as I whisper, "we need to move." I feel the warmth of her breath on my cheek the next second, and something I wasn't counting on happens. I lose it. My brain screams *look at her*, but I fight against the voice. If I listen, I'm afraid I'll feel how I did down by the water cooler, and I'm not sure if I'll be able to stop myself from kissing her this time. With one last effort to keep my breathing even, I straighten. It's a relief when she goes inside.

During the time I wait for my turn, I focus on getting myself under control. I'm having a weird day, that's all. She's my neighbour. I like her as my neighbour, and I'm only just getting used to admitting that. When the door opens again, I keep this in mind. I'm determined to walk straight past her. But then she asks if I want to walk home with her, and I realise with surprise that I do.

But I can't. "I have basketball practice." And for the first time, I wouldn't mind if I didn't.

The session isn't as bad as I thought. Unlike the coach - and my dad, come to think of it - who tells me I should only pursue basketball, or my mum, who tells me I should take anything, the counsellor listens when I say I want to help people. She runs through my options, but nothing really sticks with me.

"It's okay," she tells me. "You're still young, and you've got time to figure it out. Just make sure you do something that makes you happy. Oh, and Peter?" I lower myself back in the seat. "I know principal Eaves mentioned moving you up to Set 1, but you said no. Why is that?"

Not this again.

"Because mine is a good class." Even as I say this, I know it's not true. Set 1 is a good class - Set 2 is mediocre. The counsellor narrows her eyes as if she can read my thoughts.

"Are you sure that's the reason? There isn't something holding you there?"

My mind is threatening to go somewhere, but I don't let it. "I like it where I am."

She heaves out a sigh. "You can do better than people in Set 1, Peter. I've seen your mock test results, yet you always under perform when it comes to the real test. Being in Set 1 will help you get into a good college. If I ask you to think about that, will you?"

Of course, I'll think about it. I'm not an idiot. And if the principal had put it in the context of college, I would have listened to him more seriously, too. "I will."

"If you do want to help people," she adds as I get to my feet, "you need to help yourself first."

With this last message, I leave the room. She's right. I know that, but I can't shake the thought that moving would be a bad idea.

Matt's waiting for me inside the changing rooms. I can see he has questions for me, and I already know I'm not going to like them.

"Man, it must've sucked waiting in that line," he says, unloading his basketball kit. "You should've come with me."

I think of Emily's look of concentration and say, "it wasn't so bad."

"You're even smiling about it? Dude, you're insane. Not to mention you were standing next to Emily Clarke. I can only imagine the torture."

I try to control a sudden wave of anger. "Emily's alright. Better than most girls."

"Yeah. Right." He taps me on the shoulder as he passes, "and I'm a millionaire."

Sometimes, I wish I could drop this friend group of mine. But where else would I go? I sigh as I follow after him, joining the rest of the team by the court.

The game distracts me from all other thoughts. Ben's joined us this time, too, and if he plays good enough, the coach will add him to the team. I don't see why he won't since he's a good player. A little competitive, maybe - he hit the ball from my hand with unnecessary force - but still good.

By the time we finish, I'm almost happy to go home.

I can hear my mum complaining in the kitchen when I get there, and the happiness disappears. It sounds like she's having her daily rant about my dad. Great. At least I'm not the person in there with her. God help them.

Since I have no intention to go into *that* room, I go upstairs to check on Sammy.

He looks up from his dinosaur set with a grin. "Peter! Have you seen who's here?"

I frown at his excitement. "No. Who?"

"Go see for yourself. I know you'll like it."

Beyond curious, I take the steps back down, wondering if my dad is here. No, it can't be that. He's the subject of my mum's complaints.

I stop still when I see who it is. Emily is sitting in my kitchen, looking wildly out of place. It's like a ray of sunshine breaking through an abnormally dark cloud. I feel an unexpected jolt of happiness until I realise what the hell is happening. My eyes move across to my mum, and my stomach drops.

"You need to leave," I blurt out, feeling the panic kick in place. How much did she hear? How much does she know?

"Peter, I-,"

Something else begins to creep in, a sense of dread mixed with humiliation.

"Leave," I step back to open the door. "Now."

As she passes me, a small part of my brain registers that this isn't fair on her. But a large part is on the verge of breaking down, and I can't bring myself to call her back.

PROGRESS

Emily

Stupid cake.
Stupid idea.
Stupid me listening to Harvey.

I can feel the tears coming as I walk across the patch of grass to my house. I try to hold them off until I'm at least inside my room because I prefer to cry alone. But today, my mum calls my name as soon as I'm through the door. I ignore her as I race upstairs, feeling the first tear slip onto my cheek.

"Emily, come back down here! We have something for you!"

I retrace my steps with a groan, following her voice into the kitchen. She looks pleased about something. She obviously hasn't caught on to my mood yet because her smile doesn't fade when she sees me. I move my eyes around, wondering what she has for me, and they fall on a bike. My bike.

For a second, I'm overcome with happiness because I finally have a bike. But then remember why I wanted one in the first place and the dejection returns. The more I look at it, the sadder I feel.

"Which cousin did this bike belong to?" I quiz.

My mum's smile falters as if she hoped I wouldn't ask this question. "It was your cousin Steven's."

I knew it. I knew getting Penelope's bike was too good to be true. So this is why my aunt looked at me funny when I told her to thank Penelope for me. She knew I was getting Steven's bike instead. My problem is that Steven is about a foot taller than me.

"I'll never be able to ride this bike," I say, my voice rising as another tear falls. "It's huge!" and just like that, the floodgate opens.

I run upstairs, ignoring my mum as she calls behind me. It doesn't stop her from following me into my room.

"Emily, honey, what's the matter?" She sits beside me, running a thumb across my cheek to dry it. I bet Peter's mum has never done this for him. Thinking this makes the tears come thick and fast.

"I upset Peter," I sob.

Her hand pauses. "And this is why you're upset? Oh, sweetie, boys can be silly. He certainly doesn't deserve you to cry over him."

I shake my head. "I'm crying because it's my fault, mum, not his."

"How can that be possible?"

"I went around when he wasn't home. And his mum, his mum-," my voice breaks, and my mum heaves out a sigh.

"Let me guess, his mum said some things about his dad, and Peter overheard it?"

I blink. "How do you know that?"

"Because I've met Peter's parents. And before you say anything - it wasn't my place to tell you. Nor was it Peter's mothers." She clucks her tongue in anger, and I gulp.

"Is it bad?"

"I don't think Peter and Sammy know just how bad it is. But yes, it's not great."

I dry my eyes before scrambling to my feet. "Then I need to help them."

"Not now, you don't." My mum pins me back down with a firm hand. "Think about it, Emily. How would you feel if Peter had been the one to see your family like that? Give him some time, and let him come to you when he's ready."

I know she's right. If it had been the other way around, I would have hated it. But this only makes me more upset because I don't want Peter to feel like that.

"I'm going to go try out that bike," I say, darting to the door. "And I won't knock onto Peter's house," I add, seeing the look on her face.

Maybe if I can ride to school with him in the morning, I'll be able to cheer him up. The least I can do is let him know he has someone here who cares about him.

Even if he doesn't want to speak about it.

Wheeling the bike outside, I realise this may not be possible. It's too big for me. My short legs have a hard time getting on it. When I manage it, the bike tilts toward the ground, my knees hitting the concrete with a thud. Only when I see the blood dripping do I go inside for a plaster, calling it quits on the monster bike.

My second option is to wake up earlier than I've ever allowed myself before. Early enough that there's no chance for me to miss him. My eagerness to make sure he's alright is all I need to wake up before sunrise.

Yawning, I make my way outside, noticing that someone is already out there. Rubbing my eyes, I see Peter sitting on his bike outside his house. What is he doing out this early? Is it - I gulp - is it to avoid seeing me? I hold back. The last thing I want is to force myself on him when he doesn't want to see me. I wonder if I should sneak back inside when I hear him speak.

"Are you coming?"

My head spins toward him. Did I hear that right? When I see Peter is looking at me, I take small steps toward him, half expecting him to ride away. He holds his bag out to me when I reach him, and I wonder if this is a dream.

"What's this for?" I ask, taking his bag with shaking fingers.

Peter nods his head to the back seat of his bike, and my heart - remembering all the times I've dreamed for this day to happen - skips a beat. "I'll give you a ride if you want."

Biting my lip against a sudden smile, I attempt to climb on. But Peter's bike is bigger than the one my Aunt brought for me. Seeing me struggle, Peter hops down, holding my arm with his hands as he hoists me up.

"Thank you," I say as he holds the bike steady.

"No problem." He releases my arm as he climbs on. I hesitate for a second before I clutch the sides of his blazer.

I know our school is close, but right now it is far too close for my liking. I worry we'll arrive before I get the chance to say anything, but Peter doesn't seem to be riding as fast as he usually does.

The only problem is that I don't know what to say. How do I bring yesterday up? Should I bring it up or will he prefer it if I don't?

I think I should at least apologise to him. After all, we shouldn't pretend like yesterday didn't happen. Ignoring a problem doesn't make it go away.

I clear my throat. "I'm sorry, Peter. About yesterday, I mean. I - I shouldn't have gone to your house without you being there."

Is that an okay thing to say to him? I thought so, but then why isn't he responding? His silence stretches on, and I chastise myself for bringing it up.

"I'm sorry, too." He breaths, allowing me to relax. "I shouldn't have snapped at you. It's just- I heard what my mum said, and-," he sucks in a sharp breath. Wanting to reassure him, I give him a gentle squeeze.

"It's okay," I don't want him to feel like he needs to

say anything else. I already understand. "So we're both sorry, and we both forgive each other, right?"

He nods his head, and we fall back into a more comfortable silence. He breaks it after a while.

"My dad's never around anymore."

The unexpectedness of hearing these words almost makes me fall off the bike. Not only his words but the way he said them - like it wasn't an easy thing for him to do. Yet he's sharing it with me.

Peter's arm steadies me, and I force myself to remain calm for his sake. "When did you last see him?"

I feel him shrug. "I don't know. Before Christmas, maybe. He always says he'll come back, but he never does. I just hope he makes it to my first basketball match next weekend. He says he will, but we'll see."

He doesn't sound sure. It makes me feel a jolt of anger toward his dad because I'd never want to let Peter down like that.

"I'm so sorry, Peter. Do you know why he's doing it?" I hope I'm not crossing a line by asking this, but I also want him to know he can talk to me.

"Because of work. He's a travel worker, so I understand, but-,"

"You still want him to be there for you." How long has Peter been going through this on his own? See, when people call Peter cold, they have no idea what he's really like. He is the warmest person I know.

He sighs again. "It's not me that I'm worried about, either. It's Sammy. Without my dad at home, my mum is - well, you've seen how she can be. I worry what it's doing to him."

This is the Peter I fell for - the Peter with a heart of gold. When he and his family moved here, my first impression of him wasn't great. Actually, after our first few meetings, I decided I didn't like him. But then I saw what he did for Sammy. Peter had a comic book in his hands, waiting at the checkout to purchase it. Little Sammy ran over to him, a dinosaur set clutched in his fingers, with this big smile on his face. Peter must've only had enough money to buy one - because as soon as Sammy turned, he quickly swapped the comic book for the dinosaur set, purchasing that instead. That's when I realised Peter is the one for me, and he isn't cold at all.

"Sammy has the greatest big brother in the world," I tell him. "With you, there's no way he won't be alright."

"Do you think so?"

"I know so."

His muscles relax beneath my fingers, and I realise that he's been tensing, too.

"Thanks, Emily. You're a good friend."

I grin. "And you're the best!" Sweet sugar puff - did I seriously say that out loud? I bury my face in his blazer before he can see my face. "Please pretend you didn't hear me say that."

He chuckles. "Nah, you can't go back on it now. I'm the best." With that final statement, he picks up speed, riding so fast I wonder how his legs don't tire. I laugh as the wind rushes past my ears, causing Peter to turn to me with a grin. I've wanted to see this grin ever since I left his house yesterday.

When we reach the school gates, he slows his bike to a stop. There aren't many students around, but there's enough that several pairs of eyes are now watching us in surprise. I'm not surprised about it, either. Not many people are lucky enough to get a bike ride in from Peter.

He helps me down. As he does, there is a moment when neither of us looks away from the other. I stare into his eyes, wondering why he's staring into mine. After a second, he steps back, releasing my arm as he moves his eyes away, and I finally breathe again.

As he goes to lock his bike, I linger back to wait for him. Maybe, just maybe, there is a chance he won't go to the ramp today.

But then he turns his head, holding his phone up for me to see. "I have to take this. You go on in."

Sigh.

I head inside as he answers the call, wondering when Natasha will be here because I've got so much to tell her.

Oh, shoot - Natasha!

I've had two missed calls from her. Quickly calling her back, I pray to the friendship God above that she hasn't fallen out with me.

"I am so sorry," I say as soon as she answers the phone.

"Em? Where are you? Are you late again?"

"I'm already here," I cringe at the gasp on the other

end.

"*Without me?*"

"I know. I'm sorry, but Peter gave me a ride in-,"

"*Pete- are you pulling my leg? This is a prank, isn't it?*"

My grin is so big I'm pretty sure she can hear it through the phone. "Nope. It's not a prank."

"*What!*" I move the phone away from my ear as she screams. "*Wait - does this mean Harvey's advice actually worked? Do we need to thank him?*"

No. No, Harvey's advice did not work, and I will not be thanking him. But I can't tell her this without telling her what happened at Peter's house, and I'm not about to do that.

Instead, I say, "sort of. But it's not like he's fallen in love with me or anything. It was just him being nice."

"*But, Em, this is huge progress. I mean, since when has Peter done anything like this before? For anyone?*"

I grin because I know she's right.

Today, progress has been made. It's not the romantic kind of progress like I usually hope for, but one that is equally important to my success. Because today marks the first day that Peter Woods has accepted me as a friend.

INTOXICATED

Peter

My face is burning up. I'm not sure if the heat is from anger, humiliation, or guilt. Who knows, maybe it's all three.

I move my eyes away from where I last saw Emily and find my mum staring at me. Her head is tilted as if *I'm* the one who's difficult to understand.

"Why did you send that girl away?" She asks.

That girl? Has she forgotten her name already, or did she never ask for it?

"What was Emily doing here?"

"There's no need to sound so angry, Peter. She just came by with some cake."

I look over at the counter, spotting a pink-tinted box with flowers on it. It has Emily written all over it. Walking over to it, I allow my anger to build up. Anger that she came here, anger at what she heard, anger at my mum for what she said. Remembering my mum's words causes my anger to rise further. It's not just what she said to Emily. It's what I hear all the time. And, on top of it all, there's my dad. He's the reason for all of this.

The heat rises to a burning level. I grab the cake and walk over to the bin, slamming my foot down on the peddle. My hands shake as they hover in the air, ready to throw it in and be done with it all. *Do it*. A voice inside my head commands. I clench my jaw. *Don't*. This second voice comes from a different place, a place I'm not familiar with.

I tighten my grip on the box. As I do, the lid pops open, giving me my first glimpse of the cake inside. This cake is nothing like I expected. Nothing like those perfect shapes you see in a supermarket, with the icing smoothed around the edges. This cake is a mess. Is it supposed to be a circle? Maybe, but it's too uneven to call it that. The icing looks as if it's been thrown on at a distance, and the colour is... well, unnatural. Yet, somehow, even with the mess, it's perfect.

Emily made this with her own hands. Emily does not deserve what I did to her.

I step away from the bin with a jagged breath, putting the box safely on the counter. How could I do this to her? The answer is easy. I can't.

I turn to my mum. "In the future, can you please not say anything about dad to my friends?"

This is all I have to say to her. I turn, heading upstairs. As I'm on my way up, I see Sammy in his doorway, his eyes brimming with concern.

"Peter, what's the matter?" His bottom lip trembles as he asks this, and I try to smile.

"Nothing. I'm alright."

My eyes start to water, contradicting my words. I head to my room. When I hear Sammy following, I drop my head into my hands so that he doesn't see.

"You can tell me, Peter. I want to help."

"You won't understand."

"Why?" There's a defiance in his voice that I've never heard before. I rub my eyes on my sleeve before I look up, remembering how I used to hate it when people said *you won't understand* to me.

"I think I messed up with Emily," I cave, "and I don't know what to do now."

"Hmm." His round face screws up in thought, and my mood softens. "Whenever I fall out with my friends, we give each other one of our playing cards, and then we make up. I think you should give Emily a playing card."

I smile. What a perfect solution. "The only trouble is that I don't have any playing cards."

A light dances in his eyes before he bolts to the door. "Wait here! I'll go get you one!"

The smile stays on my lips as I watch him leave. Thank goodness I have Sammy in this house. If Emily is a ray of sunshine, Sammy is a permanent rainbow. Still, I doubt a playing card will help me make it up to Emily. But what can I do? I guess an apology is one good way to start.

Sammy returns with a card in his hands. I take it from him, spinning it over in my fingers. "Why Pikachu?"

"Because Pikachu is small and cute, like Emily."

I smile, pocketing it. "Thanks, Sammy. I'll make sure I give it to her." What *am* I going to do with this?

"At my school, if someone gives you one of these cards, it means they have a crush on you."

"Good to know." I'm about to ask if he's been given one of these cards before when we hear a loud rattling sound coming from outside.

"I bet it's an alien," Sammy says, running to the window. "Oh, no, it's Emily! Why is her bike so big?"

I walk over to the window with him, leaning against the wall. The first thing I think is that *big* is an understatement. That bike is more than half the size of her. The second is whether this means she's not upset. Hoping that she isn't, I smile and watch her attempts at climbing on it.

"Why don't you go give her the playing card now?" Sammy asks.

Maybe I should go out - not for the card, but the apology. I think this, and then I see Emily hurtling toward the ground and hear the crash of impact. I'm out of my room in a second, racing down to the front door. But, by the time I open it, she's no longer there.

My only choice is to get up early so that I don't miss her. I could catch her at school - but I prefer personal conversations to take place away from prying eyes.

And, since I'm used to waking up early anyway, it's not a stretch being out of the house while it's still dark.

I take a bite out of Emily's cake on my way out, if only to tell her I tried it. As soon as it enters my mouth, I spit it straight back out again. Yeah, it's probably best if I don't mention this to her.

I have to wait sometime before she leaves her house, but it's nowhere near as long as I thought it would be. I hope she isn't out this early for the same reason I am. If she is, I'm more of a douchebag than I thought. She takes slow steps toward me, and then she stops. Why is she stopping? It's not because I'm out here, is it?

I clear my throat. "Are you coming?"

To my relief, she starts walking again. When she reaches the streetlamps, I spot the plasters on her knees, and my stomach churns at the thought of her being hurt. I hold my bag out before I can think any further.

"What's this for?" She asks. At least she's taking it.

I nod my head to the back of my bike. "I'll give you a ride if you want." Well, that isn't something I ever expected myself to say.

I turn away as she hops on. It takes me a second to realise she's struggling. After what I witnessed yesterday, it's a second too long. Using one hand to steady the bike, I climb down. I use the other to help her on. She's as light as she looks, so it isn't any effort at all. What's surprising is that it's an effort to let go of her.

"Thank you," I hear her say, and I let my hand fall.

135

"No problem," I climb back on. After a moment, I feel her hands on my side, and my pulse quickens. It's probably the fear of never doing something like this before.

I ride slow. If it were any other day, I'd make the journey quick because what's the use in taking in the scenery when I've already seen it a hundred times. But I don't feel this way today. Today, I take in my surroundings as I wonder how to approach the subject of my apology. I want her to know it's sincere. I want her to know that it was my fault, not hers. I want-

"I'm sorry, Peter." Wait - she's apologising to me? "About yesterday, I mean. I - I shouldn't have gone to your house without you being there."

I swallow down the guilt now rising in my throat. When I know I can trust my voice, I say, "I'm sorry, too. I shouldn't have snapped at you. It's just- I heard what my mum said, and-," I suck in a sharp breath, unable to continue. Her hands tighten around me, and warmth - the kind that I've never felt before - sweeps through me.

"It's okay," she says, "so we're both sorry, and we both forgive each other, right?"

A weight lifts as I nod my head, but there's still something pressing me down. It's like there's this band around my heart, tightening a little more every day, and I can't breathe the same. I've never thought about opening up to anyone about it before because it's not something I like to do. But Emily is different from other people.

"My dad's never around anymore." There - I said it. And, to my surprise, the band loosens.

Feeling Emily move, I hold my arm behind me in fear that she'll fall. She holds onto it, steadying herself.

"When did you last see him?"

The last time was before Christmas. Has it really been that long? I tell her this, and then I tell her that he'll be coming to my next basketball match because I don't want her to feel bad for me. That's if he turns up.

"I'm so sorry, Peter," she says, and my heart clenches because she isn't the one who should be apologising. "Do you know why he's doing it?"

No, not really. But I do have an excuse for him. "Because of work. He's a travel worker, so I understand, but-" I stop. This is the part I haven't figured out.

"You still want him to be there for you." Emily sighs. I feel the band loosen some more. I'm glad someone understands me, even when I don't.

But then I think of Sammy, and everything tightens.

Whenever I think of my little brother - about what this is doing to him - I struggle to keep it together. That type of unfairness doesn't make sense to me. If it were just me, I might be able to take it. Sure, it would still suck, but it would be nowhere near as bad as seeing someone I love get hurt.

I tell Emily something like this, and her words are everything I need and more.

"Sammy has the greatest big brother in the world. With you, there's no way he won't be alright."

I hope that's true. "Do you think so?"

"I know so."

Strange how a few words can make somebody feel better.

"Thanks, Emily. You're a good friend." Even as I say this, I get the sense she's something more.

"And you're the best!" The next second, Emily's face is burying into my blazer. "Please pretend you didn't hear me say that," she groans.

Laughter rumbles through my chest, escaping into one joyous sound. "Nah, you can't go back on it now. I'm the best." I lean forward to accelerate, and now it's Emily's laughter that rings in the air. Grinning back at her, I find myself liking the sound of it. I've heard her laugh before, but there's something different about being the reason behind it.

I slow the bike to a stop when we reach the school. Some part of me wants to stretch the journey out for longer, but that makes no sense at all. When I see Emily's feet dangling high above the ground, I hop down to help her. Something possesses me as my arm encompasses her waist, and I move my eyes down to meet hers. My breath hitches as if I've forgotten how to breathe. Emily stares back at me, almost like she's as intoxicated as I am. Intoxicated - *is* that how I feel? I release her and step back, confused by my thoughts.

It's a good thing I have my bike to lock. I need a second alone. While I tie it against the railing, I feel my phone buzz in my pocket, and I pull it out to see an incoming call.

It's my dad.

I turn to Emily. "I have to take this. You go on in."

Whether she leaves or not is something I don't know. I'm too busy trying to keep my hands from shaking as I swipe to answer.

"Hi, dad."

There's a beat silence on the other end. A beat silence, and then I hear the voice I know all too well.

"Hey, Pete. Are you free for a sec?"

PLAYING CARD

Emily

Something is wrong with Peter. Ever since I left him by the school gate this morning, he's seemed upset, and I can't stop wondering if it's because of that phone call. Right now, I'm sitting at the back of English class, and I'm not the only one who's noticed something is wrong.

"It looks like he needs a hug," Natasha whispers, frowning at his back.

Harvey and Ben turn to look at the person I've been staring at all morning. The person who has caused my anxiety levels to increase with every passing second.

"You mean Peter?" Harvey asks, "he's probably just tired. It looks like he's sleeping."

"Maybe your talking did that to him," Ben teases, nudging my arm.

I shake my head at both of them. While I wish what they're saying is true, my instinct tells me it's not. All morning, Peter has been holding his head in his hands like he's defeated. He hasn't answered a single question from the teachers, which isn't like him at all.

"Are you sure nothing happened on your way in?" Natasha's eyes are still trained on Peter. I swallow down a new wave of worry because if Natasha is concerned, something is definitely wrong.

"I don't think so," I say, but in the back of my mind, I'm thinking about that phone call again. I really-, *really* hope it wasn't his dad.

When the bell rings for lunch, I expect to see Peter head straight out the door, like he's been doing all morning, but he remains seated this time. I wave the others ahead before I approach him.

"Are you alright?" I ask, feeling like an idiot because he obviously isn't.

He twists his head an inch before sinking it into his hands again. "I'm fine."

While his words should reassure me, they do the opposite. "Peter, you can speak to me if you wa-" I cut off as he gets to his feet.

"I'm fine," he says again, giving me a small smile. I don't like this smile.

I don't follow him out of the room, and he doesn't turn to see that I'm still standing here. Maybe he thinks I am following him - it's what I'd usually do. Or maybe he isn't thinking about me at all.

As soon as he's out of my sight, I grab my bag and

race toward the cafeteria.

"I'll be back soon," I tell Natasha, ignoring the questioning look on Ben's face as I race off again. I don't have time to explain.

When I reach reception, I ring the bell by the help desk, impatient in my urge to get out.

"How can I help you, Emily?" Miss Cook sighs. I'm used to this exasperation of hers. After all, I'm only ever here when I've gotten myself into trouble.

"I need to leave," I tell her. My only hope is that she can hear the urgency in my voice. But her look of exasperation tells me that I'm doomed.

"You know that I can't let you do that." She says this while shaking her head, forcing me to put on my pleading voice.

"Please, Miss. I just need to visit the shop, and then I'll be back."

"Unless I get permission from a parent or guardian, I can't let you leave. Sorry."

"But it's important!"

She turns her attention away from me, towards a pile of paperwork, and the desperation kicks in. I know full well that my mum is at work, so I can't get permission from her now. And my dad never answers his phone.

Drumming my fingers against the edge of the desk, I wonder how else I can cheer Peter up when I notice someone coming in from outside. I'm going to get into a lot of trouble for doing this. Knowing this makes me hesitate. But then I see Peter walking through the cafeteria, looking as unhappy as before, and it gives me all the courage I need.

As the automatic doors open from the outside, I take the opportunity to leap through, ignoring Miss Cook's 'Emily Clarke!' as I do so. I'll have to deal with her when I get back.

I try to be quick. So quick that I make the five-minute journey in three. Inside the store, the shop-keeper watches me as if I've just escaped from prison. I ignore the glare he gives me as I stroll through the aisles, picking up a packet of Peter's favourite crisps. Sammy once ran through a list of Peter's favourite snacks with me, and I've never been more grateful than I am now.

After the crisps, I find his favourite chocolate and move over to the fridge. Sammy also told me about his brother's love for chocolate milk. I'm sure Peter wouldn't want me to know about this, but I can't stop myself from picking one up. I think it's adorable how he tries to hide his love for it.

When I reach the checkout, I grab another one of those flapjacks I know are his favourite. The shop-keeper is still looking at me like I'm about to steal, so I give him a smile.

"Just these please," I say, but then my eyes fall on a colourful stand next to my hand. I pick out a blue eraser with a smiley face on it and, since I want to see Peter smile, add it to my pile.

I'm not surprised to find Miss Cook waiting for me when I race back inside the school. She looks like a thundercloud, ready to flood me with rain.

"Come with me," she says, stalking off into the cafeteria. My heart sinks when I see which table she stops by. This table is where all the teachers sit to eat. It's obvious why they sit here instead of the staff lounge. It's because they want to suck the fun out of lunchtime.

I sit reluctantly, moving my eyes across the cafeteria to find my three friends staring at me. Harvey and Ben have this 'why the hell are you sitting there' look on their faces, but my best friend tells me something different. Wondering what Natasha's pointed look is for, I move my eyes across the cafeteria again, this time almost knocking Miss Tarling's bottle of juice over in surprise.

Peter is still here, and he's sitting alone. In all our school years, I have never seen Peter sitting on his own before. I've wanted it to happen - wanted him to sit next to me - but he is *always* surrounded by people. Rather than being happy about it now, my anxiety for him increases.

"Sit *down*, Emily." Miss Tarling warns.

Peter's eyes flash over to mine as I fall back into my seat. For one millisecond, his expression changes into something softer, but then the sadness returns as he looks away again. I notice his food is untouched in front of him.

It's okay, I tell myself, it's okay because this is why we're here, and being in trouble is worth it if it cheers Peter up.

The bell rings, and I jump to my feet.

"Where do you think you're going, Miss Clarke?"

I turn to Miss Tarling with a smile. "To class, miss. If that's okay with you." It has to be. What is she going to do, stop me from learning?

"You can wait until every student has left the cafeteria first."

"But then I'll be late-," I start to complain.

"Maybe that will teach you to not leave the school grounds before home time."

I sit back down. Students filter from the room so slow that it's almost torture. I want to catch Peter before class, but I can already see him leaving. I wave, but he doesn't see it; I call his name, but he doesn't hear that, either.

"Stop that, Emily." Miss Tarling warns again. She's such a vampire who loves to suck out the fun.

I clamp my feet down to stop myself from chasing after Peter. Natasha approaches, but Miss Tarling sends her away before either of us can get a word in. I pout because I'll have to speak to her after history class. Natasha is in Set 1 for that.

As soon as the last student is out, I am on my feet and running. The hallways are empty, and I know there is no way I'll catch up to Peter now, so I settle on giving him what I bought during class. I'm sure I can sneak it to him.

The door is shut when I reach the classroom. It's a sight from my worst nightmare. Fighting my urge to skip it, I knock before I enter, and everyone, the teacher included, turns to look at me. I mumble an apology before I rush over to my seat, dropping the bag onto Peter's desk as I pass it. By the time I'm seated, he's staring straight ahead again, so I don't know how he reacts.

Why isn't he opening it? Time ticks by, and I worry I've made a mistake because he still isn't acknowledging the bag.

"Emily?"

I blink at the sound of my name. "Yes, sir?"

"Do you have the answer?"

Crap. "Oh, um..." I search the board for a clue to the question, but there is nothing on it. "I-, um-,"

"Somebody else? Yes – Hannah?"

"Elizabeth 1 reigned from 1558 to 1603."

"Thank you, Hannah. Emily – pay attention, please."

"Sorry, sir." I try to ignore my burning cheeks as several students laugh. When Hannah joins in with the laughter, I look down at my textbook with a grimace.

The teacher gives us ten minutes to answer some questions while he leaves the room. As soon as the door closes, I see movement from Peter, and my heart thumps when I realise that he's opening the bag I gave him. He scans the contents, and part of me worries he'll hate it, but then I see his lip pull up at the corner.

I am not imagining this! Peter Woods is finally smiling, and it's because of something I did for him. Chuffed, I watch as he pulls out the little blue eraser and twirls it around in his fingers. He places it at the head of his desk, smiley face toward him. If only he'd turn so that I can give him a smile.

Hearing the teacher return, I quickly scribble down an answer, so it looks like I've done something. I hear a loud rumbling sound and snap my head back up. What the heck was that?

Oh - the sound is coming from me.

The hollowness in my stomach makes me realise that I haven't eaten anything since breakfast. I take a sip of water, hoping it helps, but then it rumbles again. This time it's embarrassingly loud.

My eyes shoot to Peter because out of everyone in the room, I pray that his ears are not attuned to the sound of my rumbling stomach. His hand flexes, making me think his mind is on something else. I hope he isn't thinking about that other thing again.

I stay seated when the bell finally rings because I don't want to risk passing Peter when the rumbles sound again. But Peter also remains seated. I start to wonder what he's doing when he turns to look at me. And then comes the loudest rumble of all. Blushing, I dart my eyes away just as he gets to his feet. I know that he's walking toward me, and I wonder why it has to be now. The next second, some of the snacks I bought appear in front of me. I can't stop myself from looking up at him, even though my face is burning.

"Thanks for this," he smiles. "I mean it." He turns, but something stops him. Digging inside his pocket, he spins back to me. "This is for you."

"Why are you giving me a playing card?" I ask, taking it from him. It's not that I'm not grateful for it. Believe me, I am. I just didn't know Peter liked playing with them. Should I learn?

"Because you remind me of Pikachu." He answers.

I remind him-? "But why?"

A smile appears on his lips. It's a teasing smile like he knows something I don't. "I'll give you three guesses. If you figure it out, I'll let you know if you're right."

With this, he hoists his bag up and leaves the room, pausing just outside the door. When I realise it's because he's waiting for me, I scramble to my feet, clutching the playing card between my fingers.

BECAUSE
YOU'RE CUTE

Peter

I don't use the word hate often. But, right now, I hate a lot of things. For starters, I hate how your day can be ruined like a flick of a switch when you're not the one who switched it. I hate how, when you put your trust in someone, they can let you down without a single thought to how you might feel. I hate how you can miss someone to the point you feel chewed up inside when you're just an afterthought to them. And I hate my dad.

No. I didn't mean that. I don't hate him. I just... hate how he makes me feel. Is that a fair thing to say? Part of me worries it's not because maybe he does want to be at home, and maybe he can't help it. But, if you wanted to do something enough, wouldn't you find a way to do it?

I rub the back of my neck as I feel the headache coming on. I get these sometimes, often caused by stress. Great. A headache to start the day off at school, what could be better? I could go home, but I'd rather sit through class with a hammer banging against my head than go back there.

It will be bad enough tonight. By then, my dad would've told my mum that he isn't coming back, and my mum will be in full complaint mode. Doesn't she realise her complaints make it harder for us? I stuff my phone back into my pocket before I can think any further. As I pass the ramp, I hear someone call out my name. But I ignore it. Today, I am not in the mood.

Unfortunately for me, there aren't many places you can go to be alone in this school. With this in mind, I head to the one place I know I'll find solitude - the classroom. Yep, the place is deserted when I reach it. I drop my bag onto my desk in relief, dropping my head into my hands the next second.

I'm sorry, Pete. I won't be able to make it to this match, but I promise I'll make it to your next...

Do you know what else I hate? When someone makes a promise that they can't keep. No, it's not just that. It's when they *know* they won't be able to keep it, but they make it anyway. And the only reason they do that is to make themselves feel better about letting you down now. The headache is getting worse.

Hearing the bell, I turn my head to the door. I don't

realise I'm waiting to see her until I do. While she's half-hidden behind Natasha, I still catch a glimpse of the grin on Emily's face as she makes her way through the room, and I'm surprised by how it relaxes me. But that all changes when her eyes move across to meet mine. Her concern is instant. It's not the same concern I see in other people, either. It's a kind that causes a lump to rise in my throat and my pulse to quicken. I turn away from her, finding something to focus on outside the window.

But I can still feel her eyes on me. And it's too much to deal with.

Dropping my head into my hands, I wonder why I had to tell Emily about my dad today of all days. If she hasn't already figured out my mood has something to do with the phone call, she will do soon. From there, it isn't difficult to guess who called. So I do the one thing I don't want to do. I avoid her. I avoid the only person I wouldn't mind seeing today. Because, if I don't, I'm afraid of what it might do to her.

When people say a problem shared is a problem halved, I don't believe it. For me, a problem shared is a problem given. I wish I didn't think like that. I wish I could go to Emily right now and tell her everything because I know doing this will make me feel better. Getting it off my chest will make me feel better. But what I can't guarantee is how it will make Emily feel.

My neighbour is far too good a person for this world. Even when she's annoyed me, I've seen this. She's the type who'll get upset over someone else's pain. And it's not like when someone says 'I'm so sorry' and then laughs the next second. If Emily sees someone upset, she'll be the same all day. So if I show her my sadness now, she'll show it back to me. And I can't bear to see that.

Avoiding her isn't easy. By the time I reach English class, my head is pounding from the effort. I drop my face into my hands again, this time to cover myself in darkness.

"Peter!" Hannah's hand bangs down on the table. I wince away, but it doesn't stop her from laughing.

"I have a headache," I tell her.

She's silent for a second, and then I feel a hand rub my shoulder. "Aw, poor you."

Somehow, I manage to make it through the hour. I may have fallen asleep at some point because the room is quiet by the time I come around again.

"Are you alright?"

I freeze. A glance to the side confirms what I fear - only Emily and I remain in the room.

"I'm fine," I say, covering my face again. It's the only thing that will stop me from breaking in front of her. Breaking - or crumbling into an embrace I'm not sure she wants to give.

"Peter, you can speak to me if you wa-"

Afraid I won't be able to keep it together any longer, I jump to my feet. "I'm fine," I say again. A second voice screams in my head *I'm not*, and I'm sure this is the voice Emily hears. I force a smile onto my lips, hoping this will convince her to believe in the first one. When the look on her face worsens, I leave the room.

The pathetic thing is, even though I do this to escape, I can't help but hope she's following behind me. And, when I realise she isn't, I'm more disappointed than relieved.

Dude," Matt calls when I reach the cafeteria, "hurry the hell up. The nerds are about to take our table."

He barks out a laugh, and I realise that I can't deal with him today. I've already had to deal with one asshole.

"You go ahead. I want to be alone."

It takes him a second to register what I said. When he does, he frowns. "What?"

"I'm sitting on my own, so don't follow me." I stalk past him. Maybe he heard something in my voice this time because, for once, he doesn't follow.

Dropping my bag onto an empty table, I pull out my food. It doesn't surprise me that my mum's packed me another tuna sandwich, even though I reminded her that I don't like them. So I have a mum who packs me food I don't like and a dad who wouldn't be able to tell the difference, great. *It could be worse.* I sigh at the voice in my head. Yes, it could be worse, but that doesn't make me feel any better now.

"Are you doing alright, Peter?"

I snap my head up, surprised by the voice.

"I - I'm fine, Harvey. Thanks for asking."

He nods his head, pushing his glasses up the rim of his nose. I see Natasha standing beside him and Ben just behind her. Where's Emily?

"She isn't here," Natasha says, stopping my search. How did she-?

"You're looking for Emily?" Harvey drops into the seat in front of me. Funnily enough, it doesn't annoy me as it should. "I'm pretty sure I saw her make a run for it earlier."

"That's Emily," Natasha rolls her eye, and I smile because I know what she means.

"She's been worried about you," Harvey adds, taking a bite out of his sandwich. "She thinks you're upset."

I swallow down a sudden wave of guilt. "Nah, I'm just tired."

"I told you!" He grins up at Natasha, and I flick my eyes between them. I might be wrong, but I'm pretty sure he has a thing for her. From the way she looks at him, I reckon it's two-sided.

"Do you want to come and sit with us?" Natasha asks.

I hold back my surprise as I glance at Ben, who hasn't said a word since being here. Does *he* want me to join them?

"I'm alright," I say, concluding that he doesn't. To be honest, I just want to be alone.

By the time our break is ending, I still haven't touched my sandwich. I could force it down me, but I doubt I'll be able to stomach it today. I move my eyes around the room as a distraction. As I do, I see a familiar figure sitting by the teachers' table, and I do a double-take. What's Emily done to get herself stuck there? I think this, and then I notice her eyes are staring back at me. I've never seen this type of concern aimed at me before. I flick my eyes away as another lump rises in my throat, wondering why she's having this effect on me.

The thing is, I know that my neighbour cares about people. The trouble is that I sometimes feel she cares about me the most. It's stupid, I know. And, even if it is true, she'll realise that I'm not worth it sooner or later. At least that's what I keep expecting will happen.

My eyes start to blur, so I'm glad when the bell rings. Emily calls out my name as I walk out, but I can't look at her right now. I can't look at anyone. Heading to the bathroom, I splash my face with cold water, gripping the edges of the sink.

Get it out of your head that she cares about you.

Get it out of your head that anybody does.

I suck in a sharp, steadying breath as I try to bring myself back. Some days are like this. Some days, I am my own worst enemy.

In history class, I focus on nothing but a rustling tree outside the window. Someone knocks on the door, and I hear Emily's voice as she rushes inside. Something drops on my desk. I stare at the bag for a full five seconds before I look up at the teacher, waiting for him to turn his back. What is in that thing? My mind runs through several possibilities while I wait - maybe my mum's given her something to pass on to me, or she's finally giving me that textbook back, or it's some homework I forgot, or-

"Emily?"

The teacher's sharp voice forces my mind back into focus. I study the board, wondering how much of class I've missed in my distraction.

"Yes, sir?"

"Do you have the answer?"

"Oh, um..." A glance back tells me that Emily probably doesn't know the question. I'd help her, but I have no idea what it is, either. "I-, um-,"

"Somebody else? Yes – Hannah?"

"Elizabeth 1 reigned from 1558 to 1603."

A few people laugh as Emily apologises, and I glare at the one closest to me. What's so funny about it? It's not like any of *them* volunteered to answer.

At least the teacher is leaving the room now. Finally getting to open the bag, I half-expect to find homework inside - so I'm shocked when I see it's full of food instead. Did she drop this by accident? But no. Everything in here is *my* favourite. Which means it's meant for me. Suddenly, all the self-doubt I've felt today disappears. I spot a smiley face at the bottom of the bag and pull it out, twirling it over in my fingers. Is this Emily's way of sending me a message? I smile at the thought.

Sometimes, words aren't what is needed. Sometimes, a gesture speaks a thousand words.

I place the eraser on my desk, resisting the urge to look at her. If I do it now, she'll see that within this moment, I adore her.

I write some answers down before the teacher returns. As I do, I wonder when Sammy found the time to list off my favourite snacks. It must have been him. How else would she know about the chocolate milk? I'll need to have a word with him about that one. Some things are meant to be kept between brothers, Sammy. But it doesn't explain the flapjack. He knows I hate them. Don't tell me these disgusting things are special to her, somehow-

Someone's stomach rumbles, and I'm not the only one to jump at the sound. It's Emily. I don't know how I know it - I just do. Why hasn't she eaten? She found the time to get me food, but not to get herself some? I move my eyes back to the bag, and something clicks. She must have used her lunch money to get me this, and she must not have received permission to do it. That's why she was sat at the teachers' table. A sudden warmth rushes through me, encompassing me to a point I can barely breathe.

When I hear her stomach rumble again, my hand flexes automatically for the bag because I want so badly to give her some food. She could have saved some for herself, at least. But no - I doubt she gave herself a second thought.

Finally, the bell rings. I remain in my seat, knowing that she'll come to me, as she always does. But she's taking her time. I check over my shoulder to see if she's somehow slipped past without me noticing, but she's still sitting there. What is she doing?

Her stomach rumbles again, and I notice her cheeks flush pink as if she's embarrassed. Oh, she is embarrassed. Is she sitting there because she doesn't want me to hear her stomach rumble? I hold back a smile as I get to my feet, reaching into the bag for a share of the snacks. My hand pauses on the flapjack, but I let that one fall before I drop the others onto her desk.

Emily's face snaps up, just like I thought it would at the temptation of food.

"Thanks for this," I smile. Just in case that isn't enough, I add, "I mean it" because I really do.

As I turn away, I feel something inside my pocket. Wondering what it is, I stuff my hand inside, realising it's the playing card Sammy gave me. I turn back to Emily.

"This is for you."

She takes it from me, her brows furrowed in confusion. "Why are you giving me a playing card?"

"Because you remind me of Pikachu."

Her confusion deepens, and I try to fight back a smile. "But why?"

Because you're cute.

"I'll give you three guesses," I say, wondering if she'll have any idea what I'm thinking. "If you figure it out, I'll let you know if you're right."

Hoisting my bag up, I make my way out. I'm sure whatever guess Emily comes up with will be amusing. As I wait for her outside the door, I see her leap to her feet, the playing card clutched tightly between her fingers. The sight of it forces me to admit something else, something I never expected myself to think. *And it might just be because I have a crush on you.*

HOODIE

Emily

Ever since Peter gave me that playing card a couple of days ago, I haven't stopped thinking about why I remind him of Pikachu. I see him heading into the school now, and I chase after him, ready to give him my first guess.

"Is it because I'm small and annoying?" I ask, jogging to keep up.

He glances to the side, a smile tugging on his lips. "Nope."

I stop walking. Small and annoying is what Harvey guessed - and, between you and me, I'm relieved that isn't the reason. But if that's not it, what is?

"That only counts as one!" I call, realising I just told him two things.

I see him smile again, and I take it as an affirmation.

When I turn, I find Natasha and Ben walking up to me, and I fall in beside them.

"That isn't the reason."

Natasha rolls her eyes as if I've told her something obvious. "Harvey got it wrong. What a surprise."

"Let me see it again," Ben holds out his hand, and I pull the playing card from my bag with care. He tilts his head from one side to the other with a *hmm* before passing it back to me. "I still think it's because you're cute."

He's said this multiple times already, but that doesn't stop me from blushing.

"No, I'm not."

"You act as if you've never been called cute before," he laughs, and the heat rises to my ears.

Truthfully, I don't think I have been called cute by a boy before, and I doubt very much that's what Peter meant. Either way, I'm not about to waste that guess on him.

"I know what it is," Natasha says suddenly, plucking the card from my fingers. She holds it up next to my face with an evil grin. "It's because you're always getting yourself embarrassed. Look - your cheeks are as red as Pikachu's!"

"Hey!" I snatch it back from her, taking care not to damage it as I tuck it safely away into my bag. Trust Natasha to come up with that one, even if she is right.

With a sigh, I enter the school. If only *because you're cute* is what Peter thinks.

"Is it just me, or is it stupidly cold in here?" Natasha wraps her arms around herself, and I do the same when the chill hits me.

"It isn't just you," I tell her with a shiver, "it's colder in here than it is outside." I frown to myself as Ben stops walking.

"You two go ahead, I- I've got to get something from my locker." With this curious comment, he turns and darts away.

"What do you think that was about?" Natasha frowns.

I shrug, looping my arm in hers. "I'm sure we'll find out soon enough."

When we reach English class, my eyes immediately search for Peter. He isn't here yet. I drop my bag onto the table as I wait for him, ready to give him my second guess. As I do, I notice a big mound of coats has hijacked Harvey's seat. I bet he'll freak out when he gets here.

"Who gave *you* the memo?"

I look up at Natasha, wondering who she's talking to. Wait-

"Is that you, Harvey?" I bend my head, realising that the big mound is actually Harvey wearing multiple coats. *And is that a blanket wrapped around him?* "Where did you get that from?" I gasp, stroking the soft fluff with envy.

He leans back, crossing his hands behind his head as if he's some cool person. It might've worked, except that his chair is now falling backwards, with him going down with it. His smug face morphs into one of horror as he crashes to the floor.

"Are you okay?" the words, of course, come from me. Natasha is laughing her head off.

"I'm good!" He jumps to his feet, wiping his nose as he turns his face away from us. From this angle, I can see that his glasses are askew. "My dad works for the maintenance company," he continues, clearing his throat. "And he told me this morning that the heaters are broke. Which is why," he reaches down, pulling something from his bag, "I got one for you."

Seeing the blanket in his hands, I leap forward with a grin. But he doesn't pass it to me - the fluffy treasure goes straight into Natasha's arms.

"Aw, thanks, Harvey," she says, wrapping it around her as she sits.

I slump into my seat with a scowl. Maybe if I start laughing at his pain, he'll give me a blanket, too.

"Peter's here," Natasha winks, knowing just how to lift my mood.

I spin so fast that all I see is a flash of grey. The next second, a hoodie falls into my lap. Peter walks ahead, taking his seat without looking at me, but I know this came from him. It's my favourite one of his.

I clutch it to my chest with gratitude as Hannah stops in front of me.

"Peter, I think you just dropped this."

Seeing that she's pointing at the hoodie, I hold it tighter. Peter turns, his eyes flashing to me before landing on Hannah.

"No. It was meant for Emily."

A low buzz spreads across the classroom as he turns away again. I lower my face with a smile, ignoring the looks of disbelief now aimed my way. No blanket in the world is better than this.

"I'm not saying you need to thank me," Harvey whispers, bringing my attention back to him, "but I see that my tips are working with Peter."

My smile falters. "You can't take credit for this one. I'm the reason we're friends." I throw the hoodie over my head. It falls past my knees, but I don't care. This is the best thing I've ever worn.

Ben appears in the doorway. I give him a wave, the long sleeves of Peter's hoodie flapping in the air. He holds a jacket up to me with a grin, and I point at mine to show him that I have one now, too.

For some reason, his smile falters.

"Where'd you get that?" He asks, pointing to the hoodie as he takes a seat.

"Peter gave it to me." I notice that he's slipping his jacket into his bag and add, "aren't you wearing yours? You went all that way to get it."

"Oh, I-" he clears his throat, "the jog here, er... warmed me up."

I keep an eye on him for the rest of the hour, noticing his sudden change in mood. When it doesn't lift, I grab a piece of paper and draw a funny picture on it, sliding it across the table. His lips pull up as he scribbles something down. My funny face now has horns and a moustache. Holding back a giggle, I add a tail and elephant ears. We do this over and over until somebody snatches the sheet from me.

"Hey, that's-" I cut off when I see that it's the teacher.

She holds our piece of art up for the class to see, calling everyone into silence. "*This*, students, is what you're not supposed to be doing. Emily and Ben, I'll see you after class."

Luckily for Ben and me, our punishment isn't so bad. All she asks is that we deliver a pile of paperwork to another teacher, and it's sort of fun. I laugh with him as we make our way over, glad that he's cheered up again.

"You're not going to like this," Natasha says as I take my seat in math.

"What?"

She points at the board. "Our mock test is tomorrow."

My mouth drops open in horror. "But I thought it was next week! I - I'm not ready for tomorrow. They'll kick me out of set 2!"

Somebody knocks on my desk, and I look up in a panic. For a second, I'm too distressed to register who it is. When I see that it's Peter, my fear kicks up a notch because I don't want to be in a class without him.

"I need my textbook back."

I blink several times before I register what he's saying. Fumbling in my bag, I search for the textbook I've secretly been hoping to keep.

"Here you go," I say, handing it back to him.

He takes it without a word, turning to leave.

"Emily needs a tutor for the math test tomorrow,"

Natasha rushes out.

I give her a hard look before I realise she's doing me a favour. Glancing back at Peter, I hold my breath, praying his answer is yes.

"Does she?" is all he says.

Natasha shoots me a confused glance. "Will *you* help her?"

"I'm busy."

Without another word, he turns and walks back to his desk, leaving my throat to dry up.

"Have I upset him?" I whisper, a new kind of panic settling in my stomach.

She shakes her head with a scowl. "No. He's just being an ass."

My uneasiness remains, but I can't lose focus now. I can still try my hardest, even without any help. That's why, when the bell rings for lunch, I remain seated, determined to revise through the hour. Ben brings me a sandwich at some point in-between, and I wolf it down for brain fuel. When school ends, I do something that I've never done before - I head to the study hall. This is a torturous place to be, so I'm not surprised when nobody joins me. The only problem is that I do need help. The questions from here are a puzzle to me. A puzzle that reads like a foreign language.

I pull some colouring pencils from my bag, hoping a little creativity will clear my brain. My mum tells me that I like to procrastinate, but I think procrastination can work. Sometimes. Right now, it isn't working for me. I close my eyes instead because maybe I just need a nap. Lucky for me, I can pretty much sleep anywhere - more so when I need to study - and it doesn't take long before I start to doze.

A loud noise causes my eyes to snap open. I look down at my textbook, which is now sprawled on the floor, and then up at the newcomer.

Am I dreaming? I must be because why else would Peter be here? He has his back to me, but I'd recognise this boy anywhere.

"Peter! What are you-,"

"I just-," he points at the door with a textbook before shaking his head with a sigh. "I came to help. If you still want it, that is."

"I do!" I sit up straight, wiping any potential dribble from my face as I make a clear space for him.

"Okay," he sits, "so tell me where you got to."

He goes through the questions with me in detail, explaining things slow enough that I understand. The way Peter does it makes me wish I could have him for my teacher every day. Then again, maybe that isn't a good idea. Because, even though I focus for a really long time, as soon as my eyes move over to Peter, I am done. I've seen him concentrate before, but never this close up. Just this one look has me losing all other focus. I watch his lips as he talks, no longer hearing what he's saying. What would he do if I reached over and touched them? Just a touch-

"Emily?"

I blink at the sound of my name. "Hmm?"

"You've been staring at me for the past five

minutes."

Oh.

I clear my throat, darting my eyes away. When I remember what Natasha said, I turn back and say, "um, Peter?"

"Yeah?"

"Did you give me the card because I'm always embarrassing myself, and my cheeks are as red as Pikachu's?"

He smirks. "No. And that's two guesses." Hopping to his feet, he holds out his hand. I grab onto it without thinking. For a second, I stare at my hand in his, rejoicing at the warmth now wrapping around my fingers. But then I realise that he hadn't meant for me to take it. He just wanted me to join him.

I drop my hand as the humiliation hits me again. When will I stop doing things like this? "Sorry," I mumble, peeping back at him.

To my surprise, Peter is laughing. "Your cheeks do get red, don't they?" Before I can answer, he reaches over, pulling the hood over my eyes so that I'm blinded. "This suits you, by the way."

I grin. "Does that mean I can keep it?" He doesn't say anything, but I can hear a chuckle. "Is that a yes, or a no? I can't see."

"It's a *no*."

Removing the hood with a pout, I see that he's walking to the door. I follow after him, surprised by how dark it is outside.

Peter echoes my thoughts. "I didn't realise it was

this late."

"Neither did I." I shiver against the cold.

He looks down all-a-sudden, pulling something from his bag.

"Here," before I can prepare myself for what's about to happen, he takes hold of my hands, pulling his gloves up over them. When I look at his face, I see that he's smiling again. "Don't you own a pair of gloves?" He asks, pulling my hood back up. It doesn't cover my eyes this time.

"I-," whatever answer I'm about to give vanishes when I see how he's looking at me. His hands, still holding the ridge of my hood, radiate heat onto my cheeks.

"Why do you want to stay in Set 2?" He breaths.

"I-," I gulp, still unable to use my voice. *Because of you.*

A look passes behind his eyes as if he knows what I'm thinking. My cheeks flush at the thought, and Peter smiles, stepping back.

"I guess it's for the same reason as me."

Or maybe he doesn't know what I'm thinking. Because there is no way that Peter wants to stay in Set 2 because I am in it.

THE SAME
REASON AS ME

Peter

When my dad told me he wouldn't be coming to watch my basketball match, I went into a downward spiral. I'm glad to say that I'm no longer in that place. Usually, a bad mood like that will last at least a full day, but I got out of it quick this time. And I know it's because of Emily.

I swing beneath the railing, my mind still focussing on that bag she gave me. It's like I said before - sometimes, words aren't what is needed. In my case, Emily's gesture was more than enough.

"Is it because I'm small and annoying?"

I glance to the side, wondering if it's possible to conjure someone from your thoughts. When I see Emily jogging to keep up with my stride, I can't help but smile.

"Nope," I turn away as we approach the door. As I do, guilt presses in on me that this is her guess. While *annoying* may have been my answer before, I hope that's not how I've made her feel.

I open the door, allowing enough time for Emily to enter first. When she doesn't, I realise she's no longer with me.

"That only counts as one!" I hear her call somewhere at a distance.

I smile to myself. Yeah, I'll let her have those two guesses if only to hear her say it herself. *Because I'm cute.* Surely she can figure that out on her own.

Inside the school, it takes me a full two seconds before I realise something is wrong. It's the temperature. It's like I'm walking through a refrigerator. Seeing a sign on the wall, I walk up to it, groaning when I read the word 'heater' coupled with 'broken'. I don't like being cold. Remembering the hoodie I stashed in my locker, I make a U-turn. Mine is located on the other side of the school. If that isn't bad enough, it's also right next to Hannah's. And she always has her cronies with her.

"It's freezing," I hear her complain as I approach. "Honestly, why haven't they sent us home already? I could get my dad to sue this place." She slams her locker door shut, noticing me.

Keeping my eyes ahead, I stop at my locker. Maybe if I don't make eye contact, she won't talk to me. That never works.

"Hey, Peter, do you want to join us in our attempt to close the school?"

I feign coolness as I pull my hoodie out, but closing the school is the last thing I want. "Nah, I'm fine being here."

"Maybe if I had an extra layer, it wouldn't be so bad."

Noticing her eyes on my hoodie, I tuck it beneath my arm. "Right."

"I just hope I don't catch a cold," she continues, rubbing her arms with a sigh.

Emily gets the cold a lot. What was she wearing before?

"Peter?"

I clear the frown from my face. "Sorry," I say, setting off into a walk, "I'll see you in class."

What *was* Emily wearing before? I keep an eye out for her as I make my way to class, but I only find her when I get there. And, as expected, her jacket is only thin. I drop the hoodie into her lap as I pass her, mainly because I don't want to draw any attention to us. Students will gossip over anything minor here. But doing this means I miss her reaction. And, as I sit, I find myself longing to see it. Did she even want the hoodie? Is she happy I've given it to her? Will she wear it?

"Peter, I think you just dropped this."

I twist my head, my anger building when I see who Hannah is pointing at. Casting a glance at Emily, it almost softens into a smile. She's holding my hoodie as if it's a lifeline. I'll probably need to claw it from her if I ever want it back.

"No," I say, directing my words at Hannah, "it was meant for Emily."

With this, I turn away again, letting the smile surface. But it really is cold in here. I try to ignore it as I work, but that's as impossible as ignoring Jim's Jim jokes. When a shiver runs through me, I glance back, somewhat regretful that I handed my hoodie over. But then I see the smile on Emily's face as she wears it, and the regret vanishes. I guess I can be cold for one day.

I focus on the project for the rest of the hour, so I don't realise it's noisy until the teacher calls the room into silence. Looking up, I find her standing by Emily's desk, and I wonder what she's done now.

"*This*, students," the teacher holds up a picture that resembles a deformed elephant, "is what you're not supposed to be doing. Emily and Ben, I'll see you after class."

My lips pull up at the sound of Emily's name. And then they fall at the one that comes after it. I frown at the floor, wondering what the hell this feeling is about. *They're just friends,* an unexpected voice tells me. My frown deepens. Would it bother me if they're not?

I shake my head, grateful when the bell rings for break. Somehow, it's warmer outside than it is in, so I don't mind heading out to the ramp. I lean my arms against the railing, staring out in thought.

"You stressed about that mock test or something?"

I glance to my right, spotting Dec beside me. "What mock tes-,"

"Looks like the new kid's got himself a girlfriend already," Matt laughs.

My head spins so fast that a spasm of pain shoots through it. Rubbing the back of my neck, I watch Emily as she walks past us, laughing at something Ben is saying. The two *do* seem to have gotten close. And Ben *does* seem to have taken an interest in her. Enough for Matt to think she's his girlfriend. My stomach twists.

I try to reason with myself as I make my way to math. Emily can like who she wants, and I should only be bothered if the guy is a douchebag - but whatever monster this is, it doesn't want to listen to logic. In an attempt to focus, I open my textbook. But even as I work out the ratio cost of a lampshade, my mind is spinning.

Looks like the new kid's got himself a girlfriend.

I drop the pencil. On impulse, I push out my chair and stand. I have no idea why I'm doing this. I have no idea what I'm going to say when I get there. Emily doesn't look up when I reach her, but I catch the end of her conversation.

"...they're going to kick me out of set 2!"

I knock on her desk, hoping she'll elaborate. When she doesn't say anything, I rack my brain for an excuse to be here.

"I need my textbook back."

She looks at me like I've just asked her a complicated question, and I wonder if she even remembers having it. But then she searches in her bag, passing it over with a distracted look in her eye.

"Here you go."

Not sure what else I can say to her, I turn away, somewhat regretful that I'm bad on the talking front.

"Emily needs a tutor for the math test tomorrow."

Grateful to Natasha for giving me a reason to stay, I glance back.

"Does she?"

There's a second silence before Natasha responds.

"Will *you* help her?"

My pulse quickens. Stupid, since I've been alone with Emily before. I give myself a second to calm down before I respond. Within that second, a cloud of doubt passes like a shadow through my mind, telling me that this isn't what Emily wants. Wouldn't she prefer it if Ben tutored her? My throat closes as if the cloud is somehow suffocating.

"I'm busy," I manage to say, turning to leave. My muscles protest against every movement, but it's what Emily will want.

I'm out of the door before anyone else when the bell rings. Yet, somehow, I'm the last to the cafeteria.

"Peter!"

I pause, surprised to hear Natasha calling my name. She catches up to me, looking annoyed about something.

"Yeah?" I ask cautiously.

"Did you have to be such a jerk earlier?"

I glance to the side, wondering what the hell she means. "When was I-,"

"*I'm busy,*" she makes quotation marks in the air, repeating what I said to Emily. "Even if you are busy, you could have said it nicer. You know Emily only wants to stay in Set 2 because you're in it."

My eyes, fixated on the wall, shoot to meet hers. Natasha must see my disbelief because she blinks, her anger disappearing.

"Did you really not know?"

"Where is she?" I ask, ignoring her question.

"She stayed behind to study," her eyes follow me as I circle around her, "don't tell her I told you!"

I give her the thumbs up as I set off into a sprint, my heart thumping as I weave my way through an onslaught of students.

I am an idiot. An idiot who unknowingly upset the last person on Earth who deserves to be upset.

And Natasha is right - I am a jerk for it.

I pull myself to a stop when I reach the classroom, searching through the glass for a sign of my neighbour. When I find her, I realise she isn't alone. Nausea settles in my stomach when I see Ben sitting beside her. Nausea because that could be me helping her. Nausea because I did this to myself. But I still have time to make amends.

When I see Emily's friends leaving the school, I head back inside, finding her in the study hall. My hands shake as I open the door, but her eyes don't flash toward me as I expect them to. As I get closer, I realise it's because she's sleeping. My nerves vanish as a laugh breaks out. Of course Emily is taking a nap at a time like this. I continue walking toward her, ready to wake her up - but I stop myself at the last second.

She looks so... peaceful. Would it be a crime to just let her sleep? *Yes*, a voice answers for me. *Yes, because she needs to pass that test tomorrow. She needs to pass it because-*

I cut off that thought, crouching to her level with a smile. Noticing a loose strand of hair in her face, I reach over, knocking a textbook in the process. It crashes to the floor with a bang. Fearful about getting caught staring, I spin away. But a gasp has me turning back.

"Peter! What are you-,"

"I just-," I point to the door as I rack my brain for an excuse to be here. Realising that's pointless, I shake my head with a sigh. "I came to help," I admit. Then, as the doubt creeps back, I add, "if you still want it, that is."

I wouldn't be surprised if Emily is angry at me for being an ass. I wouldn't be surprised if she refused my help because of it. What does surprise me is the way she sits up. It's as if she couldn't be happier.

"I do!"

"Okay," I take a seat in relief, "so tell me where you got to."

It turns out she didn't get very far, but I don't tell her that. Instead, I go back to the start, taking her through every question in a way I hope she'll understand. She takes it in well at first. But, after a while, I notice her lose focus. A glance to the side tells me she's watching me. Is there something on my face? Why is she so engrossed?

"Emily?" I say.

"Hmm?"

"You've been staring at me for the past five minutes."

She clears her throat, and I notice her cheeks flush crimson. It takes a second before she meets my eye. "Um, Peter?"

"Yeah?"

"Did you give me the card because I'm always embarrassing myself, and my cheeks are as red as Pikachu's?"

I choke back a laugh. Now that she mentions it, why didn't I think of that? "No. And that's two guesses." Hopping to my feet, I hold out my hand. We've done enough revision to keep her in Set 2. Besides, she's smarter than she thinks.

Emily's hand falls into mine. I didn't mean for this to happen - I meant it as a gesture - but I find myself glad it has. I wrap my fingers around hers just as she jolts it away.

"Sorry," she mumbles, blushing the deepest colour yet.

I can't help but laugh.

"Your cheeks do get red, don't they?" I reach over to pull her hood up. My hoodie is big enough that it falls over her eyes. "This suits you, by the way."

"Does that mean I can keep it?" She grins. I chuckle

because her mouth is all I can see of her face. "Is that a yes, or a no? I can't see."

"It's a *no*." I head for the door, still laughing to myself as I reach outside. It's a lot darker than I thought it would be.

"I didn't realise it was this late," I say, as Emily catches up to me.

"Neither did I," a shiver runs through her, and I reach into my bag.

"Here," I take hold of her hands, pulling my gloves over them. They're big, just like the hoodie. And, just like the hoodie, the sight of it makes me smile. "Don't you own a pair of gloves?" I ask, genuinely curious. I pull the hood back up to guard her face from the cold, taking care that it doesn't cover her eyes this time. Then I do something that I probably shouldn't. Because when I move my eyes down to meet hers, I lose all thought processes, and the reason behind giving her the playing card solidifies.

Emily only wants to stay in Set 2 because you're in it.

Natasha's words catapult around my brain, forcing me to admit something I've been fighting back.

And I only want to stay in Set 2 because Emily is in it.

The admission takes me by surprise. But, when I think about it, I wouldn't want to be in a class where I don't see Emily pass my desk every day, or hear her laugh, or see that smile as she enters the room.

"Why do you want to stay in Set 2?" I breathe, wanting to hear her say it.

"I-," she gulps down her words, but I don't need

them. I can see her answer from the colour now rising in her cheeks.

I smile, taking a step back. "I guess it's for the same reason as me."

MOCK TEST RESULTS

Emily

L ater on at school, we get our mock test results back. That means I'll find out if I get to stay in Set 2. It's also the day of the boys' basketball match. If I'm honest, I'm not sure which one I'm more nervous about. On the one hand, the match is a big deal for Peter, making it a big deal for me. On the other, there is a high chance I sucked on that test, so I may be demoted by the end of the day. I don't want to be demoted. Not only do the students in Set 3 scare me - take Alice, for example - but my mum will kill me if she finds out. And believe me, she will find out.

"Emily!" I hear her call now, "it's time to come down!"

"Just a second!"

I'm currently making a poster for Peter - something I'll be using at the basketball match later on. Not to blow my own trumpet or anything, but it looks good. I've put glitter on the letter P, and I've drawn little green basketballs around his name. Green is his favourite colour, so I think he'll like it.

"Now, Emily!"

"Now schmow," I mutter, grabbing my schoolbag from the floor. After carefully packing the poster inside, I make my way downstairs, finding my mum in the kitchen with a cup of coffee in her hand. I swear she rushes me for the fun of it. "What's so urgent?" I ask, dropping my bag on the table. She nods her head to the side, and I notice my dad for the first time. Awake. Before noon. Dressed in a suit. "Wha-,"

"I have a job interview." He grins, answering my unfinished question.

"Really?" I flick my eyes between them, taking in both smiles. When I realise this must mean it's for something good, I lunge forward, enclosing my dad in a hug. "That's amazing, dad! I'm so happy for you!"

"Thanks, hon," he kisses the top of my head, and I smile into his suit jacket. "I have a good feeling about this one. It's something I've always wanted to do."

"You'll do great," I hear my mum say. The next second, an extra pair of arms wrap around me.

"Well, I best get going," my dad says, breaking us up. "Wish me luck."

"Good luck, dad."

"Good luck. Not that you need it."

He gives us a smile before grabbing his work bag from the counter. After bending to scratch Blondie behind the ear, he heads for the door, and I busy myself with making cereal. I'm halfway between pouring it when my favourite voice drifts through to me.

"Morning, Mr. Clarke. How are you?"

"Good morning, Peter. I'm-,"

Whatever my dad says next, I don't hear it. I'm too busy spilling my cereal on the floor and dropping my spoon on the counter.

"Oh, Emily," my mum says, her voice brimming with despair.

"Sorry!" after scooping the nuggets into a dustpan, I race over to the table, knocking a chair over in my haste to leave. It's a lot louder than the spoon. "Sorry," I say again, avoiding my mum's eye as I bend to lift it. Placing the chair back in its place, I throw on my coat and sprint past her.

"What about your breakfast?" she calls after me.

"I'll eat as I walk!"

My dad is still at the door by the time I reach it. Peeping around his arm, I see Peter leaning against his bike, a textbook open in his hand. A smile tugs on his lips when he sees me, and my heart does a flip.

"Emily."

"Peter," yes, I'm attempting to sound as casual as him. And yes, I don't quite pull it off as Peter does. My legs jiggle with the urge to run over to him. Giving in to it, I kiss my dad on the cheek and dart across the grass. I'm halfway across before I realise how desperate I must look. While his eyes are back on his textbook, amusement is written all over his face.

Smoothing my hair, I give him a nonchalant "morning," and his lips twitch.

"Your coat is inside out."

"What?" Looking down, I half-expect, half-hope, that he's joking with me. But no - my coat is inside out. Cringing to myself, I wonder if I can somehow pull it off as the latest fashion. "Yes, it, um, it's supposed to be like this." I look up at the sky, trying to ignore the laughter coming from Peter.

"Looks like I've been wearing mine wrong this entire time," he says. When I glance back, I see that he's walking. My mortification lasts one whole second, and then I notice that he's pushing his bike instead of riding it.

Thrilled, I fall in beside him, no longer caring about my inside-out coat. "Were you waiting for me?"

"You wish." He twists his head away as he says this, and my smile deepens. Either way, he's walking with me now. "What happened to that bike of yours, by the way?"

"What bike?" When has Peter ever seen me with a bike?

He clears his throat. "I, er, saw you on it a couple of weeks back. Well, I saw you trying to get on it."

My brows furrow. After a few seconds of thinking, it clicks. Peter must have witnessed my failed attempts at climbing onto the monster bike. Peter.

Witnessed. Monster. Bike. I cover my face as the embarrassment hits me, and my foot catches something on the ground.

"Careful," he says, just as I blurt out,

"I'm not clumsy."

"I never said you were," he laughs.

I cringe again. "I know - it's just - my mum-," I shake my head, remembering all the times I've had to say 'I'm not clumsy' to her. "Nevermind."

We fall into silence. At least, I'm silent - Peter is laughing again. I shoot him a look, and he coughs into his hand as if he's trying to cover it up. "Are you nervous?" He asks, thumping his chest, "about the results, I mean?"

Ah, the dreaded mock test results. "I think I've failed it," I shrug, "but there isn't anything I can do now, so."

Peter's eyes roam my face. After a long second, he says, "but you can do anything once you've set your mind on it. It's one of the reasons why I like you."

Hearing the words "I like you" come out of Peter's mouth sets my heart into a frenzy. I bite my lip against a smile, turning my face so he can't see this level of Peter enthusiasm. Well, I've got my mind set on becoming his girlfriend, so I hope he's right.

Thankful that he can't read my mind, I clear my throat. "What about you? Are you nervous about the match?" I would ask him about the mock test, but I know Peter doesn't have to worry about things like that.

He sighs. "I don't have anyone coming to watch, so

not really."

"But your da-," seeing the look that crosses his face, I quickly stop what I'm saying. I can tell he doesn't want to talk about it. That doesn't stop my anger from building up at his dad. Peter does not deserve to be let down like this. I clench my fingers around the poster in my bag, ready to cheer with all my might. Peter, you do have somebody coming to watch, even if it isn't who you want.

When we reach the store, I spot my best friend at a distance.

"Ooh, there's-"

"I'll catch you at school."

Before I can do anything to stop him, Peter swings his leg over his bike and rides off.

"You can still walk with us!" I call.

As I frown at his retreating back, Natasha reaches me. "What, I'm not good enough for him?"

"That's not it, it's-" I stop speaking. I don't have a good excuse for this one.

"It's that he'll only walk with you." I smile at the thought, and she loops her arm in mine with a laugh. "He might be falling in love with you after all."

"Stop it!" I turn my face away with a giggle.

"Ready to find out you aced that test?"

My giggle fades. "Please don't remind me."

Unfortunately, we don't have math until third period, which means I have to wait all morning before we get the results. I fidget my way through English, and then I accidentally play for the opposite side during p.e. To be honest, I have no idea how I managed that one. By the time I take my seat in math, I'm a nervous wreck.

"You'll be fine," Ben says, stopping by our desk.

Harvey nods his head in agreement. "He's right. You had Peter's brain helping you. How can you fail?"

I nod my head, grateful for their encouragement. But, by the time the teacher hands out our papers at the end of class, I am a nervous wreck again. I cover my eyes as I receive mine, peeping through my fingers for the score. When I see one big *70* in red ink, I let out a shriek. "I did it!" I stare at the number in disbelief.

"I knew you would!" Natasha encloses me in a hug as Harvey and Ben rejoin us.

"You did it?" Harvey asks.

"I did!"

Turning, I find Peter looking at me. I hold up my result. He smiles, giving me the thumbs up before turning away again. His face falls at the last second. I don't think I was supposed to see it, but I did.

"Let's go get Emily a treat," Ben says, hoisting my bag up.

"I-," as I look back at Peter's desk, I realise he's no longer there.

"What about me?" Harvey complains. "I think I've surprised everyone, too."

Natasha taps his shoulder. "You certainly have, Harvey. You certainly have."

As the three of them queue up for lunch, I take our usual seat, wondering what that face meant. Did Peter fail? No, that's impossible. He helped me. But what-? Seeing him walking over to a table, I call out his name. He twists his head in search before walking over to me.

"What's up?"

I tap the table, surprised when he actually sits. "How did you do on the test?"

"Alright," he shrugs.

"Alright? What score did you get? I got 70 - thanks to your help."

He smiles, but it doesn't quite reach his eyes. "It doesn't matter what I got."

"Peter," I lower my head so that I can peer into his face. His eyes flash between mine and his hands.

After a long second, he sighs. "I got 95."

"*95?!*" My mouth gapes open. "But, Peter, that's amazing! Why would you hide that?" I hope it's not because he thinks I'll feel bad about it. Sure, I'm not the smartest, but that doesn't mean I can't be happy for those who are.

"It means I'm moving into Set 1," he tells me.

Oh. My smile drops as I realise what this means, but I lift it up again. While I may be disappointed that I'll no longer be in class with Peter - very much so - I can't let that fact show. It wouldn't be fair on him. "You belong in Set 1, Peter. You're smarter than the entire school put together."

His eyes roam over my face before his lips pull up. "Thanks, Emily."

I move my eyes to the side as I try to figure out how

I can move up to Set 1. How many more marks do I need? Ten? Twenty?

"What are you thinking?" Peter asks.

"Just how I can stay in class with you." When I realise I just said that out loud, I slap my hand over my mouth. He barks out a laugh.

"What's going on here?" Natasha asks, dropping her tray onto the table.

"Nothing, I-," noticing Peter getting to his feet, I quickly reach out my hand. "Why don't you eat with us?"

"Oh, er-," he moves his eyes over to the others, and I realise that Harvey and Ben are staring at him as if they're surprised he's here.

Harvey is the first to compose himself. "Yeah, you should stay, Peter. This table needs more cool people."

"And somebody would love it if you did," Natasha gives me a not-so-subtle wink. I respond to it by pinching her arm, thankful he doesn't seem to have heard her.

"Alright then," he says, lowering himself again.

I smile into my sandwich. When he looks across at me, I shoot my eyes away, but my smile gets bigger.

"Oh, Emily," Ben says, reaching his arm across the table. "Here's your treat." A slice of cake and orange juice drops down in front of me. "Congrats on staying in Set 2."

"Thanks so much," my mouth waters at the sight of the cake. It does not, however, do the same for the OJ. I push it to the side, hoping Ben doesn't notice when I don't drink it. When I look back, I see fresh apple juice in front of me instead. Did I see it wrong? I frown, glancing up when I hear a noise coming from Peter. My eyes widen when I see him swigging a bottle of orange juice. Did he just-?

"What did you get on your mock test, Peter?" Harvey asks.

He fastens the bottle. "95."

Their mouths drop open as mine did, making me smile with pride. Yes, Peter is extraordinary.

"Are you alright?" Natasha whispers in concern. "This means-,"

I shake my head slightly, picking at my sandwich as I try to figure out how I can do better on the real test. Am I even capable of getting into Set 1? Maybe if I put in the hours, I can-

A thin sheet of paper appears in front of me. I pick it up, recognising Peter's handwriting scrawled across the inside. My fingers shake as I unfold it.

I'll tutor you

I snap my head up. Even though he's looking outside the window, I can see that his lips are curled up at the corners. I tuck the paper into my pocket as mine do the same.

I THOUGH I WOULDN'T FIT IN

Peter

Sammy has fancy dress at school today, and he's decided to go as Pikachu. I thought he might choose to go as a dinosaur, but I'm glad he didn't. If he did, I wouldn't find it as funny now.

I laugh when I see him on the landing. His face is screwed up as he tries to fasten the back of his yellow costume.

"Do you want any help with that?" I ask.

"No thanks," he sticks his tongue out in concentration, and I have to admire his effort.

"You sure?"

After another minute of trying, he drops his hands with a sigh. "Okay."

I circle around him. So far, he's managed to fasten the buttons into the wrong holes. I smile as I start fixing them. "Good costume, by the way. You make a great Pikachu."

"Thanks. I was going to go as Stegosaurus, but," he shrugs his shoulders, "I like Pikachu."

"So do I."

He twists his head around with a sudden grin. "Did you give that card I gave you to Emily?"

"I did. But she has no idea what it means." Her first guess - small and annoying - was only half correct. Her second - that her cheeks are always red - is something I wish I came up with myself.

"But how can she not know it's because she's small and cute?" Sammy asks with a frown.

"I've been wondering that myself," I tap his shoulder, "okay, we're all done. Now go have an awesome day at school."

"Thanks, Peter!" he gives me a hug around the waist before darting downstairs. I chuckle as I watch him go, more at the lightning tail than anything. After changing into my school uniform, I head downstairs myself.

"Oh, you're here." My mum says, glancing up from her bag. "Could you grab me my flask from the kitchen? I'm running late."

"Sure," I head back down the hall as she turns away

again. Seeing her blue flask on the counter, I grab it and take it back.

"Thanks. Okay, Sammy, let's go." She hoists her bag up and heads for the door, Sammy tailing behind her. I wait to see if she'll wish me good luck on the match later. When she doesn't, I let out a sigh. In all honesty, it doesn't bother me that much anymore. Maybe I've built some resistance since my dad let me down. Even though I've checked my phone every day, hoping for a message, I'm okay with the fact he isn't coming now. I guess I don't want to depend on somebody else's actions for my own happiness anymore. I've done it for too long; and, for too long, it's made me unhappy. I've learnt something since then. While I can't control how other people treat me, I can control how I treat them. And how I want to treat them - and myself, for that matter - is with more decency than my parents show me.

"I hope you win today, Peter!"

I hear Sammy's voice, but I thought that he left already. Blinking out of my daze, I see a flash of yellow as he disappears again. At least someone remembers. Smiling, I grab my coat from the front room and follow them out. I like game days. It gives me a sort of adrenaline rush in the hours leading up to it. It's as if I'm nervous, but the nerves are mixed with a dosage of excitement.

Unlocking my bike, I wheel it down the path and climb on it. I'm halfway down the street when I realise I wouldn't mind seeing Emily this morning. I turn back. Stopping outside my garden, I put the brakes on my bike and lean on it. I hope she isn't late. Then again, her leaving times are always sporadic. I could be leaving the house at seven, and so is she. Or I could leave an hour later, and she is then, too.

Just when I think she'll take a while, I hear her door unlock. I open my textbook with a sudden urge to look busy. When she doesn't say anything, I glance up to find that it's her dad who's left the house, not Emily. My heart rate steadies.

"Morning, Mr. Clarke," I call. "How are you?"

"Good morning, Peter. I'm alright. How're you?"

I like Mr Clarke. He's always smiling. Come to think of it, he's a lot like Emily in that way.

"I'm good, thanks. Do you-" I'm about to ask if he knows when Emily will be out, but a loud noise from inside the house distracts me.

"It must be my daughter," Mr Clarke says, looking toward the noise, "she's quite clumsy."

I hold back a chuckle. Yeah, I already know that.

Almost as if she heard us speaking about her, Emily's head appears beside her dad's elbow. Not her body - just her head. My lips curl up at the sight of it.

"Emily."

"Peter."

Wow, a one-word greeting. This must be a first. I'm wondering if I've done something wrong when I see that she's now running toward me, the tag of her coat flapping in the wind. I look down at my textbook before Mr. Clarke sees that I'm laughing at his daughter.

"Morning," I hear her say - another one-word greeting. Has she expelled all of that energy or something?

It's hard not to smile. "Your coat is inside out," I tell her. Probably best to get that one out of the way first.

"What?" As she looks down, I take a second to examine her face. She looks happy this morning. Even more so than usual. There's a brightness in her eyes that I don't see often. I tilt my head. When she looks like this, she isn't just cute, she- "yes, it, um," I shoot my eyes away as she continues, "it's supposed to be like this."

It takes me a second to realise she means her coat. Laughing, I wonder who else would say something like that. "Looks like I've been wearing mine wrong this entire time," I say, setting off into a walk. A glance tells me she's fallen in beside me.

"Were you waiting for me?" she asks.

"You wish," I realise I still have my bike with me and shake my head. Idiot. If I wasn't waiting, why am I not riding it?

Remembering that mammoth one of hers, I ask, "what happened to that bike of yours, by the way?"

"What bike?"

My face burns when I remember she doesn't know I saw it. I clear my throat, wishing I hadn't mentioned it. "I, er, saw you on it a couple of weeks back. Well, I saw you trying to get on it."

When she doesn't say anything, I start to panic that I've said too much. But then I see her stumbling forwards, and those thoughts vanish as I reach out to

194

catch her.

"Careful," I say, simultaneous to her,

"I'm not clumsy."

I blink, and then the laughter finally comes out. "I never said you were."

"I know - it's just - my mum-," she shakes her head, and I look over my shoulder to see what she tripped over. Nothing. There is nothing there. "Nevermind."

I fail to hold back a laugh as I imagine how many times she must fall over in front of a person who actually lives with her. By now, her mum probably uses the word *clumsy* instead of her birth name.

Emily shoots me a look, forcing me to cut the laugh off. "Are you nervous?" I ask, trying to cover it up, "about the results, I mean?"

"I think I've failed it," she shrugs, "but there isn't anything I can do now, so-"

I analyse her face for a second. Doesn't she realise she's one of the most determined people I've met? Just one day of tutoring her showed me that, and the countless times I've seen her try again after failing. "But you can do anything once you've set your mind on it," I tell her, "It's one of the reasons why I like you."

A weird look passes across her face like she's about to hyperventilate or something. She turns away, and I wonder what the hell I just said to make her react like this. She can do anything? No. I like her? Ah.

I glance back at her now-beaming face. Even though she's biting her lip like she's trying to draw blood, I can tell that I've made her happy. My heart swells all-a-sudden. Really, it's touching that she re-acts in this way to those words.

"What about you?" She asks, pulling me out of my thoughts. "Are you nervous about the match?"

"I don't have anyone coming to watch, so not really." Where the hell did that come from? I look away with a frown. I thought I was okay with him not coming now.

"But your da-," she stops what she's saying, and I'm grateful for it. But, when I turn my head, I see that her face is contorted in anger. She rarely ever looks like this. I lick my lips as a smile plays on them, turning away again. As much as it sucks, it's nice knowing I have someone like Emily to feel angry on my behalf.

When we reach the convenience store, I see Natasha walking over to us, and the panic sets in.

"I'll catch you at school," I say, swinging my leg over my bike. I don't hear what Emily says because I'm too busy riding off.

It's not that I don't like Natasha. I'm just not at all comfortable with her. If I stayed with them now, I wouldn't have a clue what to say, which will probably make me look like an idiot in front of- I shake my head, accelerating my speed.

When I arrive at the school, I bump into the school counsellor. I say "bump into," - but it's been happening far too often for me to call it a coincidence now.

"Morning, Peter. Are you ready for your results?"

I busy myself with locking my bike. The last time she "bumped into" me was to ask, again, if I'd move up into Set 1. I said I would, but only if I got the mark for it.

"I'm ready," I say.

"Did you try your best?" She gives me a look that makes me think she doesn't trust me. I guess I don't blame her.

"I did."

She smiles. "I'm proud of you, Peter. You've made the right choice."

As she turns to leave, I quickly ask, "what score do you need to be in Set 1? Is it still 85?"

"Yes. Are you confident you got that?"

"I am. I'm just thinking about someone else." As she leaves, I busy myself with my bag as I try to push it from my mind.

I've been trying not to think about it ever since I took that test. Even while taking the test, I tried not to think about it. Because if I did - if I reminded myself about what I was losing - I wasn't sure if I could do it. And I needed to do it - for me.

I know class won't be the same without Emily, but I didn't think that should be a reason to stay. It isn't what I'd want for her if the tables were turned. Here I go again - thinking about it. I sigh as I head into the school. What's done is done now.

When the test results are given out in Math, I notice the teacher smile as he gives me mine. Still, I clench my fists into balls as I brace myself for the result, my heart thumping as it always does in the seconds leading up to it.

95.

I stare at the number for a second, and then I exhale. It's good knowing that I'm capable of this, and maybe more. Stuffing the test into my bag - I plan on studying my mistakes later - I hear a shriek come from the back of the room, and I smile. Looks like Emily did well, too.

Harvey and Ben are at her table when I turn. I watch as they congratulate each other. It's nice to see, so I'm surprised by the sudden ache in my chest. I push the feeling away as Emily meets my eye, holding up her test paper. Hope simmers in my stomach. I give her the thumbs up, searching for her grade.

70. It's enough to stay in this set but not enough to move up with me. I turn away as the realness of it hits me. I'll be leaving this class. And she'll be staying in it. How do I tell her?

I leave the room before she can catch up to me because I need time to think. By the time Emily calls me over in the cafeteria, I still haven't figured it out.

"What's up?" I ask, although I already know what's coming.

She taps the space in front of her, and I eye it for a second before I sit. "How did you do on the test?" she asks.

"Alright."

If I thought that would appease her, I thought wrong.

"Alright? What score did you get? I got 70 - thanks to your help."

I smile at the memory. "It doesn't matter what I

got."

"Peter," she brings her face closer to mine. The sudden nearness almost makes me tell her.

I flash my eyes away, but they get drawn back. I sigh in defeat. "I got 95."

"*95?!* But, Peter, that's amazing! Why would you hide that?"

Doesn't she see?

"It means I'm moving into Set 1," the words are like tar in my throat.

"You belong in Set 1, Peter," she says, calming me down. "You're smarter than the entire school put together."

I analyse her face as she smiles, wondering if she's saying this for me or if she's genuinely happy. I return it, hoping it's the latter. "Thanks, Emily."

We stay in silence for a second, and then I notice the thoughtful look on her face. "What are you thinking?"

"Just how I can stay in class with you."

I look at her in surprise - a surprise that she mirrors. As the words soak in, I feel a sudden burst of joy. It escapes in laughter.

"What's going on here?"

For a moment, I forgot that other people sat here. For a moment, I forgot that other people existed. When I see Natasha, Harvey, and Ben standing in front of me, I get to my feet.

"Why don't you eat with us?" Emily asks, reaching her hand out to stop me.

"Oh, er-," I look over at her friends, convinced they

won't want me here. There's an uncomfortable second where they all just stare at me. But then Harvey asks me to stay, and I'm surprised that it sounds genuine. "Alright then," I retake my seat, glancing over at Emily. At least she looks happy.

It's weird. I've sometimes thought about coming over and sitting here, but I always stopped myself because I thought I wouldn't fit in. But, now that I'm here, I feel strangely at home. Nobody is acting any different. It's as if I've been here from the start.

"Oh, Emily," I glance at Ben as he reaches across the table. "Here's your treat. Congrats on staying in Set 2." He drops something in front of her before looking over at me. I hold his stare for a second, wishing my stomach would stop clenching. Does he have to look so smug?

I look at what he's given her. When I see that it's orange juice, I smirk to myself. Emily hates oranges. I don't know how I know this - I just do. I think I saw her bite into one once - and it made her look nauseated. A lot like now, actually.

Swapping her juice for mine, I quickly swig it down before she projectile vomits on me.

"What did you get on your mock test, Peter?" Harvey asks.

I fasten the bottle, moving it slightly so that it's out of Ben's sight. "95."

As they stare at me in surprise, I catch the sound of Natasha's low whisper.

"Are you alright? This means-,"

I move my eyes over to Emily. Why does she look sad all of a sudden? Her shoulders are slumped, and she's picking at her sandwich as if she's lost that appetite of hers. The wheels turn in my brain. She wasn't smiling because she was happy before. She was smiling for me. My chest contracts. Wondering what I can do, my mind stops on one idea.

I pull paper from my bag and scribble down *I'll tutor you* before sliding it across to her. I see her smile from the corner of my eye, and I do the same. Because even if I'm not in her class anymore, I'm glad I have another way to spend time with her.

SAMMY
TOLD ME
SOMETHING

Emily

"**Y**ou do it."
"No, you."
"No, you do it."

I stop nudging Natasha as Peter's front door swings open. His mum pokes her head out, her eyes narrowing when they see me.

I swallow hard. "Hi, Mrs Woods. Is Sammy home?"

"He-," she halfway twists her head before turning back to me. "Why do you want Sammy?"

"I-," I swallow again. *Do it for Peter.* "I was wondering if I could take him to watch Peter's basketball match at school. He's playing soon."

"Oh. He's playing that today?" A strange look passes behind her eye as I nod my head. She turns away. "I'll just go get him for you."

"Thank you," I swing back on my heel, ignoring the pointed look Natasha is now shooting me.

"She doesn't know he has a match?" She whispers.

"She's been busy," I nudge her away as Mrs Woods reappears at the door. Sammy squeezes his way to the front, looking adorable in his yellow costume. It takes me a second to realise that he's dressed as Pikachu, and I smile because it reminds me of the card Peter gave me. I still have no idea why he gave me that.

"Can I really come with you?" he asks, hopping down the step with a grin.

"Absolutely."

He twists his head to look at his mum. "And I can wear this?"

"Of course, sweetie. Just make sure you're good for your brother."

"I will!"

After reassuring Mrs Woods that I'll take care of him, I follow Sammy out of the garden. Natasha holds her hand to her heart as she watches him totter ahead, smitten already. He is a miniature version of Peter, after all. How can he not be adorable?

"Okay, he's the sweetest," she whispers. "Are you sure they're related?"

I hit her arm as Sammy turns his head.

"Does Peter know I'm coming to watch?"

"No. It's a surprise!"

"Peter loves surprises!" He claps his hands together, giving me all the enthusiasm I need. Honestly, I think I'm as much jealous that Peter has Sammy as I am that Sammy has Peter.

"I have another surprise," I tell him, stopping by his side. "Look here," kneeling down, I unzip my bag and pull out the posters I've made for Peter. Sammy's eyes widen as I give him one.

"Wow. Did you make this?"

"Yep. And you can keep that one because I've made two more." I also made one for Ben because I think he'll appreciate the support, even if he's on the bench.

I bend to fasten my bag again. As I do, a few of the flapjacks I've stored fall out, resulting in a loud gasp from Sammy. Looking up, I see that his eyes are on the flapjacks like mine would be a chocolate bar. I hold one out to him. "You can have it if you want."

"Really?" His eyes light up as he takes it from me. "Thanks, Emily. You're the best."

Could he be any cuter?

"You're a lot like your brother, you know," I say as we start walking again. "Flapjacks are Peter's favourite, too. And he likes Pikachu. He even gave me this Pikachu card, look-," I pull it from its safe spot and hand it over, but Sammy shakes his head.

"No. He gave you that because he thinks you're cute."

I stop walking. Sammy, oblivious to that fact, continues ahead - nibbling on his flapjack like he hasn't just told me gigantic news.

Peter thinks I'm cute? Peter. Thinks. *I'm*. Cute?! Luckily, I have Natasha here with me. If I didn't, I might stay stuck on this spot forever.

"Did you just say Peter thinks Em's cute?" She asks, tugging my arm until I move. I stumble forward, waiting trance-like for Sammy to answer.

"Oops. I don't think he wanted me to tell you that."

I open my mouth to ask questions, but the look of guilt now on his face stops me from pressing it. Still, it's all I can think about as we continue walking. That *cannot* be why Peter gave me the card. No way can I be that lucky. Right? Or has Peter finally fallen for my Emily charms? Maybe I should give it as my third guess and find out. But what if Sammy got it wrong-?

We reach the school, and I'm so distracted by my thoughts that I face-plant the door.

"That's going to leave a shiner."

I stick my tongue out as Harvey walks over to us.

"Do you want any help with your bag?" He asks, stopping beside Natasha.

"I'm fine, Harvey."

"Are you sure?"

"I can carry my own bag."

What is going on with these two? I'm about to ask, but then I notice he's turning his attention on Sammy. I step in front of them. "Don't you scare him away."

"I wasn't going to!" He holds his hand to his heart as if I've wounded him. Crouching down, he extends his hand to Sammy. "Hi, there. I'm Harvey. Peter's best friend."

"No, you're not!" The words come from both Natasha and me. Sammy giggles, but Harvey's cheeks are now tinted with pink.

"Soon to be," he mutters, turning into the school.

By the time we reach the gym, it seems like the entire school is already seated. Manoeuvring our way through, we manage to find some empty chairs at the back. I take the one next to Sammy before Harvey can try to become his best friend, and he holds his Peter poster up high with pride.

"This one's for you," I hand another Peter poster over to Harvey. "Natasha, you get the Ben poster, and I get this," holding mine up like Sammy, I indicate for them to do the same. They give it a half-hearted effort. "Come on, you-" as the room erupts into cheers, I turn my attention to the front, searching eagerly for a sign of Peter.

Ben is the first one out. He doesn't go to the bench as I thought but heads straight out onto the court. I nudge Natasha's arm. "Ben's playing. Raise your poster."

I don't bother to check if she does because my favourite player comes out next. Somehow, Peter manages to outshine every other person on the court. Maybe it's the way he holds the ball beneath his arm with confidence, or the way his basketball kit hangs off his tall frame, or the way his hair falls in waves on his forehead, but he looks insanely hot.

"Do you think he'll see us?" Sammy asks, wiggling in his seat.

"I'm not sure," looking back, I see that Peter has his winning face on - which means his brows are furrowed and aimed at the floor. "Why don't we cheer?" I suggest. "If we do it loud enough, he might hear us." When Sammy agrees, I raise the poster higher, cheering as loud as I can. Peter's eyes search the stands, stopping on me. My heart does a leap when I spot that smile on his lips.

When his eyes move over to Sammy, the smile widens into a grin.

"He's happy I'm here!"

"Of course he is," I glance back at Peter as he runs to take his starting position, my heart thumping at the thought of him thinking *I'm* the cute one.

My eyes stay glued to him throughout the entirety of the match. He's obviously the best player out there, which is why the other team surrounds him so much. I get angry at that. Especially when one boy knocks him to the ground.

"Hey!" I call, but Peter jumps straight back to his feet. The only thing that calms me is the fact he scores three goals after that.

"We're tied for points," Harvey whispers, staring at the scoreboard with his mouth hanging open. "Peter needs to score again."

"He can do it," I cross my fingers as I lean forward, too fidgety to sit still. When Peter gets the ball again, I cheer along with the crowd, but he doesn't shoot like I expect him to. He just stands there facing the hoop.

"What is he *doing*?" Natasha leans forward with me, gripping her poster like it's a stress ball.

"Why is he passing the ball?" I croak, watching as he tosses it to someone else.

Ben catches it. The room falls silent as he shoots - all eyes on the ball as it spins around the hoop. And then, just when it looks like it'll fall out, it goes in.

"Yes!" I jump to my feet as the last whistle blows, sharing a high five with Sammy. Turning to do the same with Natasha, I find her with her arms wrapped around Harvey. There is no way I'm getting in between *that*. "Let's go find Peter," I whisper, grabbing Sammy's hand.

Peter is sitting on the floor with his head down by the time we reach him. I'm not surprised if he's exhausted. If it were me out there, I'd probably need to be carried out on a gurney.

He gets back to his feet, his eyes searching the stands before falling on us. A cascade of butterflies let loose in my stomach as he starts walking.

"What are you doing here?" He asks, picking Sammy up into a hug.

"Emily brought me."

"She did, did she?" He looks over at me, and I have to remind myself to stay calm. "Thank you."

"You're welcome. Congratulations on the win!"

"I couldn't have done it without these posters." He points to the one in my hand, causing the butterflies in my stomach to go wild.

"Anyti-" before I can say anything else, somebody nudges me out of the way. Rubbing my shoulder, I look back to find that the popular crowd now surrounds Peter. A crowd I don't belong in.

"Em, come here," Natasha grabs my hand, pulling me away from the person I want to be with. She stops in front of Harvey and Ben.

"So," Ben grins, "how did I do?"

Remembering the winning goal, I hold my hand out for a high five. "You did great."

"So great that you'll come to the arcade with us to celebrate?"

"Yes!" I glance back, wondering if Peter will want to come. "You guys go ahead. I'll be right there."

He's still far too surrounded by people for me to get close to him, but I manage to catch his eye. Pointing to the door, I mouth arcade. Then I cross my fingers behind my back as he speaks to his friends. After a long minute, he gives me a nod.

"Let's go!" I grin, pulling them outside with me.

I fall in beside Natasha as Peter joins the boys. Harvey bombards him with compliment after compliment, making me think he really is trying to become his best friend. Well, good luck to him. I've been trying that for years. After a few minutes of discussing our favourite foods, the sound of Sammy's laughter distracts us. We look over to find him on Peter's back as they run ahead.

"Is it just me, or did Peter just get a whole lot hotter?" Natasha asks.

I watch as he runs in a circle, making Sammy laugh louder. And then I pinch Natasha's arm as I realise what she said. "Hey, find your own man."

"I will," her eyes drift over to Harvey as she says this, and I don't let it go unnoticed.

"You do have a thing for Harvey, don't you?"

"No." She walks ahead, but the colour in her cheeks gives her away. I jog after her, looping my arm in hers.

"I won't say anything else."

"He has a girlfriend, anyway, remember?"

Actually, I often forget that fact.

When we reach the arcade, the first thing I see is the Valentine's Day stand. Excitement replaces my desire for food. Racing over to it, I touch the pink heart-shaped balloons with a grin.

I love Valentine's Day. There's just something about this day that makes me all mushy inside. Not that I've ever had a Valentine myself - but that doesn't mean I can't find joy in it. Besides, maybe this is the year that Peter will be mine.

"Out of everything here," Ben says, stepping beside me, "what would you want the most?"

"Hmm," I turn away from the Valentine's stand, searching the arcade games. Spotting one with Harry Potter plush toys inside, I point to it. "Definitely something from there."

Ben's eyes follow my finger. "Oh yeah? Which one?"

"Hagrid," I catch Peter's eye as I say this, and I wonder if he remembers that time with my hair.

"Why Hagrid?"

Peter's lips pull up. I clear my throat, hoping he isn't thinking about my frizz-bomb. "I just like him."

"So do I," Peter walks past us as he says this. I watch him go, wondering what he meant by that.

His movement sets everyone else into motion. Following Ben to the claw machine, I witness his many failed attempts as he tries to win me Hagrid.

"It's fine," I say, dragging him away. "I don't want him that much."

We find Natasha inside a shooting game. Joining her, I soon discover that I'm terrible at it, so I take myself off to another one instead. I win my first prize there. Holding the bracelet-making kit in my hands, I lean against a wall. What will I do with this? The colours are all too dark for me, so I doubt I'll make it for myself. Natasha, maybe?

Somebody nudges me. Looking up, I find Peter leaning against the wall beside me.

"Here," he says, holding out a bottle of juice.

"Thanks," I take it with a smile, moving the box out of the way so I can open it.

"I like the colours on that," he notes.

"You do?" I look back at the box, wondering if I should make him the bracelet for Valentine's Day. Yes, that's a great idea. Tucking it into my bag, I spot a stray flapjack at the bottom. I pull it out for him. "Here. You must be hungry after the basketball match."

"Oh - er - do you not want it?"

"I don't like them." The sudden frown on his face makes me realise what I just said. "I mean, I like them,

I just - don't want one now." Shoot - I don't want him knowing that my mum only gets these for me for him.

"Okay," he peels back the wrapper, taking a bite. "Yum."

"Emily, come here!" Seeing Ben waving me over to the dance-mats, I drop the drink down. How does he know I love them?

"Coming!"

We play on that for a while, but then I see Natasha stalking past with a gloomy look on her face.

"What's wrong with you?" I ask, holding my arm out.

"Nothing. Can we leave now?"

"Okay..." I grab my bag and scan the arcade. "Where's Peter?" I can just see Sammy by the bench with Harvey. I search around for his big brother, but he's nowhere to be seen.

"He went to the bathroom," Harvey says when we join him. "But that was a while ago."

"I'm here." We all turn at the sound of Peter's voice. I step beside him, relieved that he's alright.

Harvey is the first to leave. We walk Natasha to her house next, and then I'm left alone with Peter and Ben. And Sammy, but he's now asleep on Peter's back. As we walk in silence, I steal glances at Peter, wondering if I'll be able to give him my third guess tonight. I can't give it now. Not in front of Ben. I'm not sure if I can give it at all.

"I'll walk you to your door," Ben says, turning onto our street.

"Oh, I-,"

"I can do it."

I hold Peter's eyes as I nod my head. "Yeah, Peter can do it. We live on the same street, after all."

Now's your chance, I think as Ben leaves for his house. You have to say it now.

"Do you have something to say to me?" I hear him ask.

"No!" I shake my head. Why am I such a coward?

"Okay," he moves his eyes to the front. My feet slow with every step we take to our houses. Is his slowing for the same reason as mine? "Well," he says, slowing to a stop. "I best get Sammy inside."

"Goodnight!" Without another word, I race over to my house, only stopping when I reach the front door. When my fingers curl around the handle, I finally feel brave enough to say something. "Sammy told me something," I blurt out.

I scrunch my eyes shut, wondering if Peter's gone inside his house yet.

"Yeah?"

I suck in a sharp breath. And then another. And then another. On the fourth, I let the words roll out in a huff. "He said you gave me the Pikachu card because you think I'm cute."

As soon as the last word escapes my lips, I run inside my house, slamming the door behind me. I don't stop until I'm inside my bedroom. Taking a second to slow my racing heart, I begin pacing. Should I have said that? What will he think of me? What is he thinking now? Is he laughing? Maybe - if Sammy got it wrong. Did he get it wrong?

These thoughts whirl inside my head until I hear my phone ping. It's odd enough that I pause because I rarely ever get a text. If I do, it's usually for one out of two reasons. Either I've done something to annoy my mum, or Natasha is telling me that I'm late. Wondering how it could possibly be either of those things now, I grab my phone from my pocket. I almost drop it when I see Peter's name on my screen.

With shaking fingers, I click on the message, my heart pounding with every second I wait for it to open.

You were right before. It is because you're cute

...

Goodnight x

SHE WON'T
WAIT AROUND
FOREVER

Peter

As the captain of the basketball team, it's my job to give everybody the pep talk. You probably know enough of me by now to discern that I don't like talking in front of big crowds, but I'm different when it comes to basketball. In basketball, I'm in it to win. I look out at the sixteen faces looking back at me, and all I want is for them to believe in themselves as I do. We can win this match. We will win this match. The only thing that can stop us is ourselves.

I say something like this to them, and then we do that break thing we do every time before a match. Seeing Ben turn away, I catch him by the shoulder. "We're a player down," I tell him. "Are you ready to get out there?"

His face, blank a second ago, splits into a grin. "Heck, yeah, I am. Let me go stretch."

"Great," I watch him leave with an increasing sense that I've made the right choice. Even though Ben is our newest player, he has a love for the sport that I admire. He deserves a shot for that reason.

"Peter, your phone's been buzzing."

Turning, I find another one of our new players warming up by the bench. I give him a nod before grabbing my bag, wondering who it might be. Maybe it's my dad telling me he's decided to come. It's not. But it is my mum. I open the message, mentally preparing myself for whatever it is she wants now.

Good luck with the match today. Sorry I didn't say it sooner.

Wow. What made her remember? Sammy, perhaps? Whatever the reason, I'm glad about it.

I quickly reply with thanks as the coach calls us out.

"Okay, team. It's crowded out there, but don't let that put you off. As Peter said earlier, you've got what it takes to win this. Just believe in yourselves."

"Yes, coach!"

We make our way out onto the court. The coach was right about it being crowded. It's so busy that all I can hear is the sound of cheers. I keep my head down as I walk, not wanting to be distracted by it. While I try to drown out the voices, there's one that I can't block out. I doubt it's a voice I'll ever forget.

When I search the stands, I find Emily bobbing up and down at the back. Crazy that I'm able to find someone so small in a crowd this big. Even crazier that I could make out her voice in it. She's waving something around in her hands. Squinting, I make out my name drawn on it. She even went to the extent of adding glitter.

The realisation that she's not only here to support the school, but to support *me*, causes a lump to rise in my throat. I smile through the sudden emotion, but I have to grip the ball beneath my arm to stop myself from going over to her. I move my eyes away before I can do something rash like that, and then I almost drop the ball altogether. Is that Sammy with her? What is he doing here?

"Peter. You coming?"

"Yeah," I cast a glance back at Emily as I make my way to the centre of the court.

Even though my mind remains half-preoccupied by the girl in the stands, we still manage to get ahead on points. The other team defends me the most, and, with my height, that means I can pass the ball to someone who isn't marked - freeing up room for them to score.

In that sense, it's great - just not so fun for me. I may as well have a target on my back. Literally. One guy even goes as far as to knock me to the floor. That annoys me off at first. But then my ears, weirdly attuned as they are, hear Emily's voice again, and I jump back to my feet with a smirk. What's a five-foot girl going to do against a team of twelve?

With a sudden surge in determination, I manage to get a few shots of my own in. But then the other team switches up strategy. Instead of marking me, they spread out. Our confusion enables them to bring the points back. Running ahead, I spot Dec with the ball and indicate for him to pass it. When he does, I realise that I'm too awkward an angle to shoot.

Searching, I find Ben open. For a second, I don't want to pass it. But that makes no sense, and it certainly isn't fair. I toss it before I can make a choice that might cost us the game. When he shoots, I hold my breath. It seems like everyone in the room is holding their breath.

Go in.

Go in.

I punch my fist into the air when the ball settles in the hoop. The crowd erupts into cheers, but it's not over yet - we've got two minutes on the timer. I race to the bottom of the court as the other team gives it their all. So, when the last whistle blows, it feels like one hell of a victory.

I collapse to the ground as the exhaustion hits me. Multiple people clap my back, but I'm too tired to see who they are. When I regain some energy back, I pull myself to my feet. I hear a girl say my name, but I'm too busy searching for somebody else.

I don't find Emily in the stands as I did before. Instead, I find her a few feet in front of me. Walking toward her, I feel my mood lift in a way that has nothing to do with winning.

"What are you doing here?" I ask, focussing on Sammy first.

"Emily brought me."

"She did, did she?" I move my eyes over to her, my pulse quickening. "Thank you."

"You're welcome. Congratulations on the win!"

Remembering how it felt when I saw my name earlier, I point to her hands. "I couldn't have done it without these posters."

"Anyti-," whatever she's about to say gets disrupted. Instead of having Emily standing in front of me, I now see Matt and the others. I peer over their heads to check that she's alright. Only when I see her walking away with Natasha, unhurt, do I look away.

"Some of us are going back to mine to celebrate," Hannah says, taking a step toward me. "you'll come, right?"

Not a chance. I'm wondering what excuse to give when Sammy speaks for me.

"I want to go with Emily."

I hold back a smile as I look down at him. "You do, do you?"

"Yes! Can we please see where she went?"

As the others try to convince me to go with them, I look over their heads to find her. Luckily she's standing near us - nodding her head when I meet her eye.

I think she's also mouthing something, but I'll be damned if I know what.

"I'm taking him with Emily," I announce, looking back at the group.

I spend the next minute trying to convince them to move out of our way. They can't seem to understand why I'd prefer to go wherever it is with Emily when I can go to a house party with them. To me, the choice is easy.

"Let's go," Emily grins when we reach her.

I still don't know where it is we're going.

"To the arcade to celebrate," Harvey tells me when I join him. "Good win, by the way. The way you- and then you-," he hops from one foot to the other, stopping with a sigh. "It was awesome. You know, you might just be cool enough to be my best friend."

"Thanks?" I'm not sure if I should be taking that as a compliment or not.

"Don't worry about him," Ben whispers. "He's always like that."

I laugh as Harvey continues talking. In this sense, he's a lot like my neighbour - a.k.a. an absolute chatterbox who has an endless amount to say.

After listening to him for a while, I notice the bored look on Sammy's face and crouch down. "Get on." His face lights up as he wraps his arms around my neck. Don't ask me why, but he always laughs when I do this. I run in a circle, and his laugh gets louder. "Ready to beat everyone in the arcade?"

"Let's do it!"

When we reach the place, the first person inside is Emily. Just when I think it's because she loves arcades, I see that she's running straight to the Valentine's stand. I shake my head with a smirk, turning away from her.

"Out of everything here," I hear Ben ask, "what would you want the most?"

I glance back, careful not to look at them. "Hmm... Definitely something from there."

Something from *where*? Could she be more specific?

"Oh yeah? Which one?"

"Hagrid." Now I can't help but look. Catching her eye, I wonder if she's thinking about that time with her hair.

"Why Hagrid?"

I smirk as the memory of her hair flashes through my mind. "I just like him."

"So do I," holding back a laugh, I walk past them. It's true. Ever since that day, he's become my favourite.

"Can we play this?" Sammy asks, pointing at a machine.

"Sure."

As the machine loads up, I move my eyes over to Ben. It looks as if he's trying to win that Hagrid for her. Why is he doing that?

"Peter," Sammy tugs on my arm. "Peter, it's ready. Are you alright?"

"I'm good," I clear my throat as I pick up the other controller.

We play until Sammy tells me he's thirsty. Leaving

him with Harvey, I head over to the nearest store and grab him a drink. It crosses my mind that Emily might also want one, so I choose one for her, too. When I get back, I find her alone for the first time, standing by a wall and examining some box.

"Here," I say, giving her a nudge as I lean against the wall beside her.

"Thanks," as she readjusts the box in her arm, I get a better glimpse of it. Looks like some kind of bracelet-making set.

"I like the colours on that," I tell her. She looks back at the box in a way that makes me think I'm going to get one.

"You do?" Yeah, maybe I shouldn't have said that. As she puts it in her bag, she pulls something out, and I realise that I definitely shouldn't have said anything. "Here," she says, passing me a damn flapjack. "You must be hungry after the basketball match."

"Oh - er -" - I'm definitely not hungry for that - "do you not want it?"

"I don't like them." What? Then why the hell does she carry them around all the time? "I mean, I like them," she continues, "I just - don't want one now."

"Okay," I guess that makes sense. I peel back the wrapper, my mind racing for a way to get out of this. Should I drop it on the floor? No. She probably lives by the 5-second-rule. I take a bite, hoping it isn't as bad as I remember. "Yum," yep - definitely as bad.

"Emily, come here!"

As she turns her back, I quickly spit the flapjack into

the wrapper and toss it into a bin.

"What was that?" Harvey asks, walking over with Sammy.

Handing a drink to Sammy, I shake my head. "You don't want to know."

He leans against the wall. While he talks, I watch Emily absentmindedly. She's putting her max effort into the dance mat, yet she's still missing all the marks.

"Can I ask you something?" Harvey asks. I give him a nod, my eyes still on Emily. "Do you like her? Emily, I mean."

I stuff my hands into my pocket and straighten. "No."

"Oh. That's a bummer."

Something doesn't feel right. Realising it's the lie I just told, I slump back down again. "I don't know, maybe." *Yes*.

"Well, you should figure it out soon. She won't wait around forever, you know. And it looks like you've got competition," he nods his head at Ben as he says this, causing my chest to tighten.

"How would you tell someone if you liked them? Hypothetically, I mean."

"Hmm," as he folds his arms, it crosses my mind that I'm now asking Harvey Morris for dating advice. "I'd probably get her something for Valentine's Day. And if we're talking about Emily, she'd love something romantic like that." He's right - she would. But I don't do Valentine's Day. "Take my girlfriend as an example," he continues, raising his voice suddenly. "I can't wait to get her something."

"I didn't know you have a girlfriend," I frown. Noticing him staring at something, I turn my head, spotting Natasha disappearing around a bend.

"I don't," he sighs. "But Natasha barely spoke to me last year because she knows I like her. She speaks to me every day now."

"You should tell her the truth," I say. "Maybe she feels different about it." Something occurs to me then. "Um, will you watch Sammy for a sec? I need, er, the bathroom."

Rather than going there, I head back to the entrance, stopping by the claw machine that Emily pointed at earlier. After checking over both shoulders, I insert some money. It's not as easy as it looks - I'll grant that to Ben. It takes me many failed attempts before I get the hang of it. Even then, I'm at the last of my money when I finally make the breakthrough. After another check over my shoulders, I grab the Hagrid from the bottom and stuff it into my bag.

Everyone is crowded together when I get back, ready to leave. There's a frantic look on Emily's face that vanishes when she sees me. I stand next to her, pleased by it.

As we walk - with me now carrying a flat-out Sammy on my back - it doesn't escape my notice that Emily keeps looking at us. It makes me wonder if she has something to say to me. If she does, why isn't she just saying it? I look at Ben, wondering if it's because he's here.

When we reach our street, I relax because this means he's leaving now. But, instead of doing that, he offers to walk Emily to her door. I realise that I can't let that happen.

"I can do it."

I hold Emily's eye, hoping she'll want that. "Yeah, Peter can do it. We live on the same street, after all."

I exhale. Ben gives me a funny look before he leaves, but I don't care. I'll get to hear what Emily has to say now. If only she'd say it. As we continue walking, she doesn't say a word to me. Yet she's looking at me like she wants to.

I need to ask. "Do you have something to say to me?"

"No!" Even though she's shaking her head, I get the sense that she's lying. What is she hiding?

"Okay," I continue walking. When we reach my house, I slow to a regretful stop. "Well, I best get Sammy inside." Will she say anything now?

"Goodnight!" She sprints across to her house before I can do anything to stop her. Just as I'm about to call out her name, she pauses, bowing her head like she's bracing herself for something. "Sammy told me something."

Sammy? I glance back at him, but he's still fast asleep. What could he have said for her to act like this?

Emily doesn't elaborate, so I feel the need to prompt her. "Yeah?"

"He said you gave me the Pikachu card because you think I'm cute."

Before I can respond - or even process her words - she disappears inside her house.

I stay outside for a long minute, staring at her door. Remembering that I still have Sammy with me, I head inside, tucking him into bed before heading over to my room.

So, Emily knows now. How do I feel about that? Nervous, I realise. But it's a kind of nervousness that I've never felt before. One that I like. Leaning back against one arm, I pull out my phone. I'm about to type a message to her when I see the last one she sent me.

Peter! A log just tripped me over. Do you know which log I mean? It's located just around the corner from our street. Beware of the log!!!!

I smile to myself as I scroll through our messages. Most of them are from her - telling me something random like how her mum banned chocolate from the house. Occasionally I'll reply, but it's nothing compared to her long paragraphs. She texts as much as she talks.

I sit up straight. It's weird being the first to text, and I have no idea how to start it.

Hey, it's me.

No - that's lame. I hit the delete button as I try to think of something else.

You forgot about the part where you're small

No - that's even worse than before. I scratch the back of my neck as I hit delete again.

Come on, Peter. *Think.*

You were right before. It is because you're cute...

Goodnight x

I hit send before I can sabotage myself with something worse. Then I throw my phone into a drawer because I can't bear to look at it anymore.

MISUNDER-STANDING PART ONE

Emily

I t's Valentine's Day! And yes, I'm excited. Who wouldn't be, right?

"Who wouldn't be?" Natasha scoffs when I voice this out loud. "Me, that's who."

I look over at Peter, who's walking in with us, hoping that I'll get some support.

"Don't look at me," he shrugs, "I'm with Natasha on this."

"You two are just-," I shake my head before moving my eyes over to Ben.

He, at least, is on my side. "Of course I love Valentine's Day. What kind of strange person doesn't?"

"Right?" I look at Natasha and Peter as I say this. Natasha sticks her tongue out at me while Peter bites his lip like he's trying not to laugh.

"I think they need to embrace the spirit more," Ben continues.

"Exactly! And I have just the thing," rooting through my bag, I pull out two of the heart-shaped badges that I made with my mum.

We make them every year, call it our one and only tradition. I just won't say that to my mum because we have tonnes of traditions according to her. Like knitting a jumper at Christmas. Or going on our bi-annual mother-daughter bonding experiences. I didn't agree to any of them - especially not the jumper. A few years back, she made me one so hideous that I actually got laughed at while wearing it. By Peter, nonetheless. If it weren't for him half-covering it up with his scarf, who knows if I would've lived it down. I still wear it every year, just to please my mum. And he still chucks me that scarf of his whenever he sees it. I best not tell him that he's half the reason why I wear it.

As it stands, this Valentine's tradition is one that I don't mind keeping.

"You are not making me wear one of those again," Natasha says, pushing me and my badge away.

I hold it back out to her. "Oh, come on. Embrace the spirit."

"You make me wear one every year, and I am *not*

229

feeling it this time." She folds her arms, and I know that there's no use in arguing.

So, I turn to Peter. "Will you wear one?"

"Not a chance," with his hands in his pocket, he walks ahead.

"But it'll look good on you," I call, following after him.

"Nope."

"I made it myself."

"Nope."

"It'll make me happy?"

He spins to look at me. After staring at me for a long second, he huffs out a sigh. "Fine, put it on."

"Yes!" I attach the heart to the front of his blazer, giving him a tap once done. "See? I told you it'll look good on you."

"Great." He turns away again. As he does, I spot Harvey by the school gate, holding a rose in his hand.

"Aw! See, look at Harvey - he's got the right idea." Lucky girlfriend, I think with a smile. Or not. To my horror, he extends the rose out to Natasha. This is not in the spirit of Valentine's!

"Why don't you give that to your girlfriend?" Natasha says to him, knocking the rose away before storming through the gate.

"She's right," I say, "how could you do that to your girl-" before I can say anything else, somebody pulls on my backpack. I look up to find Peter standing behind me, shaking his head with this warning look in his eyes. "But-,"

He shakes his head again, leaning close to my ear. "Trust me."

"Okay..." what does he know?

My plans to find out before school starts get thwarted as Harvey grabs his arm.

"I need you," he says, pulling him away before I can swat at him.

I'm surprised Peter isn't swatting him away himself. Instead, he casts one look back at me before following him through the gates. What is happening here? Since when did Harvey need Peter? And since when did Peter listen to Harvey? I shake the puzzling thoughts away as Ben extends his hand.

"Badge, please."

"You want one?" I grin. Soon, these hearts of mine are going to be a trend.

We find Natasha in English, looking out the window in anger.

I sit cautiously. "Are you alright?"

"No." She sighs. "Yes. Anyway, show me this bracelet you've made for Peter. I need a distraction."

I pull it from my bag as Jenna's voice drifts over to us.

"You got them imported from Belgium?" she asks Hannah.

"Yep. They were super expensive, but Peter deserves the best for Valentine's, right?" Hannah waves what I notice to be a box of fancy chocolates around in the air.

I look back at my bracelet. This isn't fancy. In fact, I got it for free.

"Peter's here," Natasha whispers.

I quickly hide his gift away as he takes his seat. Today is his last day in Set 2. I'm trying not to think about that.

"Emily, are you sure you want to give it to him?" Natasha has asked this many times already.

I understand where she's coming from - after all, Peter has never accepted a Valentine gift from me, even though I've given him one every year. But he doesn't accept them from anyone. And believe me, he gets a lot. But that's just how he is. Besides, this year is different.

I wait until Harvey and Ben are talking before I pull out my phone. "Do I need to remind you about the text he sent?"

"No. You've shown it to me a thousand times."

I show it to her again anyway. "See? Peter thinks that I'm cute."

She tilts her head with a frown. "Emily, why are you telling Peter that you burnt your tongue on a burrito?"

"What?" I turn my phone back to me. Oops. I'm showing her the wrong text. "Point is," I say, fighting a blush away, "Peter thinks I'm cute. And do you know what that means?" She gives me a blank expression. "It means that he might just be this cute person's Valentine."

"But anyone with two eyes can see that you're cute. I'm serious," she adds, seeing my expression. "I just don't want to see you getting hurt again. But, if you're set on it, I'll support you. What's more, if he rejects you again, I'll kick his ass."

I laugh until the teacher walks through the door. Seeing her puts an immediate stop to my merriment.

We spend the majority of class voting on each other's posters. If I told you that ours came in last, would you believe it? I suspect foul play is involved, but Natasha doesn't believe me.

"No. It's because you and Harvey slept through half the lessons. Even with Ben's addition, we couldn't make up for your lack of focus."

"At least we got one vote," I mutter. And, if I'm brutally honest with myself, we were lucky to get that. Who was blind enough to vote for our catastrophe?

Seeing Peter leaving the classroom, I quickly shove my textbook away and chase after him.

"Are you walking straight to math?" I ask.

"Yep."

"Then I'll walk with you." When he doesn't protest, I fall beside him with a smile. Wondering if he's still wearing my badge, I peek around him. I can't see anything from this angle. If I could just- leaning on my toes, I lose balance and fall to the side.

"Watch yourself," Peter says, catching my arm.

He pulls me back. The force of it has me falling into *him*. As my cheek hits his chest, I realise it's the perfect position to see if he's still wearing it. Twisting my face slightly, I search his blazer. My heart-shaped badge is still pinned there. Seeing it has me smiling into him.

"I'm not taking it off," he says, stepping away from me. I stand still for a second, wondering how he knew

233

what I was doing.

"Peter!"

We both turn our heads in the direction of the voice. Hannah's voice - *eurgh*. She barely acknowledges me as she stops in front of him.

"Have you got a minute?"

No, Hannah. No, he has not.

"Not really."

Hah!

"Please - it's important." As she pouts her lips, Peter's eyes flash over to me.

"Sorry, but I'm walking with Emily."

Why does Peter have to be so cute? To my one, he probably gets a thousand Valentine's. Then again, if Peter is my one, I'm the one who's winning.

"*Please*?" Hannah says again. Jeeze, doesn't she know when to quit?

Peter's eyes flash over to me again. "Meet you in Math?"

I nod my head, but I watch them leave with sadness. When I see the chocolates that Hannah got imported sticking out of her bag, the hole that holds my insecurities deepens. I hope he doesn't accept that.

In Math, I walk straight over to Peter's desk and stop in front of his desk-mate.

"Can we swap desks?" I ask.

"Why would I do that?"

"Because it's Peter's last day in our class, and I want to sit with him."

"Why don't you join the queue with the other girls

who've asked me to swap desks with them? Guess what? He doesn't want to sit with you."

Wow, somebody's cranky today. "But-" I stop arguing when I see that Peter's arrived.

"What's the matter?" He asks, looking between us.

"I was just asking if I could swap seats since it's your last day in here today."

He looks over his shoulder at something behind us. "Natasha, can I swap desks with you?"

"Sure."

"Just don't distract me," Peter tells me as we sit. Me, a distraction? I would never.

As Peter unpacks his textbook, I try to see if Hannah's chocolates are inside. Did he accept them? If only he'd move his bag to the left a bit so I can see-

"What are you doing?"

I jolt upright. "Nothing!"

I try to concentrate as the teacher starts his lesson. After all, I won't be moving up to Set 1 if I don't. But my sleepless nights are catching up on me. I lean my chin against an upstanding textbook as my eyes begin to droop. The next thing I know, I'm being jerked awake by my chin falling downward. I blink several times before my eyes fall on Peter. His are focused on his workbook, but I can see a smirk on his lips. Have I been drooling?

I wipe my chin as I look at the clock. "Is it really that time?"

"Yep," he answers. "You slept the hour away." He packs his things away while I let that soak in.

"Are you coming to the cafeteria?" I ask, hoping to make up for lost time.

"Can't," he zips up his bag. "I told Harvey I'd meet him somewhere."

Harvey? Again?!

"Can you meet me after it? I - I have something to give to you." I think of the bracelet nestled inside my bag and wonder if he'll accept it.

"Alright. I'll find you in the cafeteria."

Five minutes later, I'm sitting in the cafeteria as a nervous wreck. Waiting to give Peter this gift sends a whirl of butterflies through my stomach as if there's a cyclone in there.

"You need to chill out," Natasha tells me as she nibbles on her muffin. "Either he accepts it, or he doesn't - what's new?"

"I know. I just really hope he accepts it this time." I really, *really* hope.

"Why wouldn't he?" The confusion in Ben's voice gives me a confidence boost.

"What do you think of this?" I ask, holding up my finished bracelet. "Pretty nifty, huh?" A lot better than my trial runs, that's for sure.

"Looks great," Ben answers. "What about those? Can I have one?"

Seeing that he's pointing at said trial runs, I frown. "You seriously want one? They're terrible."

He ties one around his wrist. "I like terrible."

Spotting Peter walking through the door, I stuff the bracelet and its terrible counterparts into my bag. He takes the seat opposite me. I might be mistaken, but he looks slightly traumatised.

"What did Harvey do to you?" I ask.

"I didn't do anything!" the assailant defends.

"Just talked my ear off," Peter mutters this so quietly that I think I'm the only one who heard. I exchange an amused smile with him, but then I see the chocolates sticking out of his bag, and my smile drops. Those are Hannah's chocolates. And this means he accepted them.

I jump to my feet. To my confusion, so does Peter. We each have a frown on our faces as we stare back at each other. What does he have to frown about?

I start walking. When he does the same, I speed up. So does he. Is he following me? Doesn't he realise that I'm upset right now?

When we reach the exit, where you can either go left or right, we look at each other again. There's an annoyance in his eyes that flares it up in me. I'm not the one who accepted a Valentine's gift from somebody else! With a huff, I turn right. A glance back tells me that he's gone left.

Natasha finds me in the toilet sometime later. After asking me what's wrong, I fill her in on the Peter-accepting-Hannah's-chocolates details.

"That ass!" She huffs as we walk to p.e. "He never accepts anybody's Valentine's gift, but he accepts hers? Weasel."

"Don't call him that."

"I thought we were angry with him?"

"We are, but I still like him."

She nudges my arm and nods ahead. "Speak of the devil."

Following her pointing, I spot Peter walking beside Harvey. "Look at the two of them, walking like the best of friends." I don't say this in what would usually be my cheerful voice. I say it in my petty one.

Natasha doesn't join in with my pettiness. Actually, she no longer looks annoyed. I thought she was angry at Harvey? As I think this, I notice Peter coming to a stop. Stephanie, a girl in the year below us, holds out a card to him. My heart soars when he shakes his head. But then I remember that I'm annoyed with him. *Sorry, Stephanie, but he only accepts gifts from Hannah.*

My petty mood still thrives when the last bell rings.

"Wait," I stop still when I notice something sticking out of Natasha's school bag. "Did you accept that?" I point to the rose that Harvey tried to give her. The rose I thought she rejected.

She freezes. I watch as her eyes dart in every direction but my face. "No!" with that firm denial, she speed-walks ahead.

"Nata-" I'm about to chase after her when my backpack gets pulled like it did this morning.

I lurch back, but Peter catches me. Even though I'm upset that he accepted Hannah's gift, I'm still happy to be looking into his face.

"I wouldn't do that," he says, looking down at me.

I frown. "Do you know something I don't?"

"If I did, it's not for me to tell you. They'll tell you

when they're ready."

Excuse me? "*They*?"

He circles to my front. "I have something for you."

As he unzips his bag, excitement shoots through me. But then I see Hannah's chocolates again.

"I don't want it."

His hand pauses on the zip as he looks up. "You don't?"

I fold my arms, looking away. "Hannah got those imported from Belgium, you know."

"What are you talking about?"

I peek at his face. He looks thoroughly confused.

"Those chocolates Hannah gave you?" I elaborate, "she got them from Belgium."

He looks down at his bag, his confusion deepening. But then it clears as he lets out a laugh. "Hannah didn't get them me," he pulls them out to tap me on the head with them. "Harvey did. It's a long story," he adds, seeing my confusion.

I scratch my ear. *Oops. I got that wrong.* "I guess I misunderstood the situation." And thank Cupid that it is a misunderstanding. Of all the great things on Valentine's Day, he didn't accept anyone's gift!

I gulp. "I got you something. Well, I made it for you." I pull out the bracelet and hold it out to him. Is he going to reject it like he does every year? He is, isn't he?

"Thanks," he takes it from me. Trying it on, he smiles. "It looks good."

"I knew it would suit you!"

He turns it over. "Did you make one for anyone

239

else?"

"No." Of course not. "Ben did take one of my terrible practice ones, though. But this is the one I stayed up late making. Just for you."

He twists his head away. When he turns back, I notice something in his hands. "This is for you. It's, um, nothing special, but-"

Seeing the Hagrid plush, I let out a squeal of excitement. "He's perfect!" I hug it against my chest. Perfect because it's from Peter. Wait, does this mean-? "Am I your Valentine?"

"I-,"

"I am, aren't I? Am I? Am I? Am I?" I want to stop talking. I do. But my heart is too joyous to co-operate with my brain. "Does this Hagrid represent your love for me? Did you spend a lot of time getting it? Did you-" Peter, I realise, is now standing with his arms folded. There's a small frown on his face that tells me not to continue. Like my joyous heart can listen. "Am I-,"

He lifts his hoodie over his head. My eyes widen and then dart away when I see his exposed torso. Taking a step closer, he wraps the hoodie around my arms and ties it. And then he walks away.

"Eh, Peter?" I wiggle. "Peter, can you untie me? Peter?"

"You don't walk with your arms."

Oh, he's right. I chase after him. "Is this another Valentine's gift?" I ask. He rolls his eyes, and I hold back a laugh. I'm now saying this to tease him. "Am I your

Valentine? I am, right? I'm-,"

He stops in front of me. It's so abrupt that I almost walk into him. Grabbing my shoulders, he bends his head so that it's close to mine. "*Yes*, you're my Valentine."

Yes? Yes- *yes*! You heard it here - Peter Woods just confessed to being my Valentine. My Valentine is walking ahead again. Realising this, I follow after him with a smile. A glance tells me that he's smiling with me.

MISUNDER-STANDING PART TWO

Peter

It's Valentine's Day. Unlike most of the students who seem to hype over this day, I'm not a fan. What's the point in showing "love" to someone one day out of the year? Shouldn't you be showing it every day?

Not everybody agrees with me on that. Take, for example, my mum and dad. I'd bet money that my mum will receive flowers today, and she'll be happy. Then, when the morning comes around, they'll be arguing again. It's a lie.

But I'm not going to say any of this out loud. I'm afraid I'll get attacked by my neighbour if I do. Emily loves this day. I'm actually surprised she isn't sporting an 'I heart Valentine's' t-shirt. She has, however, voiced her excitement about ten times already - something that's making me wish I'd brought my bike. But I am glad she doesn't have a reason to hate this day as I do.

"Who wouldn't be?" I hear Natasha answer. "Me, that's who."

I smirk to myself as I continue walking. Natasha, it seems, has the same idea as me.

Realising that Emily has now turned her attack my way, I quickly hide my amusement. "Don't look at me. I'm with Natasha on this."

"You two are just-," she shakes her head and looks at Ben.

"Of course I love Valentine's Day," he says. "What kind of strange person doesn't?"

He isn't serious - but my neighbour doesn't understand sarcasm the same way as I do.

"Right?" she frowns at Natasha and me. When I see Natasha sticking her tongue out, I bite my lip to stop myself from laughing. The fear of getting an Emily attack is real today.

"I think they need to embrace the spirit more," Ben says.

Again, Emily doesn't hear the laughter in his voice. Instead, she takes it as an encouragement to root for something in her bag. My amused smile turns into one of endearment as I watch her. The way she views things differently to us is sweet, and I can understand why somebody like her loves a day like this. But, even with that understanding, I'm not going to wear one of her love-heart badges. She brings them to school every year. Given the fact that nobody else will wear one, I'm surprised she's still doing it.

"You are not making me wear one of those again," Natasha says. Damn it. I was counting on her saying yes.

Emily turns on me next. "Will you wear one?"

A small voice tells me to take it, but I fight against it. "Not a chance," before the small voice can turn big, I walk ahead.

She follows after me. "But it'll look good on you."

"Nope."

"I made it myself."

Again, "nope."

"It'll make me happy?"

I turn to look at her, hoping a third, firmer *nope* will make her give in. But I can't resist that look in her eye. With a sigh, I cave. "Fine, put it on."

"Yes!" as she attaches the heart to my blazer, I take a close look at it. She makes these herself? I always thought she bought them. "See?" she taps my shoulder. "I told you it'll look good on you."

I move my eyes away from her face when I realise how close she is. "Great."

"Aw! See, look at Harvey - he's got the right idea."

Turning, I find Harvey by the gate with a rose in his hand. I give him a warning look when I realise what he's about to do, but he's too busy holding the rose out to Natasha. Doesn't he realise she still thinks he has a girlfriend?

"Why don't you give that to your girlfriend?" Natasha says, sounding hurt just like I thought she would. After pushing the rose away from Harvey, she disappears inside the gate.

"She's right," Emily starts, "how could you do that to your girl-" I tug on her backpack before it can upset Harvey any further. It already looks like he's about to cry. "But-,"

I shake my head, leaning close to whisper. "Trust me."

To my relief, it looks like she does. "Okay..."

Before I can step back, Harvey grabs my arm. "I need you."

He pulls me away. The last thing I see when I glance back is Emily's look of confusion.

"You don't have to hold my arm anymore," I tell Harvey as we walk through the schoolyard. "I'm following."

"Oh," he lets it fall. With a frown, I watch as he wrings his hands together. "I've really screwed it up with Natasha."

"No, you haven't."

He's breathing like he's about to have a panic attack. "Did you not see the look on her face? She hates me."

"She doesn't hate you. She's just upset because she thinks you tried giving her a Valentine gift when you have a girlfriend."

"But I don't have a girlfriend."

I sigh at his look of confusion. Doesn't he claim to be some love genius? "You haven't explained that to her yet. To her, you still do. You should have come clean before handing her a rose."

His breathing steadies. "What should I do now?"

"Come clean," I tap his back as I turn for the cafeteria.

"Well, what about you? Today's Valentine's Day. Have you figured out your feelings for Emily yet?"

I turn away. "No."

"But you have got her something, haven't you?"

"Yes." Seeing the question in his eyes, I add, "it's the Hagrid plush she pointed at in the arcade."

"No, no, no," he shakes his head as if I've just told him some terrible news. "She doesn't want that!"

"But that's what she said she wanted."

"And you believed her?" He tuts. "She probably just said that because the options were limited. No," lowering his voice, he glances to the side, "meet me behind the old Science building at break. Trust me."

Do I trust Harvey? Probably not. But, as I enter English class, his words stick with me. *She doesn't want that.* So, what does she want? I glance at Emily as I think this, and she throws something into her bag as if she's hiding it. It's probably the bracelet-making kit she won at the arcade, one I've been catching her working on as if her life depends on its success. She also hides it away whenever I'm near, making me think she'll be giving it to me as a Valentine's gift. She does always get me one.

In class, the teacher has us voting on each other's posters. It's a bitter-sweet hour. Sweet - because it's our last day working on our project. Bitter - because it's my last day in Set 2. I run my eyes across the line of them, stopping on the one with an outrageous amount of glitter. Smiling, I place my vote down. I'd bet anything that it's Emily's.

Emily calls me as I leave. "Are you walking straight to math?"

"Yep."

"Then I'll walk with you."

I don't protest. Not only do I not want to, but I'm also curious about that bracelet - and when she'll be giving it to me. As I think back over all of our last Valentine's Day's - she usually tries to give me a gift when she first sees me - I notice she's walking like she's distracted by something. She can be distracted all she wants, but not in a crowded hallway. And not when she's about to walk into a group of girls.

"Watch yourself," I say, catching her arm. I frown back at the girl giving evils to Emily.

When they're out of sight, I look down. Emily is now clinging against my chest. Her eyes, I realise, are glued to the badge pinned there. "I'm not taking it off," I say, smiling as I walk ahead.

"Peter!" Hannah makes her way over to us. "Have you got a minute?"

"Not really."

"Please - it's important." I glance at Emily. While she

isn't saying anything, I don't think she wants me to leave.

"Sorry," I say when I realise that I also want to stay, "but I'm walking with Emily."

"*Please*?"

I look over at Emily again. Knowing Hannah, it will probably be easier if I just get this out of the way. "Meet you in Math?"

When she nods her head, I follow Hannah into an empty classroom. There, she pulls out a box of chocolates and shoves them into my hands.

"Happy Valentine's Day. I got these imported from Belgium, and they were expensive, so you better appreciate them."

"Sorry," I pass them back to her, "but I don't accept Valentine's gifts."

"But this is *me* who's giving it to you. *Me*."

Does she think I don't know that? "I'm still not accepting it."

She shoves the chocolates back into her bag with a huff. "*What* is your problem? When the girls told me you've never accepted a Valentine gift, I thought they were lying. And this," she flicks the badge Emily gave to me, "I know Emily Clarke gave you that thing. So you do accept gifts."

My patience is at an end. "I guess there's an exception."

She leaves the room. As I follow, I make a promise to myself to never leave Emily for her again. And *my problem* - if that's how she wants to phrase it - is that I don't want to give out false senses of hope by accepting a gift from someone I don't like in return.

I'm still annoyed when I reach Math class, so I don't enjoy seeing my desk-mate arguing with Emily.

"What's the matter?" I ask when I reach them.

"I was just asking if I could swap seats since it's your last day in here today."

Actually, I wouldn't mind that. But there's an easier way to go about it than asking Brian. "Natasha," I call over my shoulder, "can I swap desks with you?"

"Sure."

As Emily takes her seat beside me, the last of my irritation fades away.

"Just don't distract me," I tell her.

To Emily's credit, she doesn't distract me in her usual form of talking. She does, however, lean right across the desk as if I'm blocking her view of something. I leave her to it at first, but it starts to get weird.

"What are you doing?" I ask, pausing with my hand in my bag.

Her eyes widen like a wild animal caught in the headlights. "Nothing!"

Does she act like this with Natasha? I shake her strange behaviour away as the lesson starts. When I finish the third question, I realise she's been silent for too long. Glancing to the side, I see that she's fallen asleep.

How does she sleep like this? She has a power I wish I possessed. Leaning my head against my hand, I smile as I watch her. A pencil slips between her fingers. I take it carefully and place it down, noticing *E.C* ❤ *P.W* engraved on it. Smiling again, I turn back to my work.

She sleeps until the end of class. As everyone packs their bags, I decide it's time to wake her. Nudging the textbook beneath her chin, I watch as she jolts upright.

"Is it really that time?" she asks, wiping her chin in the same way Sammy does when he's drooled.

"Yep. You slept the hour away."

She sits up in a daze. "Are you coming to the cafeteria?"

"Can't," I zip my bag up with the hope that I'm not late. "I told Harvey I'd meet him somewhere."

"Can you meet me after it? I - I have something to give to you."

I pause. Is it the bracelet? "Alright," I tell her, "I'll find you in the cafeteria."

Wanting to be as quick as possible, I race over to the old science building, finding Harvey huddled next to another student. It looks like a dodgy dealing from the way they're looking over their shoulders.

"You're here," he says, grabbing my arm again.

"I'm here," I agree.

"Peter, this is Callum from third year. He has what you need for Emily."

He has what I need? I move my eyes over to Callum, who gives me a nod. After checking over both shoulders, he opens up his jacket - revealing a secret stash inside.

"Here," he hands me over a box of chocolates. It's the

same box that Hannah tried to give me.

"They're all the rave," Harvey tells me with a grin. "They look expensive, but Callum only charges five."

I fight back a laugh. "Have you sold these to many students?"

"Yep. Even the popular ones," he winks.

Either Hannah overpaid for these, or she lied about importing them. "I'm not taking them," I tell Harvey. "I prefer what I've got."

"Oh, yes, you are," he shoves them into my bag before I can protest, "because I'll be paying for them."

Well, I guess I can give them to my mum later.

As we make our way to the cafeteria, Harvey doesn't stop talking. His topic is all the good reasons why I should give the chocolates to Emily. I'm glad when we reach the table, and Natasha distracts him.

"What did Harvey do to you?" Emily asks.

"I didn't do anything!"

"Just talked my ear off," I exchange a smile with Emily, but then my eyes move to the thing tied around Ben's wrist. Emily's bracelet. My bracelet. No, not my bracelet. She's given it to somebody else.

I jump to my feet. When Emily does the same, I frown. Why is she also frowning?

I need to get out of here. I head through the cafeteria, and Emily follows. I speed up, but she does the same. When we reach the exit, I stop to look at her again. Why does it look like *she's* annoyed? I'm not the one who gave a Valentine's gift to somebody else! I turn left. A glance back tells me she's gone the other way.

After getting some fresh air, I find Harvey inside. His words don't help. "I told you this would happen. You took too long, and now she's moved on."

"That can't be it." I feel nauseated.

"That is it. Now you'll have to pull out all the stops if you want to win her back."

"I-" somebody blocks my path. It's a girl from another year. When I see the card in her hand, my heart drops. "I am sorry," I tell her. "It isn't against you - I just don't accept Valentine's gifts."

"You could at least give them to me," Harvey complains as we start walking again.

By the time I'm leaving the school, I have a different perspective on the bracelet situation. If Emily's decided to gift it to Ben, I shouldn't be annoyed with her. I should be annoyed with myself.

I find her outside. From what I catch of their conversation - and the alarmed look on Natasha's face - I get the sense that Natasha needs saving.

"Nata-" Emily cuts off as I pull her backpack toward me.

"I wouldn't do that," I say, looking down at her.

She frowns. "Do you know something I don't?"

"If I did, it's not for me to tell you." But I probably will if she asks. "They'll tell you when they're ready."

"*They*?"

I circle to her front, pulling my backpack down as I do. As part of my different perspective, I've realised that she still deserves my gift, even if I don't get one from her. "I have something for you."

"I don't want it."

I pause as if my heart's stopped. "You don't?"

She turns away. "Hannah got those imported from Belgium, you know."

Hannah? What does she have to do with anything? "What are you talking about?"

"Those chocolates Hannah gave you?" she continues, "she got them from Belgium."

Hannah-? I look down at my bag, and then it clicks. She must think that I accepted Hannah's gift. I let out a laugh. "Hannah didn't get them me," pulling them out, I tap her lightly on the head. "Harvey did. It's a long story," I add when she frowns.

She scratches her ear. I have to admit, she looks cute when she's this embarrassed. "I guess I misunderstood the situation." After a second, she adds, "I got you something. Well, I made it for you." She pulls something from her bag. It's the bracelet.

My happiness at the fact she's giving it to me is hard to control. I wait until I can trust my voice before taking it from her. "Thanks," I try it on, impressed by her effort. "It looks good."

"I knew it would suit you!"

As I turn it over, I can't help but think about the one Ben was wearing. "Did you make one for anyone else?"

"No. Ben did take one of my terrible practice ones, though. But this is the one I stayed up late making. Just for you."

I turn my face away as I grin. I guess I had a misunderstanding of my own. Turning back, I hand her the Hagrid plush that I won, trying to ignore the doubt that Harvey put into my head. "This is for you. It's, um, nothing special, but-"

"He's perfect!" she hugs it to her chest with a look of pure happiness. Just as the relief floods through me, she adds, "am I your Valentine?"

"I-" it does seem that way. But before I can give an answer, Emily goes off on one.

"I am, aren't I? Am I? Am I? Am I?" Do you remember when I said that Emily can be annoying and that she talks a lot? Well, this is a prime example. "Does this Hagrid represent your love for me? Did you spend a lot of time getting it? Did you-" I fold my arms as I wait for her to finish. "Am I-,"

Pulling off my hoodie, I tie it around her arms. There's not much use to it - it's not like it will stop her from talking - but her reaction does amuse me.

"Eh, Peter?" she says as I walk away. "Peter, can you untie me? Peter?"

This is like the time when a wasp stung her on the arm, and she started to limp. That time, all I could do was laugh. But I think this time requires words. "You don't walk with your arms."

She appears beside me.

"Is this another Valentine's gift?" She shakes the arms of my hoodie, and I roll my eyes in amusement. She's about to go off again. "Am I your Valentine? I am, right? I'm-,"

There's only one way to put a stop to this. Spinning

to face her, I grab onto her shoulders and lower my head. "*Yes*, you're my Valentine."

As I walk ahead again, Emily chases after me, stumbling on her way over. I shake my head with a smirk. My Valentine is clumsy.

I DON'T HAVE
THE COURAGE

Emily

B lanket - check. Sunscreen - check. Raincoat in
case it decides to rain - check. Snacks to-
"Emily!" My mum calls. "Have you remem-
bered to pack your permission slip?"

"Yes!" Have I? I look back at the items sprawled
across my bed, but I don't see that little white en-
velope. Where did I-? Ah. Spotting it beneath my Hagrid plush, I reach across and grab it, setting the Hagrid
back down with a loving smile. Now back to it. Snacks
to share with Peter - check. Candles to add a bit of ro-
mance - check.

After packing everything into my rucksack, I make

my way over to the mirror. Today, our year is going on its annual field trip that marks the beginning of spring. This year's theme is a picnic on the beach. Romantic, right? So romantic that I've decided to make today the day that I'll confess my feelings to Peter.

I know, I know, I've confessed to him before. And we all know how that went. Rejection. But things are different now. These days, whenever I see Peter, I get more butterflies than I've ever felt before. That has to be a good sign. Besides, I'm not just going to blurt it out to him as I did before. I've got it all planned out.

"Emily?" My mum is now outside my door. "Can I come in?"

Can she come in... I run my eyes across the room, just to make sure there's nothing anti-mum in here, before I call, "yes!"

She takes a seat on my bed. "Your dad's left for work already. He told me to tell you he hopes you have a good day." I smile at her words. Ever since my dad got that new job, he's been much happier. "So," she continues, "are you excited?"

"I am. But I'm also nervous."

"Nervous? About what?"

Crap. "Oh, nothing." *Just my undying love confession to Peter.* I spin away before she can read any of that on my face.

Somehow, my mum doesn't know about my crush on Peter. I say somehow because it really is a mystery to me. Not only has my crush on him survived over several years, but I also suck at hiding it. I think she still sees him as *neighbour Peter* - that small, polite boy with braces. She hasn't yet comprehended that he might be something more to me. Like a future boy-friend.

"Emily? Did you hear me?"

"Huh?" I blink out of my daydream as my eyes focus on the confetti in my mum's hand. How did I miss that?

"What do you need love-heart confetti for?"

"It's- it's not mine," I take it from her. "It's Natasha's."

I could tell my mum about Peter. That would be the easiest, most honest option. But it's been so long now that I'm afraid of how she'll react. And if one Clarke hasn't scared Peter away yet, I'm pretty sure this mother-daughter duo will.

"And is there a person who Natasha likes?" My mum continues.

I look down at my hands. "A boy."

"And is this boy also going to the picnic?"

"Yes."

"Well, sweetie, I hope he says yes to you." She gives me a kiss on the forehead before getting to her feet.

It takes me a second to process her words. When I do, I snap my head up, but she's already out the door. "I wasn't talking about me!" I call after her.

"Whatever you say, sweetie!"

After I stuff the confetti into my bag, I continue getting ready. I'm halfway between brushing my teeth when I get a text from Peter.

I have to get to school early. See you on the bus.

See you on the bus... what does that mean? Does it mean he'll be saving a seat for me? Or should I save one for him? This is what I ask Natasha when I meet her outside the shop.

"See you on the bus... see you on the bus..." she holds the phone up to her nose, which tells me she's really thinking about it. After a minute, she passes it back to me. "I think it means he'll see you on the bus."

"That's your conclusion?" I tuck my phone away as I follow her inside. "Is it not because he wants to sit with me?"

"It might be," she twirls a Twix over in her fingers. "To be honest, I'm starting to suspect that he likes you. But don't get ahead of yourself," she warns. "Let's get on the bus first."

When we arrive at the school, I have to sit through an entire hour of English before the bus arrives. I'm still not used to being in a class without Peter. Out of habit, I keep looking over at his old desk - but instead of seeing that cute, focussed face of his, all I see is an empty seat.

"Absence makes the heart grow fonder," Natasha tells me when the bell rings.

"I don't think mine could grow any fonder."

"But what about Peter's?" She gives me a wink, and I fight back a smile before she can tell me to stop getting ahead of myself again.

"Maybe I should disappear for a year," I say. "He might miss me so much that he'll realise he's in love with me."

"Forget about Peter - what will I do without you?"

"Eat all the food?" We laugh as we climb the steps onto the bus.

"More like the shopkeeper will go out of business with you not here," she retorts.

I pinch her arm. Somehow, I'm the one who ends up stumbling. "Did anybody see that?" I keep my eyes down as I wait for her verdict.

"Only Peter," my head snaps up. "I'm kidding!" she laughs. "But he is here. *And* he's sitting alone."

As I follow her eyes to the back, I realise that she's right. He *is* sitting alone. Why do I suddenly feel like running?

Natasha gives me a nudge. "If you don't go, somebody else will."

I gulp down my nerves as I walk over to Peter. He's looking out the window with his earphones in. With his bag on his lap, the seat beside him is free. I take it. Repositioning this hefty bag of mine, I feel him shift beside me.

"This seat is free, by the way."

Huh? What does he mean by that? I already know it's free. Unless- "do you mean I should have asked?"

"Yes."

Heat rises up my neck, but then I notice the playful smile on his lips. He's teasing me.

I flick him. "Do you really think I'm that polite?"

He doesn't answer, but his smile deepens. I turn away as mine does the same. If this were several years ago, I would, of course, have asked. But Peter always says no to things like this, so I've had to learn to adapt. Adaption: sit down without asking. It's worked a charm, really - because Peter no longer protests.

"What is in your bag?" He asks. "It's twice the size of mine."

I look down. He isn't wrong - mine is so packed that I haven't even managed to get the zip closed, and I can see the candles inside. Wait, I can't let him see them! I throw my arms over it. As I do, my hair falls like a curtain in front of my face. I pretend that it hasn't impaired my vision. "Just my blanket and, you know, a spare one." Through the cracks in my curtain-hair, I see his eyes narrow. "And food," I add.

His suspicion clears. "You do know that they're providing food for us?"

"Well, you know me," I laugh, "a lover of food."

A small smile appears on his lips as he lifts his hands. My eyes widen as he reaches across, tucking my hair behind my ears so that I can see again. "I do know you."

I smile into my bag as he turns to look out the window. My cheek tingles from where his fingers brushed against it - that's the Peter effect. Maybe one day I'll have an Emily effect on him.

When the bus arrives at the beach, the Peter-effect still has me smiling.

"Okay, students," Miss Gardner calls out to us, "I want you all to stay here while we sort the bus. Don't cause any trouble!" As she turns to leave, an excited murmur spreads through my classmates.

"What should we do?" one of them asks.

"Play a game?"

Ooh. I perk up at that one. A game on the beach sounds perfect to me, but not everyone feels the same. Not on my watch.

"You're playing," I say to Peter, pushing him from behind. I must be stronger than I think because he actually moves.

The game we decide on is one that I haven't played before. Its purpose, Dec says, is to see how many couples can be made. We all get into a circle - I pull Peter with me so he can't try to escape - and then Dec gives us a command.

"First," he says, "go stand next to the person you're closest to." I peek at Peter as I stay beside him. He doesn't move. "Now stand next to the person you *want* to be closest to." Again, I remain still, smiling when Peter does the same. "Now stand next to the person you have a crush on." Is Peter even playing? My legs lock into place, and I'm surprised when Peter stays beside me. But there are many girls beside *him*, so there's no saying he's here for me.

"Peter and Emily haven't moved," Jim says, pointing at me like it's an accusation.

"You two can do the forfeit."

But I haven't moved for a reason!

I stay quiet when I hear what the forfeit is. We have to stare at each other for one minute. For one whole minute, I get to look into Peter's eyes. He smiles when

I turn to look at him. And, as the minute ticks by, I forget that anybody else is around.

"Okay, you've had your fun," Miss Gardner interrupts us. "You can go set up your blankets now. Peter, Chloe - can I borrow you?"

My wobbly legs almost buckle as his eyes leave mine.

"Natasha," I breathe when he's gone. "Can you hold me for a sec?" I don't know if she can hear me or if she's even near. But I need some support right now.

"I'm here," she grabs hold of my elbow, and I let my weight fall. "What's wrong?"

"Pete- Pe- I've melted."

"Did Peter's eyes do this to you?" She laughs. "Well, did you see how he was looking at you? I'm pretty sure you melted him, too."

"Really?" I hadn't noticed that.

"You even had him blushing, Em." She moves her hands from my elbows to my shoulders. With a determined look in her eye, she says, "I think it's time."

"Time?"

"For your confession. I'll set it up with Ben, and I'll make sure Harvey is ready with his speakers. You make sure you're ready for when we get back."

I nod my head. It's all I can manage because my wobbly legs are turning into jittering nerves. What if he says no?

When Peter returns, he walks straight past me and joins the opposite side of our disjointed circle.

Come on, Emily, you can do this. You've confessed be-

fore, and you can do it again.

Can I?

Yes.

Am I sure?

No.

"*It's ready,*" Natasha's whisper makes me jump. "Behind the old restaurant, next to the port. There's nobody there."

I suck in a deep breath as my eyes re-focus on Peter. He's standing to the side of everybody else, wearing this look on his face that makes me wonder what he's thinking about. Seeing him gives me courage. Taking small steps toward him, I stop when I'm close enough to whisper in his ear. He moves his head slightly, making it easier for me. "Meet me behind the old restaurant in five."

He turns to look at me. My heart starts to race again, but I force myself to hold his eye. After a second, he nods. I take a step back. And then another. And then another. I hold his gaze long enough for the courage to return, and then I turn and run.

The blanket set-up looks beautiful. Far better than I thought it would. Really, I'll need to thank Natasha and Ben ten-fold for this. And Harvey - the music he's chosen is soft and romantic. It's perfect.

After lighting the candles, I sit back and wait. Five minutes pass, and there's no sign of Peter. Ten minutes pass, and there's still no sign of him. After a further five minutes go by, the panic kicks in. Did he only nod to get rid of me? What if, somehow, he found out about my plan - and now he's disgusted? He's not going to come.

As this painful realisation hits me, a sudden wind blows my blanket into chaos, sending things rolling across the sand. Relighting the candles first, I reach around for the fallen items. But, before my fingers can wrap around the water bottle, somebody beats me to it.

"You're here," I breathe, looking up at Peter.

He sets the water back down and sits. "Sorry I'm late."

"That's okay," I quickly flatten my hair before pouring us both a drink. It isn't easy - since my fingers are shaking. Peter is here, and so is my chance to confess.

"This is nice," he tells me. "Better than being with everyone else."

"That's what I thought!" Okay, Emily, it's time. But how should I start this? And *is* now the right time?

"So," he sets his drink down and meets my eye. Unlike before, it doesn't give me courage. It gives me a nervous whirl of butterflies. "Why did you do this?" *Because I wanted this confession to be special.*

I don't voice this thought. It gets choked back by a sudden vision of our future. If I confess now, he might reject me like before. And I'm not sure I can handle a second rejection. No, it's more than that - I'm not sure if I'll have the heart to keep trying, and I don't want to give up on Peter.

So, I lie. "It's to say congrats on doing so well on your tests."

A frown appears on his face, but it's gone in a flash. "Oh?" He clears his throat. "Thanks."

Harvey's piano music continues playing in the background, and I realise how ridiculous my lie sounds. And the love-hearts - why didn't I listen to Natasha when she told me they were too much? And the candles-

The candles-

Seeing how close one of them is to Peter's jacket, I open my mouth in silent horror.

"Peter!" I lurch toward him, but then something happens.

Instead of me ending up on top of him, he ends up on top of me. His face presses against the side of mine as his hands pin me to the ground. After a long second, he lifts his head to look at me. I can feel a heart pounding, but I can't tell if it's mine or his.

"Emily Clarke!" Somebody calls. "Is that you over there?"

Peter jumps to his feet. Seeing that he's extending his hand to me, I take it. My eyes don't leave his face as he pulls me up.

"It is you," Miss Gardner stops in front of us. I'm not looking at her, but I know she has her cross face on. "What are you doing here? The rules are that we stick together. And what is all of this?" She doesn't let me answer - which is good, come to think of it because I'm not sure what I'd say. She continues her angry rant at me for another minute, and then Peter speaks up.

"It was me."

My eyes widen in surprise.

Miss Gardner, it seems, is also surprised, but for a different reason. "Oh, hi, Peter, I didn't know you were here. You say this was you?" She moves her eyes to the blanket, and I frown at the injustice. Why isn't she ranting at him? Peter's lips twitch, and I can tell he's thinking something similar. "How romantic."

"I've been known to be that," Peter says.

A laugh bursts from my lips. I don't mean to do it - it's just the way he said it. He laughs along with me.

"Well, sorry to break up the party," Miss Gardner continues, "but can you please pack this up and rejoin us? And blow out the candles."

As I turn to do as she says, I realise something. I don't have the courage to confess my feelings to Peter. Because I don't have the courage to lose him.

I HAVE A
CONFESSION
TO MAKE

Peter

It's our annual school outing today. Usually, this kind of stuff doesn't excite me, but I woke up feeling different this morning. This morning, I find myself strangely looking forward to it.

I'm not quite sure what's caused this difference, but I'm glad about it. So much so that I got up early, and now I'm pacing around my room with time to kill. Then again, pacing is a waste of time. It's better if I go down now before my mum decides to get up.

I do just that. In the kitchen, I pour myself a glass

of juice and chug it down. Sammy's dinosaur set is sprawled across the table. Packing it away, I sit down to eat. There's still a lot of time to kill.

Grabbing my backpack, I make my way upstairs to get some revision in. I'm tackling a Math question when I remember the new teacher wants me in early today. With this in mind, I throw on my hoodie and head out.

Emily's bedroom light is on. I pause when I see it, wondering if she'll be waiting for me. We have been walking in together a lot lately. For this reason, I pull out my phone and text her. A little bit of my excitement falls away when I hit send. I guess I prefer to leave my bike at home these days.

The school is deserted when I reach it. Why Mr Redman wants me in this early is a mystery to me. I just hope that it's not because I'm failing.

"Morning, Peter," he grins when I reach his classroom. "Thanks for coming."

I pull out a chair. "Can I ask why you wanted to see me?"

"Well, why else? It's because I'm impressed with you." He drops something in front of me. A glance tells me it's one of my workbooks. "And also to ask why you haven't been in my set sooner."

I let the image of Emily into my mind as I look back up at him. "I'm not sure why."

"Hmm," he goes over to his desk. When he returns, I see something else in his hands. "Do you mind trying to answer this equation for me? I know it's a lot to ask, especially at this time, but I'm curious."

"Okay..." I glance at the clock. When I see that there's enough time, I start working through it. I keep going until the first bell rings, and then I drop the answer onto his desk. "Let me know if I got it right later?"

We have history first. As I enter the classroom, I look over at Emily's desk. No, not her desk. When will I remember that?

Class is boring without her. I never realised just how much light she brings into a room until now. Not that I have anything against my new classmates - they're alright. But they don't eat food loudly at the back or laugh at their own mistakes; their cheeks don't flush when they get in late, and I don't have to speak to them ten times a day because they stop by my desk and don't know boundaries. They aren't Emily. On the plus side, I'm getting a lot of work in. Who would have thought that Emily held half of my attention all this time?

When the bell rings, I pack my things away and head straight to the bus. Our class is the first to arrive. I take a seat at the back, putting my bag next to me so nobody can sit there. I prefer sitting alone, and I'm alright with admitting that. But that doesn't stop people from asking. A lot. If there weren't so many empty seats around, I might say yes. But there's plenty to choose from. In the end, I plug my earphones in and look out the window. That's when I see Emily coming out. As if the sight of her has activated my automatic mode, I shift my bag from the spare seat onto my knee, keeping my eyes out of the window as she gets on the bus. I know it's her getting on because out of the corner of my eye, I see somebody fall - and only Emily is that clumsy. I smile to myself. It's like being in her class all over again.

She takes the seat beside me. Unlike everybody else, she doesn't ask first. It should probably annoy me, but I find myself amused by it.

Unplugging my earphones, I turn to look at her. "This seat is free, by the way."

My words confuse her at first, but then a blush creeps up her neck. "Do you mean I should have asked?"

"Yes." I fight back a laugh as her eyes scan my face.

She actually flicks me. "Do you really think I'm that polite?"

I know she is with everybody else.

As she turns away, I notice her bag for the first time. It looks like she's packed her entire room into there. I ask what's inside, and she reacts by throwing her arms over it.

"Just my blanket," she says, "and, you know, a spare one." I narrow my eyes. There's a chance she can't see it since her hair is now covering her face. "And food," she adds.

Ah. Food. Why did I have to ask? She probably knows this already - she loves food so much I bet she carries it around everywhere - but I remind her anyway. "You do know that they're providing food for us?"

"Well, you know me," she laughs, "a lover of food."

I smile because that's what I just thought, and then my automatic mode kicks in again. Raising my hand, I reach over to tuck her hair behind her ear. "I do know you."

My hand tingles in a way that I've never felt before. I look out the window as I clench it, wondering why I keep doing actions like that without thinking. Even stranger, I find myself wanting to do it again.

When we get off the bus, the teachers leave us to our own devices while they go off to speak to someone. And what do my classmates want to do when left to their own devices? Play games, obviously. I'd prefer to sit out, but I'm with the wrong person for that.

"You're joining in," Emily says, pushing me from behind. Even her full force isn't enough to move me, yet I walk anyway.

We spend the next five minutes arguing over what game to play. If I have any luck, the teachers will get back before we land on a decision.

I don't have that luck.

"I have an idea," Dec says. "Everybody, get into a circle." As if she's afraid I'll run away, Emily drags me with her. But her excitement has already made me want to stay. "First, go stand next to the person you're closest to." Well, this is easy. I remain beside Emily because she's the person I'd choose to confide in out of everyone here. That makes his next demand easy. And his next. I stay beside Emily, up until the one that makes my ears feel warm. "Now stand next to the person you have a crush on."

I turn my eyes to the floor, acutely away that Emily isn't moving.

"Peter and Emily haven't moved," somebody accuses.

"You two can do the forfeit."

The forfeit, if that's what Dec wants to call it, is to stare into each other's eyes for a minute. Easy, if you ask me. I turn to her with a smile. It's hard not to smile at the situation we're in. But then the seconds tick by, and something changes. Have her eyes always been this brown? And the pink tint to her cheeks - is that permanent? Has she always looked this innocent? Looking at her now, I don't think I've ever seen a face so pure as if it holds nothing but honesty and sweetness.

I hear someone call my name, which is the only reason why I'm able to tear my eyes away from Emily. Following Miss Gardner in a daze, I'm that much out of it that she has to call me back when I walk ahead.

"Are you alright, Peter?"

My eyes can't focus. "I'm fine. Do I not look alright?"

"You look out of breath."

I place my hand against my heart. I'm surprised when I feel it pounding. "It's- I'm-," I clear my throat, "I'm fine."

The reason why she's called us over, she says, is because she needs people who she can trust to collect the food order. I agree to it, but I think I'd agree to anything right now.

When I get back to the circle, I force myself to walk

straight past Emily, stopping when I reach the other side. Something tells me that my heart will pound again if I go near her now. But it doesn't escape my notice that she's up to something. It's when Natasha returns and whispers into her ear that I realise she's been gone for a while. What are they-?

No. I need to refocus. I need to stop thinking about her. So why am I happy that she's walking over to me?

As she leans on her tiptoes, I tilt my head because, whatever she has to say, I get the sense it's private. "Meet me behind the old restaurant in five."

I turn to look at her in full. She's nervous, I think. Nervous and excited. Why? I nod my head, holding her eye as she steps back. When she turns to leave, it's as if a spell has been broken, and I can finally move again.

Something between us is changing. Or, at least, something is about to change. If I go with Emily now, we won't be the same again. If I go, it's because I don't want us to be the same. I step forward.

"Peter, are you ready?" It's Miss Gardner. With Chloe beside her, I'm reminded that I agreed to go get food. Why did I do that?

"I-," I glance over my shoulder at where Emily disappeared. "I can't now. I have somewhere to be."

Her brows furrow. "Where?"

Damn it. If I tell the truth, there's a high chance Emily will get into trouble for breaking the rules. How quick can I be?

I try to be quick, but Miss Gardner was wrong about the order. It isn't ready. I tap my fingers against the counter while I wait, and Chloe notices.

"Are you in a rush?" she asks.

I stop my tapping. "No. Sorry."

"Then, can I ask you something?"

"Go for it."

"Were you not moving away or something?"

I blink. "Sorry, what?"

"That's what I got told. I was actually going to ask you out before, but I thought there wasn't any point because you were moving."

I bite my lip to stop myself from laughing. One guess at who told her that. "I'm not moving, but there is someone I like." For the first time, that doesn't feel like a lie.

When we get back to the others, Emily's absence tells me that she's still waiting for me. I drop the food down and make a run for it, pulling myself to a stop when I find her. If she's angry at me for being late, I can't tell. She's currently scrambling around the place, looking for who knows what. I smile as I walk toward her. Despite the frantic look on her face, everything about this is perfect.

Getting closer, I see that she's reaching for something. Her head snaps up when I grab it for her.

"You're here!"

"Sorry I'm late," I set the water down and sit, sucking in a deep breath to control my nerves. This setup further solidifies my belief that things are about to change.

"That's okay," she hands me a drink.

"This is nice," I say, taking a sip. "Better than being with everyone else."

"That's what I thought!" She doesn't say anything else, and I wonder if it's because she's as nervous as I am.

"So," I set my drink down as my fingers start to shake. "Why did you do this?"

"It's to say congrats on doing so well on your tests."

"Oh?" Is that really the reason? I clear my throat as my idiocy - and disappointment - hits me. "Thanks."

But what's with the love-heart confetti? And Debussy? If she wanted to congratulate me, wouldn't she have done it without all that? As this thought crosses my mind, I notice her expression shift to panic.

"Peter!" she lurches toward me. I have no idea what's caused this panic, but I have a sudden urge to protect her.

I fling my arms over her and wait for the impact. Nothing happens. I raise my head. Emily is looking back at me with that wide-eyed expression of hers. It's stupid to forget that there might be danger behind me. Stupid, yet I can't look away.

There's someone I like - I repeat the words in my head as if they hold the answer to something. *There's someone I like. I like-*

Suddenly, it all becomes clear. There's a reason why my heart beats ten times its usual speed whenever I'm close to Emily. There's a reason why I do things for her that I'd never do for anybody else. And there's a reason why I look forward to seeing her every day.

I like Emily.

"Emily Clarke! Is that you over there?"

Glancing over my shoulder, I see Miss Gardner walking toward us. She looks angry enough that I jump to my feet, pulling Emily up with me. "It is you. What are you doing here?" As she goes off on one, shouting at Emily about *the rules*, I wait for a chance to say something.

It's a while before I finally get the chance. "It was me."

Miss Gardner blinks as if just registering my presence. "Oh, hi, Peter, I didn't know you were here. You say this was you?" She looks down at the blanket, and I catch Emily's eye. It's hard not to laugh at the expression on her face. It screams: *why isn't she angry at you?* "How romantic."

"I've been known to be that," as soon as the words are out, Emily laughs. The sound makes it impossible to hold mine in.

"Well, sorry to break up the party," Miss Gardner continues, "but can you please pack this up and rejoin us? And blow out the candles."

As I help Emily pack everything away, it dawns on me that she won't be making a confession if that was ever her intention. But that's okay. Because I have a confession to make to her.

NEVER BEEN KISSED

Emily

I can still remember Peter's very first day at my school. I was excited because, by that point, I already had a big crush on him, and I wanted my friend to see why.

My best friend back then was a girl named Ellie. Natasha actually disliked me for reasons I'll pretend aren't obvious. How we became friends is another story altogether - but it starts with our mutual dislike for bullies.

I walked in with Peter on his first day. And, when Ellie met him, her reaction wasn't what I expected. She couldn't understand what I saw in him. He was cute, yes, but his personality was 'nothing special'. Why isn't he speaking? Why is he so unfriendly? Why does he sit alone when he can join in and play?

It didn't take me long to realise that she wasn't the only one to speak like this. But that's when I realised it. My classmates haven't seen the vulnerable side to Peter. The side that swaps his toy at the checkout so he can buy a dinosaur set for his little brother.

So, while my fellow classmates left Peter alone, I had the luxury of finding him alone. And what I saw was something that would change my temporary crush into something that still lasts today.

Peter will always be the first to offer help if somebody needs it. But, because he doesn't shout out about it, people don't know this. He's also never sent me away, even when I've annoyed him. Unlike my other classmates, something in Peter's eyes told me I had a friend.

Of course, as we got older, Peter got adopted into the popular crowd, and I rarely found him alone then. I almost gave up on him because of that. But when I did catch him alone, those wild butterflies still thrived, and I knew there was something special about him.

Maybe it's because we're neighbours as well as schoolmates, but I'd like to think that we're close, and that I can determine his mood. And, if it's a bad one - like when he's angry or upset - I'm able to figure out why.

Until now.

"Is he still acting weird?" Natasha asks. We're currently sitting in the cafeteria eating lunch - just her, Ben, and me. Harvey has gone off with Peter.

I pick at my bagel. "If by acting weird you mean he's avoiding me, then yes."

"Wait, he's avoiding you now?" Ben frowns.

I put my bagel down. "I haven't seen him at all this week, so it seems so."

I know Peter is in a different class now, but that doesn't explain his disappearance. Up until this week, he was eating lunch and walking in with me. He even waited outside my class so that we could walk to the cafeteria together. And now, without a word, he's vanished.

"He's done a complete 180," Natasha throws her back against her chair as she says this. "But why? What's so different about this week?"

I shrug my shoulders. "I wish I knew the answer to that."

Usually, I'd just outright ask him, but I haven't been able to find him for that. Or, if I have, he's turned away before I've had the chance to speak.

"Is it-," Ben gives us both a look. "This is only a guess, but it's not because it's prom week, is it?"

Prom week - a.k.a. the traditional week that the students of our school will ask someone to prom.

"But why would Peter avoid Emily because of that?" Natasha asks. "Are you saying that Peter doesn't want her to think he'll ask her to prom?"

"It's only a guess," his eyes turn apologetic. "Or

maybe he's scared Emily will ask him."

"That is something I'd do," I panic. Actually, after a sudden return in courage, I almost asked him at the beginning of this week.

I'm relieved when Natasha disagrees. "No," she shakes her head. "I don't think that is it. Ever since the school picnic, he's been acting as if he likes Emily, right? Maybe he isn't avoiding us. Maybe it's Harvey."

For a second, my hope lifts. But then I catch the look in her eyes, and I know she doesn't believe it. I slump in my seat as the bell rings.

"Hey," Ben says, holding up my bag, "how about we ditch study hall and have some fun? I'll cheer you up."

"No, no, no," Natasha waves her arms in front of us, "free period is there for us to study, and you two need to study as much as Harvey does."

I laugh at the offended look on Ben's face. "It's fine, honestly. I'm alright. Besides, maybe Natasha is right. Peter's disappearance may have nothing to do with me." A big part of me believes that. After all, he has been acting extra nice to me recently. Not only has he dropped snacks into my bag every day last week, but he's helped me with my homework and permanently handed over his hoodie. I just hope he'll speak to me soon.

As I think this, I swear I see Peter's silhouette from the corner of my eye. I freeze when I realise it is him and that he's heading into a classroom.

"What's the matter?" Natasha asks.

"Come on," not wanting to miss this rare opportunity to speak to Peter, I pull her to the classroom with me, stopping outside of it.

"Emily, what-,"

"Shh," holding a finger to my lip, I peek around the door. Peter isn't alone in there. He's with Alice, I realise.

"So," she says to him, "I know you've not got a date to prom yet, and neither do I. We should go together."

Hasn't he already told you he doesn't like you, Alice!

I crane my neck, but Peter has his back to me, so I can't see his expression. "Actually," he scratches the back of his neck. "I do have a date."

No!

Did I just say that out loud? I smack my hand over my mouth as Alice looks over at me. Her eyes are brimming with annoyance. Still not over my fear of her, I grab Natasha's arm and run.

"What was that about?" Natasha breathes when I pull her to a stop.

I clutch my chest. "Did you not hear Peter just then? He already has a date to prom! Do you-," my voice goes small, "do you think he's avoiding me because he thinks I'll get in the way of it?"

She shakes her head. "Not a chance. He just said it to get rid of Alice." I nod in agreement. If Peter likes someone enough to take them to prom, I'm sure I'd know about it. "Why don't you ask him out yourself?" She continues. "Find out once and for all if he likes you."

"Me? I can't, I-,"

"I know, I know, you don't want to lose him. But, Emily-," she stands upright, "you deserve to like someone who likes you back. You know that, right? If he says no to going to prom with you, then you can move on."

I gulp. Natasha is right. I know she is. But that's what I'm most afraid of. "Alright, I'll do it." I turn to look over my shoulder. Seeing Peter coming out, I run over to him.

"I have something to ask you," I say, jumping to his front. He looks down at me with his mouth slightly open. I try to ignore the expression that tells me he doesn't want me here.

"I have to go," he turns to leave. Why is he trying to escape?

"Wait!" I hop in front of him again. "Will you-," *it's now or never*, "I mean, do you want to go to the dance with me?"

There, I've said it. But my relief only lasts for one second. Because, in Peter's eyes, I can see that he doesn't want to say yes. He takes a step back. And then another. And then another. His eyes stay glued to mine, looking what I can only describe as panicked. He turns a corner, disappearing from my sight again.

I let myself fall to the floor.

"*Emily!*" It's Ben in front of me. He helps me back to my feet, holding my arm steady. "What happened?"

"What did he say?" Natasha asks, catching up to us.

"He said no." I shake my head, "no, he didn't even say that. He just walked away without saying anything."

"He just *walked*?" Natasha sounds appalled.

I duck my head as a tear rolls onto my cheek. I wipe it away with a sniff. "I must've startled him. It's not his fault."

"Hell no," hearing the anger in Natasha's voice, I look up. She's already storming down the hall.

Ben puts an arm over my shoulder as I try to call her back. "He really just walked away? Jeeze." He shakes his head, and I realise that he's angry, too. I've never seen Ben angry before. "You deserve someone better than him, Emily. Someone kind, and warm, and loving. Like you are."

I try to smile, but my lips refuse to move. "Peter is all those things too," I say. With another sniff, I hold my head high. "But I'm fine. You can't force someone to like you, right? I can move on now." Before I can crumble again, I add, "I need to go. I forgot I told Miss Gardner that I'd help untangle decorations in the gym."

Ben doesn't follow me as I make my way down the hall. I'm thankful for that. I don't want anybody to see me cry. I'm crying because I know what I have to do now. I have to move on. Because loving someone who doesn't love you back is too painful, even if that person is as special as Peter.

But... I don't want to move on.

With my head down, I open the door to the gym. There's already a number of my classmates helping inside. Miss Gardner hands me a box as I walk past her, and I take it over to the stage so I can be alone.

The methodicalness of untangling fairy lights is a

good distraction for my brain, but it's not enough to loosen the tightness in my chest. Will it ever be loose again?

I hear somebody say my name, and I look up for the first time. Hannah and Jenna are standing near me, laughing about something.

"Look at her," Jenna says, "it's so sad."

Hannah's eyes move over to me, and I realise that I'm the source of their amusement. "Did she really think Peter would say yes to her when he's already turned down Alice and me?"

As they laugh again, I look back down at the decorations in my hand. Tears splash onto them.

Stupid prom. Stupid decorations. Stupid me getting my hopes up. Somebody's hand touches my cheek, but it only alarms me for a second. I recognise this hand.

"Don't cry," Peter says, brushing my tears away with his thumbs.

I blink up to find him crouched in front of me. There's a smile on his lips, but it doesn't match the sadness in his eyes. "What are you doing?" I ask.

The sadness deepens. "I don't want to see you cry anymore."

This - Peter - the way he's holding my cheek - I don't understand it. "But I thought-," I swallow against the lump in my throat, and then it all rolls out. "I thought you wanted me out of your life, and that's why you've been avoiding me. And-," remembering how he walked away earlier, I have to swallow again, "that's why you rejected me."

"No," he shakes his head as if he's in pain. "I can't imagine my life without you in it. I didn't walk away because I was rejecting you. I walked away because *I* wanted to be the one to ask *you* for a change." He lets out a laugh, which only adds to my confusion.

"Wha-," Is this really the truth? I search his face for some sign of a lie, but all I see is sincerity.

"Ah," he says suddenly, pulling out his phone. When he passes it to me, I have to blink several times before knowing what I'm looking at.

"What is this?" I can see that it's an order confirmation for a necklace, but why is he showing it to me? I tilt my head to the side. Something about this necklace looks familiar. Wait- "This is the necklace I wanted," I gasp. "How did you remember?" I showed it to him last Christmas, but I thought he hadn't paid attention. There's a butterfly on it that's the same shade of his eyes. "Wait," I add, realising there's a more pressing question, "*why* did you order it?"

Peter's lips pull up into a smile that isn't sad anymore. "I wanted to give it to you when I asked you to prom. It's not come yet - that's why I haven't asked. And that's also why I walked away from you earlier - I didn't want to reject you, but I couldn't accept."

My mouth hangs open as I process his words. He wanted to ask me to prom? And the necklace - he's been avoiding me because he wanted it to come first? I search his eyes. As soon as I find the truth in them, my lips stretch into a grin.

Something shifts in Peter's expression. He leans

forward, and my heart races when I realise what's about to happen. My eyes, wide in fear and excitement, move to his lips as they get closer to mine.

I've never been kissed by a boy before. But, even if I'd had the opportunity, I would have saved it for Peter. As his warm lips press against mine, my heart swells in happiness. It's as if there's a warm glow encompassing me - expanding and stopping when it's safely wrapped around Peter.

Could it be better than this? I don't think so. As my excitement defeats my fear, I relax into him, my lips moving to the rhythm of his. His hand moves to my face, his thumb brushing against my cheek as if *I'm* somehow precious to *him*. In a daring move, I lift my arm to his shoulder and hold the back of his neck. His hair is softer than I could have imagined.

When we break off, he leans his forehead against mine for a moment. I stare back into his eyes as I listen to the sound of our breathing. I start to hear whispers coming from behind, and I remember that we're not alone. Peter must notice it too because, with a smile, he interlocks his hand in mine and stands up straight.

As we leave the gym together, my eyes stay glued to his. And, incredibly, his are filled with love.

MY EXCEPTION

Peter

My first day at school here didn't go as expected. By then, I'd already met Emily, and I thought I'd scared her off. So I was surprised when she knocked on my door in the morning, asking if I wanted to walk in with her. I didn't, but I was too young then to know that honesty pays off. I told her that I wasn't ready yet, and what did she do? She waited outside my gate until I came out. That's when I got my first taste of Emily's tenacity.

When I got to school, I was surprised to find that she wasn't popular. With her outgoing personality and friendliness, it seemed a sure fit. But she only had one friend - and even she didn't treat her nice. Everybody else made fun of her. I decided that she wasn't my problem. After all, we might be neighbours, but that didn't mean I needed to look out for her. At least, that's what I kept telling myself.

It's not often that my behaviour contradicts my judgement. Emily, in many ways, has always been my exception. While I sat away from everybody else, I couldn't help but watch her. And what I saw was a girl who, while annoying, had only good in her. A girl who doesn't just talk but listens. A girl who, for whatever reason, I liked seeing smile.

Ever since then, I've been looking out for her without even knowing it. If I heard somebody badmouth her, I'd tell them to stop. If Emily dropped something out of her clumsiness, I'd place it back onto her desk before she realised it was gone.

Thinking back, it might seem ridiculous that I've only just realised my feelings for her. But, while I've always felt her pull, I don't think it has always been romantic. That side happened slowly. Slowly, but with enough force that I'm now irrevocably taken away by it. And now it's time to tell her.

"Remind me again," Harvey says, sitting on a step with his sandwich, "why you haven't told her yet?"

I resist the urge to shake my head. "As I said, I'm waiting for the right time."

"And why is now not the right time? Sorry," he holds his sandwich up as I frown. "I'm just saying, haven't you waited long enough?"

I take a frustrated bite out of my own sandwich. We're currently eating outside the old science building in an attempt to hide from Emily. "I know I've waited long, I know *she's* waited long, but that's exactly why I want to do this right." Restless again, I jump to my feet. "Do you remember what she did for me at the picnic? How much effort she put into it? I think she deserves that in return."

"She does," he agrees slowly. "But I miss eating my lunch with Natasha. And Ben - he's not happy I've ditched him. If that necklace hasn't arrived by tomorrow, I'm going back."

I kick a stone. I'm with him on that. Not only do I miss sitting with Emily, but I also miss seeing her altogether. But I'm afraid if I bump into her, she'll ask me to prom before I get the chance to ask her. And she deserves to be the one getting asked for a change. It's only for one more day.

"How do you even know she'll ask you?" Harvey asks. I give him a look, and he nods his head. "Yep. She'll definitely ask."

With this week being the "traditional" week to ask, there's a high chance she's planning it. I would have asked her already if this damn necklace had arrived. It's something she told me she wanted a while ago because she liked the butterfly on it. I didn't get it for her then - but I'm fixing that.

"That's the bell," I pick up my bag and help Harvey to his feet. "What are you doing in free period?"

He rubs his hands together with a smile. "Finding Natasha and then taking a nap."

I chuckle. Now that we're at the end of our last year, we get multiple *free periods*. We're supposed to use them to study - I do - but Harvey sees it as a chance to rest.

"I'll see you later," I tell him as I head for the library. I barely make it down the corridor when somebody calls out my name. Turning, I see that it's Alice. "What's up?" I ask her.

She leads me into an empty classroom. From experience, this is a bad sign.

"So I know you've not got a date to prom yet, and neither do I," she shrugs her shoulders. "We should go together."

I scratch the back of my neck. "Actually, I do have a date." *I hope.*

"Oh?" Her eyes frown at something behind me, but when I turn, there's nothing there. "So you've asked someone?"

"Not yet."

"And who is this mysterious person you like?"

I smile. "Emily Clarke."

Her eyes widen in surprise, and it annoys me. Why is it surprising that I like Emily? What's surprising is that she likes me.

"Well," I point to the door, "we have some revision to do, so..."

Phew. Relieved that that's over with, I head out, where I come face-to-face with none other than Emily. Of all the times for her to appear out of nowhere.

"I have something to ask you," she says. She's wearing that look on her face that I saw at the beginning of the week. A look that says she's going to ask me to prom.

"I have to go," I turn to leave, but she hops in front of me.

"Wait!" Even though I want to escape, I can't help but feel happy at being this close to her again. "Will you- I mean, do you want to go to the dance with me?"

Oh no.

In my state of panic, I take several steps back, turning when I'm far enough out of her reach. I try not to think about the look on Emily's face as I race to the library.

Is she upset now? I run my fingers through my hair as a new panic takes over. No, she'll be fine. It's not like I voiced a rejection. I take a seat as I try to convince myself that I'm right, but it doesn't sit well in my stomach. Unable to take it, I jump to my feet, but my exit's blocked by an angry-looking Natasha.

"You asshole!" she yells in a voice more aggressive than usual.

I ask this question even though I think I already know the answer. "Why am I an asshole?"

My heart races as I wait for her to answer.

"Emily is crying over you. *Again.*"

I wince at the last word. When have I made Emily cry before? "Where is she?"

"You know what, Peter, I actually thought you liked her. I even told her that she should hope this time. Damn it! I guess you were just leading her on."

It's hard not to defend myself against her accusations, but Emily is the only thing that matters right now. "Can you tell me where she is?" I ask again.

"You don't deserve her."

I already know that. "*Please*," I beg, "where is she?"

Her eyes scan my face for a long, painful second. Maybe she sees the sincerity in it because she lets out a sigh. "I don't know. I left her outside the cafeteria, but I doubt she's still there."

I huff out a sigh of my own. All this time talking could have been spent searching. "I'll find her."

As I turn to leave, Natasha calls me back. Her expression is less angry than before. "I'm sorry for calling you an asshole," she says. "You're not. It's- Emily has liked you for a while."

I nod my head. "I get it. You're looking out for her. But I like Emily back, and you can trust me on that."

When she gives me a nod, I turn for the door and run.

If I were Emily, where would I hide? I check outside, but she isn't there; I check the stairway - I've caught her hiding there before - but she's not there, either. By the time I'm scratching my head at a loss, I run into Ben.

I don't have any time to waste with formalities. "Do you know where Emily is?"

"If I did, I wouldn't tell you."

I run my eyes over his face as he folds his arms. "You do know, don't you?" When he doesn't answer, I add, "can you just tell me? Please. She's upset because of me."

"I know she is, and that's exactly why I'm not telling

you." He scoffs. "You know, when I first moved here, I couldn't believe that a girl like Emily likes a guy like you. It didn't surprise me to find that you hung around with jerks like Matt. I've seen it all before - the nice girl being hung up on a guy who doesn't deserve her."

That's the second time I've heard this today, and, along with his other words, I'm not surprised. I know what people think when they first meet me - cold, heartless, an asshole. Half the school probably still thinks that. But Emily is the only one who's stuck around long enough to figure out that I'm not.

"Tell me one good reason why I should tell you," Ben continues.

I rack my brain for a good answer, but I can't think of one. I sigh instead. "I don't have a good reason. You're right. I don't deserve Emily. Yet - miraculously - she likes me." I let out a single, disbelieving laugh. "*Still*. I can't tell you how grateful I am for that. I can't tell you how grateful I am for *her*."

Ben doesn't say anything, so I continue,

"Do you think I know why she likes me? I have no idea. She's better than me in every way, and I'm just waiting for her to realise it. But, somehow, she still greets me as if I'm her favourite person. I guess I just want her to know that I feel the same."

Some of the tension in Ben's face disappears as he unfolds his arms. "She's in the gym, helping with decorations."

"Thank you," I set off into a run. Did I expect my words to change his mind? No. If anything, I thought that they'd solidify his belief that he's doing the right thing. But I'm glad they didn't.

I pull myself to a stop when I reach the gym. It's busy inside, mostly with people trying to untangle decorations. As soon as I open the door, I spot Emily sitting on the stage. It looks like she's struggling the most. Something about seeing her sitting there calms me down. I smile to myself, but it drops when I see who else is here. Hannah and Jenna are doing that thing I sometimes see people do when they laugh at someone who's right beside them. And the person they're laughing at, I realise, is Emily. That does it for me.

As I walk past them, Hannah and Jenna go silent. But I don't spare them a glance. Instead, I crouch down in front of the only sweet person in this room. It's her sadness that makes me do it. Raising my hands, I place them gently onto her cheeks and wipe her tears away.

"Don't cry."

She blinks up at me. As her eyes widen, I force a smile onto my lips, but it's not easy with this lump in my throat. "What are you doing?" she asks.

"I don't want to see you cry anymore." The truth hits me like nothing else before. I never want to see this girl cry again.

"But I thought-," she swallows against a sob. "I thought you wanted me out of your life, and that's why you've been avoiding me, and," she swallows again, "that's why you rejected me."

"No," I shake my head. The thought of not having

Emily in my life now is painful. "I can't imagine my life without you in it. I didn't walk away because I was rejecting you. I walked away because *I* wanted to be the one to ask *you* for a change." I let out a laugh because I've never said anything like this before in my life, and it feels good to say it.

"Wha-?" It looks like she doesn't believe me. How do I make her see?

"Ah," pulling out my phone, I open up the order confirmation for her necklace. As she takes it from me, her nose twitches in that way it sometimes does when she's concentrating.

"What is this?" Her eyes scan my phone from side to side. After a minute, they widen and look back up at me. "This is the necklace I wanted. How did you remember?" Funnily enough, I remember a lot when it comes to Emily. "Wait," she adds, "*why* did you order it?"

I smile. "I wanted to give it to you when I asked you to prom. It's not come yet - that's why I haven't asked. And that's also why I walked away from you earlier - I didn't want to reject you, but I couldn't accept."

Her mouth is hanging open. Just when I hope it's because she's absorbing what I'm saying, it stretches into a smile. Not for the first time, I'm reminded of the sun breaking through a cloud. You don't know how much you want to see it until you do. And, when you do, it fills you with so much warmth that you can't look away.

It happens then. The urge overpowers me, and I

lean in to kiss her. She doesn't respond at first, and I fear that I've made a massive error in judgement. But then her lips relax against mine. I move my hand back to her cheek, brushing my thumb against where it always blushes, and she moves hers to my shoulder. Her fingers run through the back of my hair.

Have I ever felt completely at ease before? Right now tells me that I haven't. Right now tells me that, up until this point, my axis has been tilted, and Emily sets it right.

We break off, and I realise that Emily's breathing is as heavy as mine. I lean my forehead against hers for a second, listening to the sound of it. Our classmates are whispering behind us, but I don't care about them. Entwining my fingers in Emily's, I take a second to appreciate who I have in front of me before standing upright. My eyes stay glued to hers as we leave the gym together. Together - I like the sound of that.

PETER ENTHUSIASM

Emily

"**I** can't go to prom like this!" leaning close to the mirror, I stare at my lips in horror. No amount of scrubbing will get this red lipstick off. In fact, it's the scrubbing that's made things worse.

"Relax," Natasha says. She's sitting cross-legged on my bed with her make-up sprawled in front of her. "It's not like we're going to the real prom."

She's right. The five of us – Peter, Ben, Natasha, Harvey, and me – decided to ditch the actual prom and hold one of our own. It made more sense to celebrate the end of our school year with the people we cherish the most. But still.

"Why do I listen to my mum?" I complain. *"Red lip-*

stick will look good on you, Emily. You should be more daring, Emily. Where did she even buy this stuff?" I scrub at my lips again, but all it does is smudge it around.

"Hey, it's not your mum's fault you put lipstick on like a five-year-old. Why don't you ask Peter to bring Sammy over? I'm sure he'd-," a sponge to her face cuts her off.

"Do that again," she reaches across my bed for something, "and Hagrid gets it."

Seeing my beloved plush in her hands, I quickly back down. "You don't want to hurt him."

"Or- do I?" she wiggles her brows at me.

Despite my lipstick fiasco, I can't help but laugh. "No, it's not funny. We're leaving for prom soon, and I look like a clown."

"Clown or not, Peter will think you're adorable."

My lips twitch. "Do you think so?"

"Just as long as you change out of those pizza pyjamas. And you *stay away* from those heels."

Ah, the heels. They're another thing my mum picked out for me. "But they'll make me taller for Peter," I say. She gives me a look, and I know what it means - yes, but they will also kill you.

Natasha's argument is that I'm far too clumsy for heels. I don't want her to know this, but I have tested them, and I have fallen over.

"Emily!" my dad calls from downstairs, "Peter is here!"

"He's early!" scrambling to my feet, I race to the top

of the stairs, knocking my hairdryer over in the process. Peter is standing at the bottom, looking far too handsome in this dark green suit of his. I take a second to appreciate my fortune before calling out, "you're here!" and thundering down to meet him.

"Ooft," he stumbles back at my impact, and then his arms wrap around me. "I've missed you, too."

I give him a squeeze. "You look handsome."

"You look... I like your pizza pyjamas."

My eyes widen as I remember the stains and tears on them. Oh well. Peter knows I'm not perfect. I step back. "Heels or sneakers?"

"Sneakers," he brushes his finger across my lip as he says this. "If you're in heels," he adds, taking a step toward me, "how will I be able to do this?" leaning down, he plants a kiss onto the top of my hair, and I bite back a bubble of giddiness.

"Sneakers it is."

Racing back upstairs, I quickly change into my dress. I'm in a rush now that I know Peter's waiting for me.

"You. Look. Amazing." Natasha says from the door.

Catching her reflection in the mirror, I spin to face her. "Me? What about you! You look-" I'm too amazed to say. In her red satin dress, she looks gorgeous. "I can't wait to see Harvey's face," I laugh.

They've been dating for a few months now, and I couldn't be happier about it. Especially since I found out that Harvey made his girlfriend up. Natasha refused to tell anyone at first, but then the love in her eyes as she looked at him became impossible to hide. I just won't say that to her face because she might barf on me.

"But that dress-," she moves toward me, running her fingers through the mesh material. "Now I see why you bought it."

It's only a simple dress - white, thin straps, knee-high. But, as if by fate, it has green butterflies on it that match the necklace hanging around my neck.

"I can't wait to show Peter."

His reaction is better than I could have anticipated. Cool, calm, collected Peter actually stammers out his words. "You- I- you- beautiful."

I grin as we head out. "How's your mum and Sammy? Are they still coming over for dinner on Saturday?"

"They're-," he clears his throat, "doing a lot better, actually. And yeah, they can't wait."

"Good," even though he tells me they're alright - and that *he's* alright - I can't help but worry. If my dad left us, I know I'd be heartbroken.

Peter's hand wraps around mine, and the warmth momentarily calms me. No matter what happens, at least I can be there to comfort him. It might not be enough to take the pain away - but I'll do whatever I can.

"So this is what it feels like to be the third wheel," Natasha's sigh bursts through my Peter-bubble. "Can we speed up the walk?"

Harvey and Ben are waiting for us at the park.

That's where we've decided to hold our private prom. When we get there, the first thing I see is the fairy lights hanging from the trees, and my breath catches.

"This is amazing!"

"Good," I hear Ben say. It looks like he's got himself tangled up in some wires. "Because we've been here for hours."

As Peter goes over to him, I see that Harvey is now kissing a red-cheeked Natasha. I swear my new favourite thing is catching her doing PDA. She blushes more than me now.

The night flies by too quickly, but that's what happens when your time spent is perfect. Will I regret not going to the actual prom? No. Not when I'm here spending it with the people I love.

I think this, and then I spot Harvey munching my last packet of crisps, and my mouth falls open. "Hey, I was saving that!" As he sets off into a sprint, I chase after him. Both our fitness levels have us lying down in minutes.

The other three lay down beside us, and it turns into a night of stargazing.

"If you had a favourite memory from school," Natasha says after a while, "what would it be?"

We all lean up, exchanging a look between each other.

"Meeting you guys," Ben answers first. "I've never been at a school long enough to make real friends, so this is nice."

"Mine would be getting the girl of my dreams to

say yes to me," Harvey answers next. When said girl makes a barfing sound, he quickly backtracks. "Fine, fine. Then I'd say breaking my leg in our second year. I got so much time off school because of that!"

"Yes, and you wouldn't stop badgering me for weeks to help tutor you!" Natasha complains. "Mine is coming first every year at Sport's Day. That was awesome. What about you, Peter?"

"Me?" Peter's eyes move up to the sky before falling on me. His lips stretch into a grin. "I'd have to say having a little person appear in front of me twenty times a day."

Just as my heart starts to swell at his words, Natasha ruins it. "Was it not a hundred?" she laughs.

Peter chuckles. "What about you, Em?"

Hmm. What about me? I look up at the sky, but I already know the answer. "I'd say right now. Here, with all of us together. It feels like we'll be friends forever."

My words are met with silence. I look at each face in turn, wondering if I said something wrong when Natasha lurches toward me.

"My best friend is the cutest!"

She encloses me in a hug. Harvey and Ben follow. When I'm finally free, I look over at Peter and see my favourite smile playing on his lips. He opens his arms out. Will I ever refuse a hug from him? No. No, I will not.

Shuffling toward him, I press my face against his chest as he wraps me into a bear-hug. "You are cute," he whispers. I giggle as his breath tickles my ear, and his chest rumbles beneath me.

"Okay, okay," I hear Natasha say. "I think it's time to leave these two lovebirds alone. Ben, fancy a game in the arcade?"

"I guess it'll be good to beat Harvey."

As our friends leave, Peter pulls away to look at me. "Fancy some food?"

If I thought I couldn't love him more. "Yes!"

We walk around until we find a food truck that smells beyond delicious. Settling on a hotdog, we take a seat on a bench. I'm enjoying the taste of mine when Peter turns back to the food truck guy.

"Excuse me, do you have a napkin? My girlfriend spilt ketchup on herself."

It's a good job Peter's attention is still averted, or he would have caught sight of the hotdog spewing out of my mouth.

I grin as he turns back to me.

"It's not something to smile about," he frowns, leaning over to wipe the ketchup off me. "Wasn't this dress expensive? I heard they can cost a fortune."

The dress – and the ketchup spillage – is something I'm not bothered about. I do stuff like this all the time. No. I am smiling for a different reason.

"Actually," I say, "my mum got it from a charity shop, so it only cost a fiver!" wait – is that something I should tell my date?

Peter smiles. "So, if not the ketchup, why are you smiling?"

"You just called me your girlfriend for the first

time." I grin again, but then I notice the frown on his face. Had he meant to say it? "Do you- do you want me to be your girlfriend?"

Peter's frown clears as he leans forward. His lips press against my forehead. The way he's kissing me - so tender, so careful - it sends heatwaves running through me. "Yes," he answers, leaning back. "Do you want me to be your boyfriend?"

"I do!" I realise how loud I just shouted that and slap my hands over my mouth. Even the food truck guy is giving me a funny look. I move my hands to cover my face. "I don't think I'll ever be able to contain my Peter enthusiasm."

"What's Peter enthusiasm?"

Peeking through my fingers, I contemplate whether or not I should tell him. I probably should. It will make both of our lives easier if he knows the full extent of my feelings for him. "It's what I call my enthusiasm for you because it's on a different level to everything else," I admit.

He doesn't look at me like a weirdo like I thought he would. Instead, he lets out a laugh that makes me feel surprisingly sane.

As I revel in the sound of Peter's laughter, I'm reminded of something someone wrote in my yearbook. The anonymous person told me that Peter won't like me for long and that he'll find someone better once school is over. I ignored the message then, but now I wonder if he'll ever feel the same enthusiasm towards me.

"Um, Peter?" I ask.

"Yeah?"

I look down at my hands. "Do you think you'll ever like me as much as I like you?"

He remains silent as I twiddle my fingers. I'd look at him, but I don't want him to see the pain in my eyes.

"Come with me," he says suddenly, holding out his hand. I take it with a frown.

"Where are we going?"

He doesn't tell me. Instead, he leads me through the streets with a determined look on his face, all the while holding my hand like he's afraid to let go.

As we near the basketball court, I realise that we're heading toward our street. We stop outside his gate, and he leaves me with an "I'll be back in a minute" before disappearing inside.

What is he doing? He takes a while to get back to me. When he does, he has a bag in his hands. I peek inside, but I have no idea what I'm looking at. All I see is a bunch of papers.

"What is all this?" I ask. He pulls the papers out, placing them into my trembling fingers. I flick through them with an increasing sense of awe. These are our old test papers from school, but that isn't what surprises me.

"But you got ninety-plus on all of these," I say, looking back up at him. "Shouldn't you have always been in Set 1?" Instead of answering, he pulls something else out. When I recognise the old teddy bear I bought years ago, my eyes widen. "But I gave you this when you first moved here. You still have it?" Again, he doesn't answer. He pulls out an unopened flapjack instead. *Why-*

"Those are the test papers I took home to try again," he explains. "In the real test, I always scored enough to stay in Set 2."

He always-? "But why?"

"Because of you." He holds my eye for a second, and I realise my mouth is hanging open. I'm too baffled to close it. "Do you know why green is my favourite colour?" he continues. I shake my head, unsure if I can use my voice. "It's because of this bear you gave me. I can't tell you how many times I've tried to get rid of this weird thing-"

Wait- "What's weird about scruffy?" This bear was precious to me way before I gave it to Peter.

He raises his brow, but my question goes un-answered. "-But I never had the heart to do it. And finally," sucking in a deep breath, he holds up the last item, "I hate flapjacks."

"You- you hate flapjacks?" how does that even make any sense? He's always taken them from me, and I've been giving them to him for years!

"More than any other food. I've never told you be-cause-" he pauses. "Because I wanted you to keep giv-ing them to me, so I had an excuse to be near you."

He wanted to be near *me*. And I only gave him the flapjacks because *I* wanted to be near *him*!

The realisation that Peter has felt something for me - no matter how small - all these years has me grinning from ear to ear. I wrap my arms around him. "You love me!"

"I do love you," he laughs. "Of course, I love you."

I can't help but laugh with him. "I love you, too, if you didn't know."

"Really? I would never have guessed."

I need to clear something up. Stepping back, I give him a serious look. "If you didn't like flapjacks, I would have found another excuse to come over to you."

He smiles. "We should head inside. It's late."

"But I don't want to go in."

Before I can protest any further, he spins me around, wheeling me across the grass. "We'll see each other again tomorrow."

"Okay," but every step to my front door is taken with force. The only location I want to be right now is right beside Peter. I reach for the handle, but then I realise that I haven't given him a proper hug goodbye.

Maybe it's just an excuse, but I race back to him anyway, wrapping my arms around him in an embrace that I don't want to break.

And then he kisses me.

This isn't like our other kisses, either - this time, Peter lifts my feet off the ground, our lips crashing together as if we both need to somehow be *closer*. I wrap my arms around him as both love and desire burn through me. A love and desire that Peter reciprocates. His feet move beneath me, but then he lowers me down in too soon a time.

My lips stay pressed against his until the last second. It's my dizziness that forces me to stumble back for air.

"Tomorrow," I say when I catch my breath.

"Tomorrow," he promises.

That's enough for me. As I make my way inside, I smile to myself. Because tomorrow, I know that I'll get to see my favourite person again.

THE REASON
WHY

Peter

I stand in front of my mirror as I do up my tie. I've left my hair how Emily likes it, which means it's messily strewn across my forehead. My blazer is hung up on the door, and my shoes are already on.

Is it ridiculous that we're dressing up for a prom we aren't going to? Yes. But Emily insisted we make an event out of today, and who am I to resist her?

I smile as I think about seeing her again. I miss her, and it hasn't even been a day.

The green suit is to go with the patterns on her dress. Not that I've seen the dress myself because she won't let me. But her mum ran through several suits with me before I got the thumbs up for this one.

Speaking of mum's, I can hear mine shuffling outside my door. "Peter?" she asks. "Can I come in?"

I clear my throat, turning from the mirror to face her. "Yep."

She enters with hesitance, and I'm not surprised about it. We aren't used to this mother-son relationship yet. "You look great," she says, twisting her hands together.

"Thanks."

"Do you need help with your tie?"

"No, I-," seeing her face fall in disappointment, I quickly backtrack. "I mean, yeah, that would be- yeah."

So, my dad left us about two months ago. It turns out that he's been working away to *stay* away. My mum knew about his decision for a while, but she didn't know how to tell us. Instead, she fell into a dark, downward spiral. I've still not completely forgiven her, but our mutual breakdown helped me forgive her some. Actually, it's our shouting match that brought us to where we are today - with her in my room and me letting her fix my tie.

"I'm proud of you," she tells me as she works on it. "I'm proud of what you've achieved and who you've become. I know I don't say it enough, but..." she trails off.

I clear away the lump in my throat. "Thanks, mum."

"Say hi to Emily for me." She taps my shoulders with a rare smile. "That girl's really grown on me. You won't hurt her, will you?"

Even though we're on better terms now, I sometimes sense she's afraid I'll turn out like my dad. "I won't hurt her." *Not like dad hurt you.*

"Right, well, I'll leave you to it."

I grab my jacket and follow her out. "What's Sammy doing?"

"He's watching TV downstairs."

Before I leave, I make sure I check on him. One of the things I regret about our shouting match is having it while Sammy was home.

"There he is," I ruffle his hair as I sit beside him. "How's my favourite Sammy doing?"

"I'm good," he takes a bite out of something. When I see it's one of Emily's flapjacks, I shake my head.

"You eat way too many of those."

"But I love them," he takes another bite, unfazed by my barely contained look of disgust. "You won't tell Emily about what I did, will you?"

"Of course not."

What Sammy *did* was tell Emily that I like flapjacks just so he could have them for himself. Yep, he can be sneaky when he wants to be.

I ruffle his hair again as I stand. "I have to get going. We're taking you to the arcade tomorrow, remember?"

"Yep!"

As I leave the room, I hear his little voice call after me, "will you bring me back more flapjacks, please?" and I chuckle to myself. How anyone - especially a dad - can leave a kid like him is beyond me.

When I get to Emily's, it's her dad who lets me in. He's grown on me even more now that I'm her boy-friend. To my surprise, I seem to have grown on him.

"Hey, Peter, you're here. Let me call Emily for you," as he shouts her name, we hear a bang coming from her room, and we exchange a look that's not surprised. "Oh, that girl. Great suit, by the way."

I smile. "Thanks."

As he walks off to the kitchen, I remember how I used to wonder what the inside of Emily's house looked like. Now I've been inside more times than I can count.

"You're here!"

Spinning, I see Emily bounding down the stairway. She throws her arms around me before I get the chance to prepare myself. "I've missed you, too," I say, hugging her back. *A lot.*

"You look handsome."

"You look-," what is she wearing? "I like your pizza pyjamas."

She steps back. "Heels or sneakers?"

The thought of Emily walking around in heels - when she already falls over in flats - has me on edge.

"Sneakers," I answer, brushing my finger against her extremely red lips. Just in case she isn't convinced, I take a step toward her. "If you're in heels, how will I be able to do this?" and then I plant a kiss onto the top of her hair.

"Sneakers it is," as she turns away, I catch the blush on her face, and I let out a laugh. I'm finding this tendency of hers more and more adorable.

After she changes into her dress - one that has my voice catching in the most embarrassing of ways - we head outside. Harvey and Ben are already at the park. I helped set up earlier, but I promised Emily I'd walk in with her.

"How's your mum and Sammy?" she asks. "Are they still coming over for dinner on Saturday?"

"They're," - I clear my throat because that dress is having a lasting effect - "doing a lot better, actually. And yeah, they can't wait." Well, Sammy can't. My mum still gets nervous about it.

Ever since we found out about my dad, Emily's parents have invited us over a lot. It's been great for Sammy. *And* my mum - she appreciates it, even if she does get nervous. I can't even tell you how much Emily has helped me.

"Good," she sucks in a sharp breath, and I enclose my hand in hers. An act as simple as this still sends warmth shooting through my veins. It's as if I've never held hands with anyone before.

The spot we've chosen for our prom-that's-not-prom is a good one. It's in a small clearing, so we have complete privacy. Ben's done a good job hanging up the fairy lights, and the stereo that Emily once tried to serenade me with has been set up by Harvey. Yeah, Emily told me the real reason behind that picnic.

I smile as I watch her take in the scene. "This is amazing!"

"Good," Ben wrestles himself free from a fairy light, "because we've been here for hours."

I hand him a drink - he deserves it - and I clangs it with mine. "Cheers."

"Cheers."

"So," he nods over to where Emily is standing, "what's with the red lips?"

I look over at her with a smile. "Who knows? She's Emily."

Most of the night is spent talking about our dreams for the future. That, and watching Emily chasing Harvey around because he ate her last packet of crisps. I laugh because I know better than to come between Emily and her food.

When the sun starts to set, we lay on our backs and savour in our freedom.

"If you had a favourite memory from school," Natasha says, "what would it be?"

I lean up, wondering what mine is. It reaches my turn before I've landed on an answer.

"Me?" I look up at the sky in thought. There's been both good and bad times - bad being when my dad has let me down, good being when we won the basketball tournament. But there's one memory that beats even that. I turn to Emily with a grin. "I'd have to say having a little person appear in front of me twenty times a day."

"Was it not a hundred?" Natasha laughs.

I laugh along with her. "What about you, Em?"

She looks in thought, and I realise I want to know her answer. "I'd say right now. Here, with all of us together. It feels like we'll be friends forever."

Everyone remains silent. I exchange a look with the others, wondering if it's because they're feeling the same choked-up warmth I am.

Natasha breaks the silence first. "My best friend is the cutest!" she encloses Emily in a hug, and the others follow suit.

I watch the commotion as I wait for her to be free. When she finally is, I open my arms with a smile.

She crawls over to me, burying her face in my chest. "You are cute," I whisper into her ear. It makes her giggle, making me laugh in turn.

"Okay, okay," Natasha jumps to her feet, pulling Harvey up with her. "I think it's time to leave these two lovebirds alone. Ben, fancy a game in the arcade?"

"I guess it'll be good to beat Harvey."

As soon as they're out of sight, I pull away from Emily to look at her. "Fancy some food?"

"Yes!"

Ten minutes later, I'm taking a bite out of my hotdog when I notice the ketchup running down Emily's dress. She's so far unaware of it - and I have to cover my mouth to stifle a laugh. The way she's sitting there - blissfully unaware of the mess she's created - it's adorable.

I turn back to the food truck, "excuse me, do you have a napkin? My girlfriend spilt ketchup on herself."

"Sure," he hands one over to me. When I turn back, I see that Emily is now grinning. That's a strange reaction.

"It's not something to smile about," I tell her, wiping the ketchup off. "Wasn't this dress expensive? I heard they can cost a fortune."

"Actually, my mum got it from a charity shop, so it only cost a fiver!" Her eyes widen as if she's just realised what she said. Seeing the blush now on her cheeks, I give her a smile. Honestly, there's no need for Emily to go crazy on a dress. Not when she looks this good in a five-pound one.

"So if not the ketchup," I say, "why are you smiling?"

"You just called me your girlfriend for the first time."

I frown. Did I? I mean - is this really the first time I've called her it? As I think back, I realise that she's right. I guess I just thought we naturally became that.

"Do you- do you want me to be your girlfriend?" she asks.

I clear the frown away as I hear the doubt in her voice. Leaning forward, I plant a kiss onto her forehead. The gesture feels right. So right that I keep my lips there for a second longer than I intended. "Yes. Do you want me to be your boyfriend?"

"I do!" she slaps her hand over her mouth before covering her face with them. "I don't think I'll ever be able to contain my Peter enthusiasm."

Peter *what*? I need to ask. "What's Peter enthusiasm?"

She looks up. "It's what I call my enthusiasm for you because it's on a different level to everything else."

I bark out a laugh. How did I get lucky enough to meet someone with their own level of enthusiasm for me?

"Um, Peter?" she asks.

"Yeah?"

"Do you think you'll ever like me as much as I like you?"

What?

I do a double-take as I process her words. Did I hear that right? How does she not know that I feel that way about her, if not more? How does she not know that she's become the most important person in my life - the reason why I smile the first second I wake up? It occurs to me then that I haven't given her a reason to know it. As I look back into the eyes of the girl that I love, all I feel is ashamed. Of all the times I've said no to her, or ignored her, or avoided her altogether - how *could* she know?

"Come with me," I say, getting to my feet. She takes hold of my hand, but her expression is confused.

"Where are we going?"

I don't tell as we make our way to my house. I'm too focused on the need to make her see.

When we reach my gate, I say, "I'll be back in a minute," and then I race upstairs to my room. I know I've left Emily confused, but I'm hoping I can clear that up.

Skidding to a halt by my bedside table, I drop to my knees. There, at the bottom, is where I've kept a stash of all the things Emily has given to me over the years. At the time, I had no idea why I kept this stuff. But now I realise it's because I've always felt something for her.

Emily still looks confused when I go back down to her. And impatient, I realise. With a smile, I hold out the bag.

"What is all this?" she asks, peering into it. I pull the test papers out first, passing them over so she can see for herself. Her eyes widen as she flicks through them. "But you got ninety-plus on all of these. Shouldn't you have always been in Set 1?" I pass her the scruffy green teddy bear next. "But I gave you this when you first moved here. You still have it?" And then an uneaten flapjack.

She gets confused at that one, so I start to explain. "Those are the test papers I took home to try again. In the real test, I always scored enough to stay in Set 2."

"But why?"

"Because of you." Her mouth hangs open as she absorbs my words. I love this expression of hers. "Do you know why green is my favourite colour?" She shakes her head. "It's because of this bear you gave me. I can't tell you how many times I've tried to get rid of this weird thing-"

"What's weird about scruffy?"

I raise my brow. What's weird about a one-eyed, stitched-up bear named Scruffy? Many things. But I won't go into that.

"-But I never had the heart to do it. And finally," I suck in a deep breath before I tell her this one, "I hate flapjacks."

"You- you hate flapjacks?"

It feels like a weight has been lifted. "More than any other food. I've never told you because-" I'm about to tell her it's because I didn't want to hurt her feelings, but I know that's not the real reason. I sigh. "Because I wanted you to keep giving them to me, so I had an excuse to be near you."

Something flashes behind her eyes. The next second, she's lurching toward me with a smile on her face. "You love me!"

I laugh as her arms wrap around me. This is the most lightweight I've ever felt. "I do love you."

Emily. The girl who's always spilling sauce on herself and tripping over her own two feet. The girl who can appear out of nowhere and can talk for England. The girl with the brightest eyes and an even brighter smile. The girl who I'm not only in love with but have loved as a person for many years.

"Of course, I love you," I say, laughing once more at how euphoric this feels.

She laughs with me. "I love you, too, if you didn't know."

"Really?" I joke. "I would never have guessed."

She steps back. "If you didn't like flapjacks, I would have found another excuse to come over to you."

And I believe that. I smile, but then I notice her porch light come on. "We should head inside. It's late."

She pouts. "But I don't want to go in."

Neither do I.

I spin her around before I can give into temptation. If I had it my way, I'd be keeping her out all night. "We'll see each other again tomorrow."

"Okay," without looking back, she walks over to her front door. I let out a regretful sigh as she reaches for the handle. But then her hand drops at the last second. I have to admit, I'm relieved when I see her running back to me. That's when I lose all restraint.

As she pulls me into another hug, I press my lips against hers and lift her. She reacts by wrapping her arms around me, returning my kiss with the same urgency I feel. I move my hand to the back of her head with the need to somehow be closer, and she does the same with mine.

Do I have to leave her tonight? Can't we just stay out here? My feet take a step away from her house, but then I realise that I can't do that. It's with an effort that I lower her down again, but our lips stay pressed together until the last second. Still, my burning desire doesn't go away even after she stumbles back.

"Tomorrow," she recites, holding my eye.

"Tomorrow," I promise.

When she disappears inside, I wait until I see her bedroom light come on before I release another sigh. Tomorrow. I'll get to see her again tomorrow.

Printed in Great Britain
by Amazon